CONTEMPORARY AMERICAN FICTION

THE RUG MERCHANT

Phillip Lopate is the author of *Bachelorhood*, a collection of personal essays that received the Texas Institute of Letters award for best nonfiction book of 1982, and of *Being With Children*, a personal account of his teaching experience, which earned him a Christopher Medal in 1975. His first novel, *Confessions of Summer*, appeared in 1979. Mr. Lopate has also written two collections of poetry, *The Eyes Don't Always Want to Stay Open* and *The Daily Round*, and has received National Endowment for the Arts, CAPS, and Revson grants in support of his work. Since 1980 he has taught at the University of Houston's Creative Writing Program. His work has been selected for inclusion in *Best American Essays of 1986* and *Best American Short Stories 1974*.

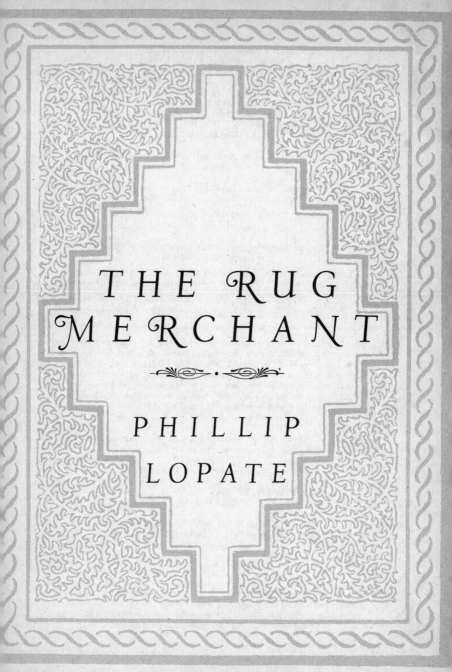

THE RUG MERCHANT

PHILLIP LOPATE

PENGUIN BOOKS

PENGUIN BOOKS
Published by the Penguin Group
Viking Penguin Inc., 40 West 23rd Street,
New York, New York 10010, U.S.A.
Penguin Books Ltd, 27 Wrights Lane, London W8 5TZ, England
Penguin Books Australia Ltd, Ringwood, Victoria, Australia
Penguin Books Canada Limited, 2801 John Street,
Markham, Ontario, Canada L3R 1B4
Penguin Books (N.Z.) Ltd, 182–190 Wairau Road,
Auckland 10, New Zealand

Penguin Books Ltd, Registered Offices: Harmondsworth,
Middlesex, England

First published in the United States of America by Viking Penguin Inc. 1987
Published in Penguin Books 1988

Grateful acknowledgment is made for permission to reprint the
following copyrighted material:

Excerpt from *Cavafy* by Robert Liddell. Copyright © 1974 by Robert Liddell.
First published by Schocken Books in 1976. Reprinted by permission of Schocken Books Inc.

Excerpt from *The Teachings of the Magi: A Compendium of Zoroastrian Beliefs* by
R. C. Zaehner. Published by Oxford University Press and Sheldon Press.

A portion of this book first appeared in *Boulevard* magazine under the title "Body, Remember."

Grateful acknowledgment is also made to the following individuals for their generous
assistance in technical matters regarding this story: Bapsi Sidhwa, David Kermani,
Robert Pittenger, Steve Null, Dr. Howard Kiernan, Elana Hoffman, and Michael M. J. Fischer.
A special thanks to Terrell James for her encouragement, advice, and warm support throughout.
I would also like to thank my editor, Stacy Schiff, and my agent, Wendy Weil, for
their sensitive handling of me. Finally, this book was considerably aided by grants
from the National Endowment for the Arts, the Charles Revson Fellowship Program
in Urban Affairs, and the University of Houston.

LIBRARY OF CONGRESS CATALOGING IN PUBLICATION DATA
Lopate, Phillip, 1943–
The rug merchant.
(Contemporary American fiction)
I. Title. II. Series.
PS3562.O66R8 1988 813'.54 87-7251
ISBN 0 14 00.9676 8

Printed in the United States of America by
R. R. Donnelley & Sons Company, Harrisonburg, Virginia
Set in Electra

THE RUG MERCHANT

1

LEAVING CARNEGIE HALL

IT WAS LATE, almost eleven-thirty, when Cyrus Irani left Carnegie Hall with the crowd at the end of Bach's Saint Matthew Passion. He noticed it had started snowing for the first time that winter. All of Fifty-seventh Street looking west from Carnegie Hall, that gray, stalwart shaft of office buildings filled with law firms, subway entrances and deserted automobile showrooms, was suddenly a whirl of wet confetti, as during tickertape parades of old.

Cyrus paused on the curb to drink in this first snow, while yellow cabs skidded to a stop in front of the concert hall. He imagined the snow's frustration, trapped between the skyscrapers' high walls as in a prison yard. Then he shook his head, disavowing the fantasy: if he were not careful, he would lose even the simplest pleasures to a preempting melancholy.

He crossed over to the discount bookstore to look at the window titles. The store was closed, which suited him fine because he did not want to go in there anyway. A better bookstore had once stood on this spot, where Cyrus used to browse after concerts. He wanted to express his loyalty to the ghost of the former management by buying as little as possible from this usurper, but force of habit kept him mesmerized by the window display of stacked books, although none of the titles (an actress's memoirs, a spy novel, a picture book on gardening, a sexual confidence builder) held any interest for him.

Presently he became aware of a sort of mocking onlooker on his right, who was watching him and making a chuckling, snickering sound. Irani peered sideways at the man's reflection: it was Aberjinnian, the round-faced auctioneer, appearing in the glass like some satanic double. (If only it *were* Mephistopheles, thought Cyrus, come to buy his soul.) Aberjinnian grinned with the satisfaction of having interrupted Cyrus in a reverie, as though catching him in the midst of a solitary sin. Still not giving him the benefit of a direct look, Cyrus stole a glance at what Aberjinnian had been scrutinizing: his own reflection, Cyrus himself (supposedly), a man of forty-four, whose kind black eyes, protuberant nose, bushy mustache and harassed noble air had momentarily stiffened into the equivalent of a death mask.

"How long have you been standing here behind me?"

"Oh, a minute or two. You seemed in a trance."

"Sorry. I just got out of the concert and was still under the influence of the music. How are you, George?"

"I am fine, and I see that you are cultivating your 'artistic sensibilities' as usual," said the auctioneer, savoring his own worldly shrewdness. Cyrus was not really in the mood for Aberjinnian's one-upmanship tonight; perhaps he could think of some excuse to get away.

"Not at all. I was bored, I had nothing to do, so I came here because it was close by."

"Don't try to be modest. You study everything: music, poetry, paintings, ballet. You are refined and I admire you for that. Now me, I am not cultured. I care only about money, sex and what I put in my stomach. You, my friend, are an idealist, and me a sensualist. What? I see you turn up your nose. You don't think I have the right to call myself a sensualist? You would probably use another word: vulgarian, *phil*istine, barbarian," Aberjinnian said with gusto, clearly enjoying Cyrus's discomfiture.

"Please, I think nothing of the kind."

"Well, even if you do, at least give me the pleasure of joining this barbarian in a cup of coffee so we don't have to stand talking in the snow like two Turkish horse traders."

"I'd like to, but—" He glanced at his watch. "It's late."

"Come on, Irani, don't tell me you don't have a quarter hour for a colleague. Please, do me the honor."

Cyrus, finding his elbow taken by the other man, was suddenly glad for the company. Even a devotee of solitude can spend too many evenings alone. They waited for several cars to pass, then crossed over again to the Carnegie Hall side of the street.

"Shall we go to the corner pancake house?" suggested Aberjinnian.

"It's too depressing there. And it reeks of griddle grease."

"Ah, finicky. Then you suggest a place."

"I don't know." Cyrus looked about. "The Russian Tea Room?"

"We're getting posh. Are you treating?"

"Ha . . . the Eternal Question. Where to go for a bite in this neighborhood that will not cost an arm and a leg? How about the Carnegie Deli?"

"A good compromise."

The snow looked as though it might stick. It dusted the shoulders of the green, boarded-up newspaper kiosks. Cyrus welcomed the cold sting of blood in his cheeks.

The two men pushed their way through the revolving doors of the sizable restaurant and waited by the front to be seated. Behind the meat counter, sandwichmen with unhealthy-looking complexions, the color of the brisket they were slicing, muttered under their breaths and popped end-bits of red pastrami into their mouths. The delicatessen manager, a florid man with curly hair and an enormous stomach that barred the way as effectively as a velvet sash, finally signaled the two men that he had the perfect table for them—conspiratorially, as though he had sized them up and picked out a special corner to suit their needs and desires. (This insinuation of more perspicacity than the situation called for was a New York disease, thought Cyrus; he did it himself at the shop.) They were seated in the middle of the room, facing a row of mirrors.

Their waiter, nervous and thin, with intense tormented eyes popping from his head (he had the look of either an unemployed actor or a disturbed relative of the owner), handed them large grease-spotted menus.

"Tea and Russian coffee cake, please," Cyrus said, snapping the menu shut.

"You make up your mind so quickly. I can never decide what is best to eat. . . . How are your stewed figs?" Aberjinnian asked absently, in his leisurely, bazaar-haggling manner.

"From a can," said the waiter, swiveling his neck around, straining like a tethered horse to break away. His black bow tie dangled from one collar.

"How about the bread pudding? Is that also from a can?"

"No, that's made here." The waiter's eyes darted to his other tables.

"Good, then I'll have a . . . bread pudding and a coffee. Do you have Turkish coffee by any chance?"

"Why should they have Turkish coffee in a deli like this?" demanded Cyrus, feeling the waiter's itch to escape.

"Well, they have 'Russian' coffee cake. It's a reasonable assumption. Don't get impatient with me, my friend. . . . I'll have the bread pudding and an *American* coffee," said Aberjinnian. The waiter left.

"You have snow on your lapel," observed Aberjinnian. "Unless it is dandruff."

"Satisfied?" said Cyrus, brushing it off.

"Don't take offense. You are always so sensitive around me."

"I'm sorry. You're right." He asked himself why Aberjinnian had that effect on him. It must be because George reminded him of his older brother. They had fallen silent. Glancing past Aberjinnian's right shoulder, he noticed several classical musicians enter, holding instrument cases. The manager made a great fuss over them, seating them near the front. With their black bow ties opened at the collar, they looked oddly like the waiters. He wondered if they had just been playing the Bach Passion.

"You seem restless tonight," Aberjinnian noted.

Cyrus shrugged. "What gives you that idea?"

"You keep looking around, you don't talk, you want me to hurry my order, you keep glancing at your watch. Do I bore you so, my friend?"

"You don't bore me at all. You weren't talking either—my friend. I refuse to indulge your craving for insult, George. It's a transparent strategy to force me into a contest, so that you can triumph in the end."

"Very good. Excellent," Aberjinnian said, grinning from ear to ear. "By the way, do you know about my auction this Sunday? You got my card?"

"I got your card. Anything worthwhile?" The waiter brought their food.

"Believe me," Aberjinnian said confidentially, leaning forward as the waiter retreated, "a whole shipment from Afghanistan smuggled through Singapore. The old families are desperate for cash, and with the Russian invasion the patriots are swapping rugs for guns, cheap. Just your cup of tea."

"All right. I'll try to come."

"Don't sound like you are doing me a favor. I'm only trying

to help you." Aberjinnian ran his hand over his head, bald except for two cross-strands.

"I understand that, and I'm grateful. No, I only hesitated because it's Sunday, and I hate to waste on business my one free day to read."

"So bring your book with you! You are so funny."

"I am glad I amuse you."

"No, you interest me. You are a complete enigma to me. No alcohol, no drugs, I have never seen you with a woman, and you don't even smoke cigarettes. A man without any vices."

"Of course I have vices," Cyrus said moodily.

"What? Name one."

"Pride, selfishness, lies, despair. Not enough compassion for my fellow human beings. A lack of faith."

"'Those are not vices, they are unavoidable—pollutants. The price modern man pays for breathing. I am talking about *vices*, that you ruin yourself over, that you throw your money away on. Like gambling or the track. Obsessions. Our grandfathers knew how to lose control—they would spend fortunes on courtesans, little dancing girls."

"I don't know about your grandfather but mine was a dyer in Kirman. Anyway, I don't need vices to ruin me. I am a small merchant, that's bad enough."

"I thought business was going well these days."

"Well, no. I sell barely enough pieces to get by. The neighborhood is becoming chic, so I have many more strollers with ice cream cones dripping onto my rugs. But they only waste my time. They don't buy any more than the old customers did, and this way I can't even read in the shop."

Aberjinnian laughed. "And women? There must be lots of chic pieces of ass that come into your store."

"So what are you trying to say?"

"I think you need to get laid, my friend."

Cyrus blushed in spite of himself; he hated for Aberjinnian

to see that he had guessed correctly. "I have, from time to time, even if I don't do it in front of you."

"But if I had your full thick head of hair, nothing could stop me. It's wasted on you, that hair."

"Maybe so," Cyrus said gloomily.

"When it comes to women, this is my theory. You have to grab them whenever you can," said Aberjinnian, tilting back in his chair. He paused a moment, as though considering whether to add something further. "Do you want some more coffee?"

"No thanks, it will keep me up all night."

"I think I will have some." Aberjinnian signaled another waiter, who was circling with a pot of black coffee. "Refill this, please." The old waiter, white-haired and stoop-shouldered in his yellow jacket, complied and moved on without a word. "I wonder if they will charge me for the extra cup."

"Probably."

"Do you know where I was tonight, before I ran into you?"

"No. Where?" asked Cyrus perfunctorily.

"Guess! Try and guess."

"I can't, but since you are going to tell me anyway I will be happy to learn."

"I went to a swing club. You go there to get laid. Only it's not a brothel, it's all voluntary. Wonderful country, America."

"This sounds like the hotel you told me about once in upstate New York. With the free-love orgies."

"No, this is right here in Manhattan. That other place, you had to put up with group discussions and cooking together and other nonsense. This is strictly 'down to business.' You come into a dark room and you fuck. They're all lying on the floor. I won't deceive you, sometimes the floors are filthy. You will need to take a shower afterwards. Anyway, you step over the bodies. Someone grabs you, you pair off. Twos, threes, sometimes it gets even bigger. Only if you want. If you're not attracted to the woman, you say no, sorry, another time. You'd be amazed though, some of them are beautiful. I don't understand why they come to such a place if they could get any man. Maybe they like it that they will never see the fellow again. No responsibilities. Tonight I had one with big tits, gorgeous, like a nursemaid. And she liked to have them sucked. I was in paradise! Just as the Prophet promised, with a beautiful houri by my side. Then I rolled over and there was another one, she wanted to lick my balls!"

Cyrus signaled the other man to lower his voice. He felt oppressed by Aberjinnian's boasting. Oh, he knew how some Middle Eastern men became like little boys fascinated with the smutty side of sex when let loose in America. But then why did he feel his own throat swelling, as though he were on the verge of tears? The more he listened to Aberjinnian's sordid escapade, the more he sensed himself endangered. Perhaps by the temptation to go there.

Finally he interrupted, trying to make his curiosity sound disdainful: "How do you find out about such places?"

"Where have you been, Irani? They take ads in the back of the *Village Voice* every week. There is a whole section on swing clubs. You really ought to try it because it would do you some good. And it's not expensive, only eighty dollars. The price of taking a woman out to dinner and a show and filling her with liquor. Even less!"

"The problem is, I don't believe in paying for sex."

"You think you are such an Adonis that you don't need to pay?"

"Certainly not. No, but—you will laugh at me, but I think it distorts the love act, which should be undertaken with affection and respect."

"Such a romantic. You never had a hard-on for a good-looking bitch you just wanted to—*vmmmmm!*—and never mind affection? Besides, you don't pay the woman, you pay the club, so it's not the same as with a prostitute. It's like dance partners choosing each other. What is the phrase they use here? 'Consenting adults.' "

"Look . . . I am glad you have found your paradise on earth, but it's not for me."

"You're a puritan. American-raised Zoroastrians are all becoming puritans. Your father should never have left Iran. But I won't say another word." They stood up and signaled for the bill. "Should I pay or should you pay?" wondered Aberjinnian, staring at the two checks.

"Let's both pay. Consenting adults."

"By the way," said Aberjinnian as they approached the cashier, who sat before a thicket of hanging salamis, "what happened to that woman, that neighbor of yours?"

"What neighbor?" asked Cyrus, presenting his bill.

"You know, the one who had something funny with her leg."

Aberjinnian was referring to an episode Cyrus preferred to forget. "Nothing happened," he said with a touch of formality.

"You mean you didn't get in, after all that?"

"Please, some other time I'll tell you."

He said a quick good-bye to Aberjinnian on the sidewalk and started walking home uptown. The snow had stopped; he wished it could have fallen a little longer.

2

THE LETTER

CYRUS HAD BEEN rubbing his mustache thoughtfully for an indeterminate amount of time as he sat behind the desk in his store. The letter, dated December eleventh, lay in front of him on crisp embossed stationery. He opened his eyes and read again the announcement that his new landlords were more than tripling the store's rent, from nine hundred to three thousand dollars a month. The bad news brought a lethargy to his limbs; a smile floated briefly across his lips. It had always been this way: whenever he found a powerful, virtually insuperable barrier in his path, one part of him grew pensive and resigned, while another seemed unaccountably relieved.

The worst had happened. Now he would be forced to act. The very thought made him sleepy. He would have to do something *different*—but what? Passive resistance seemed a pleasant alternative: he imagined himself continuing to send in the old rent (it was all he could afford anyway), just as if nothing had happened, and when the police came to evict him, going limp like Gandhi, letting them carry him to wherever they had in mind. Unfortunately, he knew, that would only be the sidewalk. He had once seen someone being evicted from the apartment house across the street. There were several police cars, an incredible show of force for one pimply, slightly built young man with two cartons of belongings. After the police had left, the evicted man sat on the curb crying. Cyrus had gone over to him to invite him in for a cup of tea. But the young man shook his head no. He seemed more ashamed of having been humiliated in public than upset that he had no home, and he quickly walked away with his roped-together boxes, making a whimpering sound. At the time, Cyrus had suspected the young man was mentally unstable. Perhaps he should have been more insistent about offering help.

Cyrus made an inventory of his own resources: he had about $8,500 in bank savings which would buy, at most, four months' stalling time. He had some money owed to him by customers, not more than $3,000 probably, and it remained to be seen how fast he could collect it. He had his small private collection of old rugs which he kept in his upstairs apartment, and which he would only part with as a last resort. He could go to his mother for a loan, which he did not want to do, or to his brother—a prospect he liked even less. He could start looking for another, cheaper location, he supposed, releasing a heavy sigh; somehow it seemed impossible for him to function anywhere else. He would never find a place which suited so well his hibernating personality. This was the cave where he had retreated seventeen years ago, and where he had been licking his wounds ever since.

WHEN YOU WALKED into the Amsterdam Carpet Store, there was a thick jumble of rugs, old furniture, dust and shadow, side by side with an impression of austerity. The dark musty corners gave customers the urge to explore, like a backstage littered with decaying scenery. After several hours the overhead fluorescents caused eye strain through their indecisive dimming and surging. Cyrus had meant for some time to install gallery track-lighting, but in the end he merely put up with the discomfort, equipping his desk with a small reading lamp.

It was his tendency in any case to adjust himself to whatever physical environment he found himself in, rather than remake the setting to suit some prior ideal of beauty or order. Even when Cyrus went away on vacation or on a buying trip (like the last one, several years ago, to Turkey and Germany), he would never complain if the lodgings were mediocre, or request a hotel room with a better view. It was almost a point of pride with him to accept the provisional as the inevitable, and to find half-hidden crumbs of aesthetic satisfaction in whatever he was given. When he heard of people tearing apart their lofts, knocking down walls and hiring architects to design the perfect living or work space, he shook his head in awe, not only at their admirable energy, but at their unfathomable belief that they could control the world around them.

Certainly laziness played a part in his adaptive passivity, but there was something else. He regarded his stay on earth as that of a subletter. He was occupying other people's domains, the transitional figure between those who had stamped the place with their pioneering ardor, and those who would succeed him, to reshape it as they willed. Even in his small upstairs apartment, where he had lived continuously since dropping out of graduate school, he had tried to preserve some of the flavor of the previous tenants, like a steward holding it for their return. The only major change over these years had been some parrot murals on the bathroom walls which an old girlfriend, Bonita, had painted to cheer herself up when she was living there. She had left a few other feminine touches: painted sea shells, table scarves, and an ebony Chinese music box, not entirely to his taste. Still, honoring the painful memory of her short tenure there, he was as non-interfering as a museum guard.

CYRUS HAD BEEN SITTING at his desk near the back of the store all morning, lost in thought. It had been a slow day so far, a good day for brooding. His desk was a Biedermeier piece with a marble-slab top, left over from the years when he had carried antiques as well as rugs. At the time it had seemed a good idea; up until the mid-1970s estate auctions had grouped furniture and carpets together, so that if one wanted a particular batch of rugs, one might as well take the rest into the bargain. The legions of chairs and dressers may have indeed attracted a few more customers and improved the cash flow, but he soon grew tired of moving around heavy objects. Moreover, the spirit of the shop felt "violated." Uncle Noshir had run the business strictly with Oriental carpets, stacking his merchandise horizontally rolled on shelves, sometimes with their triangular tongues sticking out, and keeping the center free for unrolling individual pieces. Cyrus cleared away all the antiques, except for a few sofas, and restored the shop to its traditional appearance. The one innovation he permitted himself was to install in the front some movable racks on which the cheaper rugs were hung vertically, poster-fashion, which allowed customers to browse to their heart's content without disturbing his reading.

Cyrus went next door to the pet shop, to see if Marge had also received a rent-increase notice. The two shopkeepers were friendly in a professional way, signing for each other's packages, sharing news about the street. He respected Marge. She was a solid woman in all respects. A shrewd, tough, likable merchant, with humane values and a soft spot for animals. He guessed she was a lesbian, because of certain characteristics he associated with a type of gay woman he had known: namely, her cropped hair, her chunky muscular body, her plaid workshirts and loose overalls and feminist buttons, her eschewal of makeup and skirts, and her set of cultural references and opinions. Any one of these alone would not have had him jumping to this conclusion, but together they seemed to add up to a trustworthy pattern.

Recently, however, he had begun to get the peculiar impression she was flirting with him. Not that lesbians didn't flirt with men, he realized. But it worried him that she seemed to light up almost too much whenever he came around. He could no longer be certain of Marge's story. It made him uneasy to think she might be expecting him to make a pass at her. Since Cyrus always had a hard time believing that women actually found him desirable (which was both modest and convenient on his part, especially when he himself was not attracted to the woman in question), he concluded that he must have been misinterpreting the signals.

As he entered the shop, the fecund smell of animal warmth and waste, that unasked-for yet perfectly natural intimacy, suggested to his mind something about the owner herself. For a moment he wished he were more like her—earthier, not so afraid of life—but it seemed a not entirely sincere idea, so he dismissed it. "Marge?" He paused. The shop looked deserted. Parrots squawked high on one wall, monkeys chittered in their cages. A family of Airedale puppies tussled in the window. Cyrus watched one black pup nip his brother's ear and scramble-tumble away to safety. "Marge?" At the bottom of the puppies' box, litter squares had been carefully and uniformly cut from a *Daily News*. Cyrus found himself trying to read the fragments of newsprint under the glaucous circles of dried urine. He could hear the television on in the back room—a daytime talk show, he guessed, knowing her interests. "Mar-arge!" he called out lonesomely, this time louder, feeling foolish addressing a roomful of animal auditors.

"Just a min-it!" The television sound cut off, and the pet-store proprietor parted the beaded curtains. "Oh, it's you, Cy.

Sorry to keep you waiting. I was just working in the back." Her cheeks dimpled in a smile and her green eyes sparkled. The old cliché about chubby women passed through his mind: She has such a pretty face. Marge was about his age or a few years younger, maybe forty, with brown-gray hair cut tight to her scalp like a bathing cap, and formidable breasts over which she wore a white T-shirt that said WOMEN HOLD UP HALF THE EARTH.

"Are you busy? I can come by later."

"No—what's up? Oh, did you get one of those mash notes from our landlord?" she asked.

"That is what I came by to talk about."

"Cute, eh? I thought Nussbaum was bad, but at least there were limits to his greed. His was old-style greed. Sure he neglected the building, and we didn't always have heat, but I'll take Nussbaum back any day. As soon as he sold it to those two young guys, I thought: uh-oh. The day they came prancing around in their Madras jackets to introduce themselves, all regular-guy and assuring us there would be no changes, I knew right away they were going to jack the rents up through the roof."

"I don't see how I can pay it," said Cyrus wearily, sitting down. "Why are they doing this to us? We have never given them trouble in the past, we are loyal tenants and we run clean, respectable businesses. You would think they would be satisfied to keep it that way."

"Satisfied? Assholes are never satisfied. It's this new breed of capitalist, they want to make it into the millionaire club by thirty-five. So they can retire and play squash."

"This is bad. I don't know what I can do." Marge was standing over him, and he found himself staring at her thick, blue-jeaned thighs dusted with birdseed. "I knew it was happening all along Columbus Avenue, but I never thought it would spread to Amsterdam. This is not exactly a landmark block we are renting on, it has always been relatively speaking a slum. For the past twenty years, a Puerto Rican slum. I don't know what those poor people will do. I don't know about myself . . . it could easily put me out of business."

"I'm probably the one they want to get rid of. Tony landlords despise pet shops. They claim we bring the neighborhood a bad odor."

"But why? A pet shop is so . . . so life-affirming."

"Not to them it ain't. A pet shop attracts families and they don't want families in this neighborhood any more, they want single white professionals who'll pay through the nose. They want cute little patisseries with *pains au chocolat*, or another Haagen-Dazs or Tofutti ice cream."

"We already have three ice cream shops. How can they all stay in business, especially in winter?"

"First of all, they're charging a buck twenty-five per cone, and it's costing them at most a quarter. So there's a high profit margin, a fast turnover—much faster than rugs or pets. Plus, some of these jokers don't even last through the winter, they make their pile in summer and fold up their tents. Or they skip out without paying. The landlord doesn't care—he gets to hike up the rent thirty percent more for the next tenant. He's making his dough. Meanwhile there's no neighborhood stability any more, the faces keep changing, it's become a no-man's-land."

Cyrus knew all this, but he liked listening to Marge's explanations. "Well—what can we do?" he asked with a shrug. "Have you any ideas?"

"I've already spoken to a lawyer friend. This whole building used to be rent-controlled. Now it's listed as 'rent-stabilized.' I've got to go down to City Hall and dig up the records. Once I find that out, we can appeal to the Rent Guidelines Board. It's basically a stall, they can't do anything. But we can also go to the Division of Housing and Community Renewal—DHCR. We can call in the tenants' unions. I used to be a community organizer for a rent strike up in Morningside Heights; I've got lots of contacts. We can fight this thing. We don't have to take it lying down."

"Are you sure? I was under the impression that there is no commercial rent protection in this state."

"Sure, I know that, but there's got to be *some* statute pertaining to retail we can monkey around with."

"Somehow I have the doomed feeling the answer is no."

"So, at least we can make these guys *look* bad," declared Marge. "We can go to their houses in Long Island or wherever they live and picket their lawns on Saturdays. We can call up the papers and embarrass them with bad publicity, or call that people's advocate guy on television. Damn! What's his name again?"

"I am wondering whether they will raise my upstairs apartment rent as well."

"That's a very good question. If they raise everyone's rent in the building, not just the shopkeepers—this is a big building, that'll give us a much bigger pool of protesters. Then we're really in business! It ain't gonna be a picnic. I mean, this is going to be a *struggle*." The nostalgic enthusiasm with which Marge said the word, so unpleasant to ordinary people, conjured up her radical background in Cyrus's mind. "Anyhow, that's my proposal. What were you planning to do?"

"I was thinking . . . I would write them a letter asking them to reconsider." He smiled meekly, aware of how naïve and anemic this must sound.

"I'm sure a letter will bring tears to their eyes."

"No, I don't hope for tears. But I still feel we should give them a reasonable chance to understand how bad our situation will be, and maybe change their minds, before we start picketing and bringing lawsuits. I don't claim it will help. It is just the way I have to do things."

"All right. As long as I have you on my side afterward. Everyone on the block respects you so much, Cy."

"That I doubt. But I will do what I can. Anyway, it is sweet of you to say that." He started to leave but paused, sensing from Marge's face that she still had something to tell him.

"Oh, listen. I got some real cute puppies in. Can you use a dog?"

"A dog?" he repeated, with a pained smile. "I have a feeling— not. But thank you for offering."

"Okay. Just wondered. . . . Oh, yeah, I've been meaning to say. I have this friend who's opening up a Mexican restaurant on Seventy-ninth Street. She says I can come by any time with a friend in the first few months and it's on the house. Do you like Mexican food?"

"Certainly, Margie. Thank you very much for asking." He gave a ceremonious bow of the head. "Whenever you would like. I am usually free in the evenings. Any time that is convenient for you."

"Good, it's a date."

He turned again to leave. As he was near the door, she yelled out, "Geraldo Rivera!" Cyrus looked around, startled.

"Excuse me?"

"That's the name of the ombudsman on TV."

3

MEDITATION CARPET

BACK AT HIS DESK, Cyrus made a stab at replying to his landlords in longhand:

Dear Messrs. Hahn and Dromgoole:

I am writing to implore you to change your mind about my rent increase. ("Implore" sounded too archaic and servile, reminding him of Russian novels in which serfs embraced their masters' knees. Start again.)

Dear Mr. Dromgoole and Mr. Hahn:

Today I received your notification of a proposed rent increase. ("Proposed" would keep it in the realm of fluid change; nothing definite yet.) *I must regretfully inform you that I cannot pay it. Such an increase would put me out of business in less than six months. I can show you my books as proof and will be happy to, as a matter of fact.* (Big deal, thought Cyrus). *I do not doubt your good intentions for the building, but permit me to say that because you are new here, you may not be aware of the rich family*

history and traditions connected to this shop. (He crossed out
rich.) *My late uncle, Noshir Irani, occupied these premises for
close to thirty years, and he passed the business on to me seventeen
years ago, when he retired.*

Cyrus put down his pen. He was remembering how his father
had taken him for the first time into the city, to visit his Uncle
Noshir's store on the Upper West Side. He was ten at the time,
and the familly had just emigrated from Iran to the United States.
They were living in a little rented apartment in Jamaica, Queens,
all crowded together. His beloved father would take him and his
older brother Farokh on Sunday excursions to "American things":
rodeos, comic book conventions, baseball games. His father adored
Americana, more than Farokh and he were able to. But one
Sunday a month they would take the train into Manhattan to
Uncle Noshir's carpet shop. Cyrus loved the old-fashioned, musty,
backwater atmosphere of the shop, which reminded him of Kirman, the mountain town where they used to go every summer
to visit his grandmother, before they moved to the U.S. He did
not get homesick for Teheran much, surprisingly, though they
had lived there almost year-round, but he missed Kirman and
the dry desert air, and the cypresses and the pistachio trees (once
when he was little he had eaten fifty pistachios, and naturally
gotten sick as a dog); he missed the old Zoroastrian compound
behind the mud walls, that you entered through elaborate carved
wooden doors (THE GATE OF THE UNBELIEVERS, the sign said—
because they were not Muslims, his father had explained), and
the surprise behind those gates of pools and lush gardens.

Time stood still in his uncle's shop; he would dream over the
carpets, making up stories from the figures he had learned, with
Noshir's help, to decipher in the woven patterns: scimitars, gates
of paradise, trees of life, moons, camels, scarabs—adventure tales
in which he played the hero. Cyrus would listen to the two men,
father and uncle, talking between themselves, and watch the
proprietor handle with leisurely dignity and courtesy his American customers.

At fifteen he was already bored with the shop, preferring to study at home. He had become a scholar; his good marks admitted him to Columbia. Intending to prepare for a medical career, he fell under the wonderfully benign influence of an art history professor, McPhee Davis. Davis was not one of those charismatic lecturers who convert hundreds to his field, but his patience, his gentle, selfless passion for early Italian Renaissance painting touched Cyrus and made him want to imitate the man.

It was Davis's offer to recommend him for a fellowship that convinced Cyrus to go on in graduate studies at Columbia. There he studied Byzantine art with Meyer Schapiro, and aesthetic philosophy with Ernst Cassirer.

In some ways Cyrus was an exemplary graduate student, endlessly researching obscure trails to see where they would go; while staving off his dissertation, he supported himself (barely) with a teaching assistantship. After seven years of hanging around the library he had become a sort of departmental heirloom, as familiar a presence as the worn marble bench in the lobby of Avery Hall.

Cyrus had finally decided to write his thesis on Gottfried Semper, the nineteenth-century architect and theoretician whose influential masterwork, *Der Stil*, had never been translated into English. It was Semper's contention that the walls of ancient primitive houses were not made of stones but consisted of hanging cloth, either rugs or woven mats, on skeletal frames. This hypothesis led Semper into a far-ranging study of textiles and the other applied arts. In some sense responding to the same crisis Ruskin had decried, the disappearance of handicrafts in an age of mechanical technology, Semper took a less nostalgic position, and his rationalist views, Cyrus would argue, did much to shape modern progressive design. Cyrus wavered between writing a critical thesis on Semper's "theory of cladding" or attempting a translation of the two-volume work, which was noted for its peculiar, lyrically turgid prose style. Unable to make up his mind which course to follow, he began work on both projects at once.

In the middle of this double labor, his father died. Cyrus had always felt close to his father, a gentle, witty man who ran an import-export business, read history books as a hobby, and was, for all his professed agnosticism, a pillar of the New York Zoroastrian community. The funeral hit him especially hard. At about the same time, the woman he had been seeing for years, Gina, dropped him for a younger, more stellar graduate student. These two blows precipitated what Cyrus later thought of, with a certain warm indulgence, as his "nervous breakdown."

It happened not long after his father's funeral: he began to experience ordinary life as unreal. He would be sitting in the Hungarian coffee shop, a student hangout, listening to talk at nearby tables of committees and favoritism while underlining in his book with a pale yellow marker, when suddenly an overheard conversation would grind insanely on his nerves, or even seem to be coming from inside his head—he wasn't quite sure—and the sweet cappuccino taste with grated cinnamon would fill him with a numbing, buzzing dizziness: it was as though his whole body had started to feel as one's foot does when it falls asleep. His mind was a helium balloon, and he began to walk slightly doubled over, so as to bring his center of gravity closer to the ground.

Eventually he was taken to Saint Luke's Hospital for a two-week diagnostic period. When he got out, he stayed in his apartment for weeks, wearing only pajamas. Another crisis had been brewing for some time, which Cyrus had been keeping at arm's length but which he now embraced, in the vacuum begot by lassitude. It was simply this: he doubted he had anything original to contribute to art history. Would it matter in the least if he completed his dreary thesis? Compared to the real thing—Panofsky, Gombrich, Schapiro, Hauser—his learning was pitifully shallow, his grasp of theory would always be weak. Oh, certainly, he could find a niche for himself as a bibliographical mole, writing unnecessary papers to keep his teaching position, but what was the point? He no longer had the energy to camouflage his mediocrity, or to continue fighting the Darwinian struggle of graduate school. He would have to drop out. At least for the time being.

It was then that he thought up the plan of hibernating in his Uncle Noshir's rug store for a year or so. At the wake, his uncle had talked of wanting to retire. Now Cyrus approached him with an offer to let him manage the store, and eventually, perhaps, buy him out with whatever inheritance money Cyrus's father left him. Noshir agreed. The plan appealed doubly to Cyrus: he would be joining the "real world" at last (a reproach to academia), while at the same time retreating into a tiny, protected, overlooked corner of it.

Holed up in the sleepy carpet store on Amsterdam Avenue, Cyrus discovered he had a métier for withdrawal. This appetite, which seemed to him so poorly understood by worldly, dynamic people, could only partly be explained by clinical depression or "fear of success." There was also a positive aspect often overlooked, since no one withdrew *from* without also withdrawing *to*. In his case, released from the anxiety of needing to turn every passing thought into an articulate insight, he found himself with the freedom of drift through whole interior topographies. I have always believed, he reminded himself, that the highest value in life is introspection. Now I am merely acting on it.

At the beginning he kept telling himself, "I need time to think, I need *peace* to think." It was unclear, even to himself, what the goal of such speculative reveries might be: he sensed only that there was a dark, empty stillness he was trying to reach. In fact he did achieve states of gentle repose for hours at a time, when he didn't give a fig about anything. At other times, however, the demons of meditation would pay a friendly visit: vivid memories of his own shameful mistakes and other people's treacheries; "temptations" in the form of sexual fantasies or daydreams of success (a clever critical thought would suddenly sprout a dazzled audience, rising to its feet with astonished applause); obsessional list-making (works by favorite artists he had seen, concerts attended, books read) to keep the abyss at bay.

At night, he would review his conduct over the last twenty-four hours from a vantage point which allowed Cyrus to extract the maximum moral comfort a guilty conscience would permit. Sometimes he was overly harsh on himself. Other times he would gild the mundane, viewing, for instance, his lack of commercial prowess as a sort of heroic reserve, his powerlessness as integrity. It was as if he sought to console himself for the poverty of his life by saying: "I am all right. I cannot fail, because I attempt nothing." He even entertained the whimsical ambition of leaving no mark on the world whatsoever. In aspiring to this commonest of fates as though it were something perverse and unique, he betrayed the degree to which an old desire for recognition had not been totally eradicated.

He sometimes imagined himself a knight of culture. All through the world, he fancied, there were these "superfluous men," scholars without institutions like himself, brothers and sisters scattered in China, Russia, Europe, South America, Africa, whose mission it was to keep reading alive in a postliterate age, and to remember all the beauty that was in danger of being forgotten. Lesser-known but worthy artists slipping into obscurity had a particular hold on Cyrus; choosing them for study, he felt virtuous, like a volunteer soldier defending the homeland of culture. But if all of it was locked in his head, how would he perpetuate this knowledge, this good taste?

For a long time he clung to the hope of finishing his thesis on Semper while managing the shop. He imagined startling his old professors by returning with an unassailably researched, brilliant, footnoted dissertation manuscript under his arm. Even after he had abandoned the Semper project, he continued to take notes on articles he hoped to write for journals like *Hali* or *Oriental Rug Review*. One projected essay was to be on the evolution of the meditation carpet; another, on flatness and depth in Oriental rugs, and that paradigm's possible influence on modern abstract painting. But the frequent interruptions of customers and the general narcotizing influence of the shop prevented these fragments from ever reaching completion. Nor could he, after the first flush of inspiration, convince himself that it would make any difference one way or the other if he were to finish the essay. He had only to wait patiently, and a few years later he would see some other article writer tackling the same idea with which he had flirted. If the scholar did better than he might have with the same premise, he would be relieved that he had not rushed into print and made a fool of himself; if the treatment were less satisfactory than his might have been, he would feel a pleasure of another kind.

So the years passed. Cyrus put on a stomach paunch, while his eyes developed dark pouches underneath them, sometimes from insomnia, sometimes from oversleeping; and he developed that sad, teasing half-smile that often puzzled new customers. It was an attractive smile, drawing in the more sensitive stranger: a smile compounded of resignation, kindness and some mysterious superiority. The émigré smile, the smile of someone guarding a secret. But though a part of him might have felt he was in disguise as a shopkeeper, that he was still the protégé of McPhee Davis and the student of Meyer Schapiro, another part of him recognized that he had become, for all practical purposes, simply a rug merchant.

My late uncle, Noshir Irani, occupied these premises for close to thirty years, and he passed the business on to me seventeen years ago, when he retired. Since then I have been a reliable tenant, always paying my rent on time, never causing a problem. As you know I also rent an apartment from you two floors above the shop, and have maintained there as well an impeccable (he crossed out *impeccable*: occasionally he had been late) *dependable record of payment. The rug shop itself is quiet, dignified and caters to residential needs, as one would think especially appropriate for the ground floor of an apartment building such as yours. I might add that the garbage my business generates is minimal and non-odorous.*

He was already losing heart that this letter would serve any purpose. The wheels of real estate rolled on, seeking the greatest rate of return. How useless to tell speculators who had invested venture capital that they should demand less than the market could bring them, simply because of humanistic considerations. Cyrus could not bring himself to feel that Dromgoole and Hahn were even evil. They were doing what people did in that situation. He liked to believe that there was a time in New York, not so long ago, when landlords settled for a more reasonable profit. As recently as the early sixties, the tone of the city had seemed more blue-collar, more down-to-earth; the typical New Yorker may have been rude but he was also generous with the little he had; people here were proud of their expansively gregarious natures. Then this housing shortage had come along and distorted the character of New Yorkers, making them, for the moment, grasp-ingly opportunistic, suspicious and mean-spirited. But perhaps it had always been this way and he was simply romanticizing the past. Had he been fortunate to miss the worst of that normal brutality which the city was famous for, by having lived off the beaten path? In any case, he would no longer be so protected.

Up and down Columbus and Amsterdam avenues, expensive new stores sported elegant signages, white modular cube decors, hot pink neon waterfalls, cut vases with amaryllises and tiger lilies, papier-mâché opera sets for the display of boots or food. Cyrus's carpet shop looked like a mousehole in the midst of this packaging renaissance. Up to a point, being visually trained him-self, he liked the sophistication of display, but nothing could convince him to join in.

Now we come to the main point. Just then the doorbell tinkled and someone entered. Cyrus hid the letter in his desk.

It was Arnie, one of his rug fanatics. Cyrus had known many of these eccentric characters over the years, and some had even become borderline friends of his. A goofy lot, paying little attention to personal appearance, they saw the universe in the contracted form of woven rectangles. He could always spot these odd birds, usually male, the first time they entered the shop, because they would go right over to the most threadbare rugs and begin feeling them and sighing; they would squinch up their noses distastefully while cruising the newer, mass-marketed carpets. All this was an elaborate pantomime to impress the storeowner, who was then supposed to spend the balance of the afternoon trying to excite the connoisseur with his choicest wares. Most of the time these aficionados bought nothing—or if they did, it was usually on the installment plan. Their greatest delight was to talk knotting techniques, provenances, dyeing peculiarities, the differences between similar designs, and the nomadic patterns of rug-producing tribes.

Today Arnie was wearing an old torn oatmeal sweater and paint-stained gray corduroys. His Adam's apple was unusually large, or perhaps his bony, equine profile made it appear unfairly prominent.

"Where is your winter coat, Arnie? You will catch cold without it."

"It's not that bad out."

"Yes, it is. I worry about you," Cyrus said with a teasing smile.

"Thanks. You and my mother are about the only ones. Have you got any new stuff in?"

"I doubt it. When was the last time you stopped by?"

"About three weeks ago."

"Then I think you are acquainted with all my stock, I am sorry to say."

"Well, I needed to bring by the down payment anyhow."

"Of course. It is always a pleasure to see you." Cyrus accepted the two ancient twenty-dollar bills. "Would you like some Turkish coffee? Or a cup of tea?"

"Sure, either one," Arnie said distractedly, looking around

the shop. "No, better make that herbal tea. I'm trying to cut down on caffeine. Everyone tells me I'm too intense."

Cyrus noted Arnie's right knee hopping up and down while he sat, a curious nervous habit. "This will just take a moment," he said, and went to the back-room sink to fill the pot with water. He always enjoyed making tea or coffee for customers, a gesture which, so un-American in its prolonging of transactions, made him feel connected to the old bazaar rituals his uncle had practiced: the leisurely haggling, the offerings of food, the little spoons spinning like dervishes in the cups, the umbrage taken at a customer's "ridiculous" price, the slow arrival at a compromise figure. Most of this psychologial game did not suit Cyrus's nature, but he clung to the tea-making ceremony.

"Here you are. I think I have some figs as well." He dug around in his desk for a box of fruit and placed it on the chased silver tray. "So. How have you been?"

"*Mezzo-mezzo.* What do you know about the origins of the Lotto carpet pattern?"

Cyrus shrugged. "Just what the books say."

"I've been thinking a lot about animal carpets. And I came up with this theory that animal imagery actually forms the basis of the Lotto pattern. You know the experts only discuss Lottos in terms of abstract lozenges. Let me show you." Arnie reached across the desk for Cyrus's copy of Murray Eiland's *Oriental Rugs* and opened it quickly to an illustration. "Now if you look at one square at a time, you can see shapes that duplicate almost the dragon figure. Or here's a lion or a griffin, if you look at it from a certain angle. I also found two sunbirds and a serpent. Can you see them?"

"I am trying to . . ."

"At first it's difficult to. But then you start seeing them all over the Lottos. The trick is to take it one square at a time. It's fascinating!" Arnie drained his teacup in a gulp. "Nobody's ever pointed this out before."

"Mmm," said Cyrus, squeezing his chin doubtfully. "What would be the significance of such a discovery?"

"Well, it would mean there's a lot more persistence of the old animistic religions in the later carpets than anyone thought. But because there was a prohibition against human or animal forms at the time by the imams, the weavers who still clung to animistic beliefs had to camouflage them. It would mean all the books have to be changed."

"Have you consulted Schuyler Camman yet?"

"I'm going down to the public library this afternoon to look up Camman's 1972 article and a few other things. But I think I've stumbled across something."

"Good work, Arnie!" Cyrus stood up. "Can I get you some more tea?"

"No thanks. I've been thinking about that Turkish kilim you showed me a while back. Do you still have it?"

"I believe it's still here. Why?"

Arnie suddenly seemed nervous, as his knee jumped several times. He usually became that way when discussing costs or asking for a favor. Cyrus wondered which it would be this time.

"I was wondering, I was wondering if you would consider letting me exchange the Beloush I bought from you for the kilim."

Cyrus thought for a long moment. "I would need to see them side by side."

"I was going to bring it in, but I wanted to find out what you thought about it first—if you were against trade-ins on principle."

"No, I have only a few principles, and that is not one of them. Of course I would *prefer* if you bought the kilim separately. I will never get rich this way, letting customers exchange one rug for another when they are tired of the first. How much did I charge you for the Beloush?"

"Something like three-fifty. Three-seventy-five."

"I will have to go back and check my records."

"Meanwhile, can I see the kilim again?" Arnie asked tensely.

"Certainly. I just have to go in front and get it."

Cyrus fetched the kilim and rolled it out in front of them. It was rather frayed, with a tear in the top quadrant and the bottom selvages eaten away. He remembered a time before the fashion in kilims and antiquities, when most self-respecting buyers would have rejected such a piece right off on the basis of these flaws. But that shabbiness was precisely what appealed to Arnie, who would have disdained a robust, bright, thick-piled Persian in excellent condition. What lured him into loving this battered kilim, understandably, was the mellowing process, the inner glow of latent hues concealed under dirt, and the charm of the *abrash*, where the dye had unevenly faded, transforming the once-uniform marine blue into four separate sections like a color chart.

"It will look great once it's washed," said Arnie.

"We can repair the ends for you."

"I don't mind doing it. I'd be hanging it on the wall anyway. Is it okay if I put it on my lap?"

"Please, go ahead."

Cyrus regarded Arnie, fingering the kilim's back, with the sympathy of a man who has fallen out of love with a hobby— philately, say—watching another for whom the paper stamps are still magic. In the old days, he himself had spent his money foolishly on that small collection of rugs he kept upstairs; but the fever had passed long ago. The way Arnie stroked the kilim, petted and sighed over it, made Cyrus think that for many men, rugs were feminine. Perhaps it had something to do with the fact that the weavers were often young women, with their small nimble fingers.

"I love that greenish cast. . . . What do you think?" asked Arnie.

"I think it's a fine piece."

"No, I mean, can we work out an exchange of some kind?"

"Bring in the Beloush, and I think we can arrange some accommodation. Meanwhile, I'll reserve this one for you."

"Please! Don't let anyone else walk off with it."

"I shall hold it for you till the end of the month," Cyrus said with a smile.

AFTER ARNIE HAD LEFT, Cyrus opened automatically the book he had been keeping on his desk for distraction, the Goncourt brothers' *Journals*, and read a few entries. He found himself pausing at this one:

Flaubert, who was even more than usually verbose this evening and kept throwing out paradoxes, not with the ease of an Indian juggler like Gautier but with the clumsiness of a professional strongman or rather just an egregious provincial, declared that copulation was in no way necessary to the health of the organism and that it was a necessity created by our imagination. Taine pointed out that even so, when he who was no débauchée indulged in sexual intercourse every two or three weeks, he was relieved of a certain anxiety, a certain obsession, and felt his mind freer for work. Flaubert retorted that he was mistaken, that what a man needed was not a seminal discharge but a nervous discharge; that since Taine went to a brothel for his love-making, he could not possibly experience any relief; and that he needed love, emotion, the thrill of squeezing a hand. Whereupon we pointed out to him that very few of us were in that happy position, seeing that those who did not go to a brothel for satisfaction had an old mistress, a passing fancy or a legitimate wife, with whom there could be no question of an emotion or a thrill; the result was that three-quarters of the human race never had a nervous discharge, and that a man was lucky if he experienced it three times in a lifetime of copulation. From copulation we went on to spleen. Taine deplored this ailment. . . .

Cyrus thought how rare such "nervous discharges" had been in his case. He felt he had missed out on love, that he had not had much luck with the opposite sex. Yet over the years a number of women had been good to him, he had to admit. It usually started by their hanging around the shop until even he, the self-doubting one, understood they were interested. He sometimes forgot that he could be quite distinguished looking and attractive—exotic, perhaps—to certain American women. Drawn also, maybe, by the challenge of his kind, remote manner, they would feed him meals, listen to his dreams and disappointments and, in the end, fall in love with him. Then why did all these affairs seem so somber in retrospect? Because none had awakened his passion (except for Bonita). For the most part he had slept with women he had not been that sexually attracted to, doing it more out of "kindness" or self-consolation. But after all, Cyrus asked, what sort of woman would be drawn to an ineffectual man like me, if not someone frightened by a real show of worldly power and manliness—in short, a depressed creature, wounded in her own femininity. A Marge.

He pictured Marge in bed with him. What right had he to be so picky about physical standards? No, it had nothing to do with rights: he knew enough about himself to realize that, however lonely he was for a woman now, it would not work out with Marge. He would end up hurting her—and feeling cheated himself again. She was probably not interested in him anyway. He would go through with their dinner "date," and that would be the end of it.

From Marge, he found himself thinking about Kathleen, the woman Aberjinnian said had something funny with her leg—the woman Cyrus used to call in his own mind "the lame girl." That was an embarrassing business. Not that so much had happened. And yet, its very minimalness was somehow characteristic of his amorous situation recently. . . .

Embarrassed with these musings, Cyrus cut himself off and rummaged around for his accounts book: he wanted to see what he had charged Arnie for the Beloush. Inside his desk he saw a yellow legal pad with his handwriting on it. He had completely forgotten about the letter to his landlord. He read what he had written so far with almost disinterested curiosity. *Now we come to the main point.* Yes, what is the main point? He was lost in thought for some minutes. Then he picked up his pen, hoping that the feel of it would dictate something to him.

In this city, we are daily losing pieces that we care about, the cherished places that hold memory and continuity. A sense of tradition that makes it possible to live in and love an environment is disappearing, only so that the maximum dollars can be squeezed out of every property. You know this, and I know this. Not only are small businesses like my own affected, but ordinary tenants, poor people, are being pushed into homelessness, and ballet schools and other cultural necessities are being forced to close. Why are we doing this? What purpose can it serve in the long run? We will be destroying the very qualities of the city that have traditionally made it so attractive and desirable, and we will be left with a posh sterility.

It seems to me that disasters come in two categories, avoidable and unavoidable. The glass is rolling off the table—but it is not too late to keep it from crashing in this particular case. We can still compromise, so that you can go on with your way of life and I with mine. This is my own neighborhood, my place of work. Don't force me to leave it. I am sure it is only because you have no idea of the suffering you would cause—not only to myself but to the other storeowners—with this tripling of the rents, that you propose it. You have not thought it out sufficiently, you have not put yourself in the other person's shoes. If you do, you will see that it is not too late to avert catastrophe. To you, maybe, it would mean a minor loss. But for a man like me, close to forty-five, to have to start a new life—where would I go, what would I do? Please reconsider. Do not hesitate to call me at the above number if you want to discuss it further. You will find me a reasonable man, one willing to cooperate in every other way I can.   *Very sincerely yours,*
                                                 Cyrus Irani

4

THE
LAME
GIRL

CYRUS LIVED two flights above his rug shop. The building itself was a broad six-story walkup, and he knew many of the other tenants in it, by sight and enough to say hello. The old man directly beneath him had been a shoemaker. Cyrus used to listen to him clearing his throat of phlegm in the middle of the night.

Over a year ago, in late August, Cyrus had closed up his shop and gone away for two weeks. When he returned from vacation, Marge told him that the shoemaker had died and the apartment had already been rented. The new tenant was a nice young woman who wore a leg brace, according to Marge, and who had some sort of muscular illness whose name she had forgotten.

One night, Cyrus heard slow, deliberate footsteps on the staircase beneath him. He was anxious to meet his new neighbor, whom he already thought of as "the lame girl." This poeticized label conjured up something charmingly nineteenth-century: the consumptive courtesan, the lame girl, the sorcerer's daughter unable to leave her garden—fit objects of passion a hundred years ago. Cyrus was old-fashioned; moreover, it took very little to start him fantasizing about meeting the love of his life. But, since the hour was close to midnight, he thought it would frighten the girl too much to come upon him in a stairwell.

In due time he would meet her. A few nights later, he heard music from the apartment below and, unable to wait any longer for chance to perform its work, he grabbed a bottle of red wine and rapped on her door. It was six-thirty, a more suitable hour.

This way of introducing himself might not have been a very bold thing for another man to do, but to Cyrus it was garishly brazen. The wine in his hand appeared to him almost a professional seducer's implement.

"Who's there?" a frightened-sounding voice cried out.

"It's your upstairs neighbor, Cyrus Irani." He waited. Eventually a complicated round of police locks snapped and the door sprang open. A gaunt, redheaded woman about thirty years old, with a piercing stare behind tortoise-shell glasses, managed a gracious smile.

"Welcome to the building. I am Cyrus Irani, the man who runs the rug store. I live right above you."

"I hope I haven't been too noisy for you with my opera records at night."

"Not at all. I love good opera."

"I'm Kathleen, DeVoti. Half-Irish half-Italian."

"Please. I don't want to disturb you, but I thought you might like a glass of red wine."

"Oh, that's lovely. Won't you come in?" she offered, taking the bottle and looking around for a corkscrew. "I'm afraid I'm still unpacking and this place is a mess."

"On the contrary. It's beautiful, what you've done here." Wooden mini-blinds blocked out all exterior light, making the bare room dark and cool. In its center was a plum-colored Chinese rug, a tasteful one, and above it a ceiling fan rotated slowly. The bookcase, he saw at a glance, contained many oversized volumes on the world's great painters. Her interest in culture reassured him. At the same time there was something almost too sealed-off and timeless about the room. He associated its sepulchral air with her illness, though later he learned another reason: she was a night person, and, as with other night owls, her interior decoration was dominated by the need to create a chamber impervious to the sun.

They chatted for a half hour about the neighborhood, the building, the landlord and the wine. Then Cyrus left, feeling rather tired. It was the very particular weariness of one more amorous disappointment, followed by the need to make pleasant conversation.

Just as it took little to inspire Cyrus with romantic hopes, it took equally little to scare them away. In Kathleen's case, it had been the reality of a voice too strident, a face too eaten by physical pain. Nevertheless, he decided, she would make an excellent neighbor and possible friend.

So the next time they were thrown together by the mailboxes, and Kathleen invited him in for coffee, Cyrus accepted immediately, although he had been looking forward to an evening by himself. This time Kathleen was wearing shorts, and the metal brace over a withered leg was not easy to ignore. As if to acknowledge its presence, she began telling him the story of her illness. She had been twenty-five when she first fell ill, four years and twelve operations ago. "I was working as an office temp at a big law firm. I bent down to pick up something, and a time-bomb went off."

Cyrus thought at first that she had detonated some sort of letter-bomb, but a moment later he realized she was speaking metaphorically, probably echoing the language of her doctors. "My family has a genetic predisposition to this disease. It kills me to think of my younger sister getting it. She's already starting to have problems with her arm. You can be going along perfectly and then, boom, your leg gives under you. Or your back snaps out, and your whole life changes. It gets to where you're completely crippled. I'm lucky, I've come back from much worse. I can walk now. But I never know from day to day whether I can depend on my body."

"That must be very hard for you," murmured Cyrus.

"Oh, yes, but there are good things that come out of it too. Before it happened, I was drifting around confused about careers. Thanks to getting sick, I discovered what I want to do in this life!" she said, her face beaming suddenly. "I started drawing in the hospital, I had lots of spare time. And I felt like *I'd finally found myself*. I'm not saying Leonardo, but good enough to be a commercial illustrator."

"That's wonderful, Kathleen."

"Unfortunately, since then my arms have snapped out of alignment, so it's been too difficult to draw these last six months. . . ."

"How do you support yourself now, if I may ask?"

"I proofread a little. I edit trash. Odd jobs, piece work. It's better than welfare. I hated being on welfare. You can't imagine how degrading they make it. And having to go to the welfare office—sometimes when I was most debilitated, it would take me two hours just to walk the five blocks from my house to the center. I'd feel all my strength giving out. But I'd scold myself: What are you going to do, Kathleen, quit? Fall down in the gutter and stay there? One thing you discover: you've got that extra strength inside you! Another good thing: one *hundred* percent of your brain is taken up with reality. There's no room for phony sentiment or daydreams, you've got to concentrate on what's in front of you. Just make it another fifty feet to that lamppost over there. I also learned I could survive on very little money. Fortunately my little Italian grandmother, she taught me practical stuff like how to cut up a chicken and make it last for a week. I eat better than most people, and on very little money.

I've also learned you don't have to worry so much. Before I got sick I was always anxious about how I was going to pay the bills. You know something? It comes! Somehow the money arrives just when you need it."

"You have a wonderful attitude," said Cyrus. He excused himself soon after, feeling dizzy. Inspirational sermons always had that effect on him. Why was she giving him this pep talk? he wondered. Did he strike her as so beaten down that he needed confidence-building? He knew he wore a depressed, defeated air at times—not always, however. Probably she simply had this one story to tell, and felt obliged to squeeze in all the moral lessons, no matter who the listener. Well, she had a right to be proud of herself. What did he know about living with such acute physical pain? Still, he felt put off by her didactic, nutritionist's manner. Kathleen had once again refused to be the lame girl of his imagination.

EARLY OCTOBER is apple-gathering season. City-dwellers drive upstate to pick sacks of apples—for a few hours, and for a fee, transforming themselves into migrant workers. Kathleen's sister rounded her up in a borrowed car and drove her to one such orchard on a Saturday morning, with the idea that it would be good exercise. The next day, Kathleen knocked on Cyrus's door.

"You like apples?" she asked.

"Certainly!" he lied. In truth, he was not very fond of them. "Take as many as you want. I've got bags full."

Cyrus invited her into his rooms and picked out a dozen of the little brown-spotted apples. They were smaller and duller than the McIntoshes in the supermarkets, but for that very reason seemed more authentic. He thanked her again and again, casting about for something to do in return.

Kathleen was talking about a recent terrorist bombing in the Middle East, and how scary the headlines seemed lately. "I don't even like to read the newspaper any more. I wouldn't buy it at all, if it weren't for the music reviews."

"It must be difficult for you to walk to the newsstand sometimes when the weather is cold. . . ."

"It's not so bad."

"I could drop off the entertainment section of my newspaper on your doorstep after I'm finished with it. That way you won't have to waste your money or go out when it's snowing."

"You don't have to bother, that's too much trouble," she said.

"But I would like to," he said.

So they traded neighborly courtesies, rooted in misunderstandings. Kathleen kept bringing him small dented red apples from the country which sat at the bottom of his refrigerator, and he kept leaving his newspaper on her doorstep in the evening, although he suspected she had already bought her own copy. It would be even more ironic if his intended kindness should rob her of one of her few excuses for getting out of the house every day.

ONE NIGHT KATHLEEN KNOCKED on his door, asking if he would help her move something. Her favorite picture, by a friend, had developed a crack in its glass frame and she was afraid it would fall down on her head, or be ruined. As he followed her downstairs and into her apartment, he noticed that her voice was close to hysteria; tears filled her eyes when she pointed to the picture hanging on the wall. Cyrus took it down, assuring her that there was very little chance it would burst into a million pieces as she had feared. On examination, he saw the crack was a minor one; something else must be making her so agitated. The portrait was an idealized charcoal sketch of her, looking soft and young with hair down to her shoulders; he guessed it must have been done by an old boyfriend. It was the old Kathleen, before illness had left its shriveling mark. He reglued a wooden splinter in the back, more to calm her than out of strict necessity, and told her to take it to a frame shop if she was still worried; in the meantime she might lean it against the wall, on top of her dresser, instead of putting it back on the nail.

ONE SUNDAY AFTERNOON, he was entertaining Aberjinnian in his rooms. They were drinking tea when they heard a knock on the door. It was Kathleen. "I have some pumpkins from the country. I thought you might like one."

"Yes, certainly, thank you, that's so nice of you!" he said, the profuseness of his gratitude at the door in direct proportion to his eagerness to get rid of her. He did not want to expose her to his companion, who made crude come-ons to anyone in skirts. Or perhaps the reason was less chivalrous: he did not want to be seen with a semi-crippled woman in front of Aberjinnian, who always bragged about his conquests.

"You can eat it as a vegetable, or cut out the eyes and mouth and put it in your window as a jack-o'-lantern for Halloween. . . . Oh, excuse me, I didn't realize you had company!" said Kathleen, peering over Cyrus's shoulder. "I'm very sorry, I'll come back some other time."

"Please, don't be silly, what is there to be sorry about? Please come in and meet my friend." Cyrus ushered her into the flat, where his tea things had been set on the table, and introduced the two of them. "Charmed," said George, kissing her hand. "You didn't tell me you had such a beautiful neighbor, Irani. That's just like you, keeping her to yourself."

"Won't you please join us for tea, Kathleen? There are plenty of cakes left."

"No thanks," she said, looking flustered. "I just came by to bring the pumpkin. I'm in the middle of something."

"It's a pity you won't stay," said Cyrus, suddenly meaning it. "Sometime soon I would like to have you up for tea. Next weekend, perhaps?"

"Fine, if I'm around," she said, going out.

Kathleen had no sooner closed the door than Cyrus began explaining in an excited whisper: "She's shy because she is lame—she has something wrong with her leg."

"That I didn't notice. But I did notice that she has the hots for you."

"Don't be ridiculous. I knew you would misunderstand."

"Don't tell me ridiculous. That woman wants to sleep with you. The signs are unmistakable. This pumpkin, for instance, is her symbolic offering. You are to scoop out the vulva—"

"The trouble with you is that you cannot understand any motivation other than sex."

"What other motivation is there?" asked Aberjinnian.

"There are people who just try to make things better, kinder. She brings me fruits from the farm but she gives them also to the woman in the pet store. People live such lonely lives in these apartment houses—I am including myself—that there is no way to demonstrate connection. We have lost the vocabulary, there is nothing intermediate any more between aloofness and sex. Except for certain good people like her, who go around making things a little less bleak, a little friendlier . . ."

"Thank you for the sermon. That has nothing to do with the look that girl gave you," Aberjinnian said with a smirk.

"Maybe you're right," admitted Cyrus, sitting down. "Maybe you're right." And, pleased at the implied compliment, distressed at the prospect that he might someday have to reject her, he thought about the mess he had gotten himself into. It was all because of that damned wine bottle, which had given off the wrong signal.

AFTER THAT, Cyrus never passed his neighbor's door without a pang of guilt. At the same time he stopped leaving the paper for her. That gesture was too much one of pity, he decided. She must have come to a similar conclusion, it seemed, because there were no more knocks on his door.

A few weeks after Aberjinnian's visit, he passed Kathleen in the street. "Hello, how are you?" he called out warmly, but she gave no return acknowledgment. It was hard to tell whether she was in a fog or deliberately snubbing him. Her eyes stared straight ahead; she walked like a madwoman along Amsterdam Avenue.

Cyrus now worried that he had hurt her feelings so deeply it had unhinged her. Supposing she had been standing outside the door when he had told Aberjinnian she was lame? Supposing she had heard their entire conversation? Even if she had just heard the first part—oh, why hadn't he waited longer, at least until he was sure she was downstairs and in her apartment? Why was it so necessary for him, in any case, to blab to Aberjinnian about her disability?

Cyrus brooded a long while over the incident. If indeed she had heard what he had said, then there was no forgiving himself, he should have his tongue cut out. This blunder ranked with the dozen shameful errors from childhood onward that still had the capacity to keep him awake nights, atoning.

If, on the other hand, she had not overheard, then her failure to return his greeting in the street may have merely been a case of self-absorption. In that case, why was he being so hard on himself? He was exaggerating his importance. Did he really have so much to reproach himself for in his conduct with this woman? When he thought over their conversations, the remarks on his end had been polite and well-wishing—empty, perhaps, ultimately, but not malicious. Still, he could not get over the feeling that he had done her some unforgivable wrong.

It was a few days before Thanksgiving when he heard what sounded like Kathleen on the staircase below. He opened his door and called down on impulse: "Hello!"

"Who's there?" she yelled bravely, looking down, at first not realizing that the voice had issued from above.

"It's me, Cyrus, I'm up here!" She stared through the truncated perspective of bannisters. "It's your conscience!" he added facetiously—a strange thing to say, given the circumstances.

Kathleen broke into a beautiful smile. "Oh, how are you?"

"Wait, I'll come down." Cyrus hurried down the stairs to greet her.

"Did you hear I got a new kitty?" she said.

"Why, no."

"You must have wondered what all that noise and bumping around was. She's in the active stage. It's incredible what happened. You knew I used to have a cat, didn't you?"

"No, I didn't, but go on," said Cyrus, realizing that she was the kind of person who thought everyone knew everything about her.

"I had a cat for fourteen years, but in the end I had to put her to sleep. She had cancer. Anyway, after that happened, this was about a year ago, I decided I wouldn't get a cat to replace her right away. And now this is such a coincidence! Marge was walking her dog the other night and she heard some meowing. It was a baby kitten crying. So Marge picked her up and brought her to me. The incredible part is that she looks exactly like my old cat! My vet almost had a cardiac when he saw her. I mean, you've never seen two cats that looked more the spitting image of each other. Come in, I'll show you. I'm sure she's around here somewhere."

Kathleen opened the door and the kitten immediately ran to her feet. She picked the animal up in her arms. "Oh, kitty's been lonely? Hadn't anyone to play with? . . . She jumps on me when I'm asleep. Claws me. I don't mind. Now, you notice how there's a stripe over her face? My other cat had a stripe just like that, although this one's cuts across diagonally, and this cat also has 'boots' which my first cat didn't. But other than that they're identical!"

"That's amazing," Cyrus responded. He was glad that she was talking to him in such a friendly, chattering manner. It proved that he had only imagined offending her—unless, out of the goodness of her heart, she had willed herself to transcend her anger, the way a saint might. Whichever it was, he never found out. She moved away shortly afterward to Rochester.

5

HOLIDAY SEASON

A WEEK HAD PASSED since he'd received his landlord's letter; the store had suddenly gotten busy with Christmas Day drawing near. Sales were taking a healthy upturn. Occupied with customers all day, Cyrus put off thinking about his long-range rent problems. Irrational as he knew it to be, he hoped that the volume of business would triple and stay at that level, making it unnecessary for him to act further.

He was trying to steal a few moments with the crossword puzzle when the doorbell tinkled, as it had been doing all morning.

A shy young couple entered the store, staying put a few feet from the threshold. They looked Puerto Rican or Italian; newlyweds, Cyrus imagined. He liked them. With all his new customers, he had immediate intuitive flashes of like and dislike.

"Can I help you with anything?"

"We're not sure. . . . " The young bride looked at her husband for help.

"Fine. Take your time and look around. It might help to know what size rug you were interested in."

"It's for under a dining room table," the muscular young man said softly.

"Well, that tells me something. What colors did you have in mind?"

"I guess earth tones?" the dark-haired young woman said apologetically. "Like orange or beige. Not so much red—right?" she appealed to her husband.

"Fine. That should be no problem," said Cyrus. "And did you have a certain style or design preference?" Cyrus was going down his usual checklist, zeroing in like a medical diagnosis. Next he would ask about price.

"We don't really know much about Oriental rugs," said the young man.

"Why don't you step over here. Let's see . . . ," said Cyrus, gazing at his stacks. "It's a little hard to get away from red in the traditional Persians. But there are rugs with some red in them, and then there are *red* rugs. May I know what sort of amount you were planning to spend on this?"

The woman looked panicked. He realized he had asked the question too soon with them; it was all a matter of tact, he should have sensed it. "Well, we can just pull out a few rugs and you will see what you like anyway."

He had shown them five, and was in the midst of unrolling several other possibilities, when another couple walked in with an air of expecting immediate service. Cyrus wound up the conversation and left the newlyweds to ponder the choices alone, going over to this older pair. The woman was thin, pinched, with glasses and a mistrustful expression, as though she smelled something a little "off"; and the man was stooped, balding, also bespectacled, with a mournfully tweedy, academic appearance.

They were both very educated Upper West Side. Cyrus was not sure he liked this particular example of the species.

"We're just at the beginning of the shopping pwocess. We'd like to see something with an ivowy gwound," said the man, in a professorial English accent which turned *r*s into *w*s.

"We want to stay away from a central focus. No medallions in the middle," the woman said scornfully.

"We're not interested in a pwain open field with a medallion," her husband explained. "You see, we have a firepwace that's the center of attention. So we don't want too dwamatic a wug, with too centwal a focus. We'd pwefer something that will—in a manner of speaking—fade into the backgwound, yet not be too innocuous."

"And what sort of design or style, may I ask?"

"Geometric. Angled, not floral," the woman said sourly, as if he were trying to sell her yesterday's fish.

"You see, we have wather modern furniture."

"About how big is your room, please?"

"I don't think we can get much wider than ten feet because we start wunning into the firepwace."

"And it would help if I knew the approximate price range before we start. . . . "

"Oh—anywhere from five hundred to five thousand. To add to our awea of indecision, we could either go to a high quality Persian or—an imitation."

Cyrus began showing them some of his better rugs. The woman kept saying, "I'm not crazy about that green" or, "I'm not wild about that rusty red," in a hard, carping voice, while the man asked him questions. Usually Cyrus enjoyed playing the pedagogue—it was a role required of any rug dealer in America—but in this particular case, he sensed the man was picking his brains so that they could go armed with knowledge afterward to the rug district on lower Fifth Avenue. They had no intention of buying anything from him. "Excuse me for a moment, I must attend to my other customers."

The young couple had narrowed their choices to three. Now they asked the prices, and were pleasantly surprised that the rugs seemed to be within their budget—or, at any event, not far beyond. Cyrus helped them to settle on a favorite, and the young man wrote out a check. Why could not merchandising always be this way?

"Thank you so much. If you have any problems, just bring it back and exchange it for something else."

"Oh, no, we love it."

"I am glad. I only say that because sometimes the colors appear different when you get it home than in the store. I also recommend that you put a pad under it. That can double the life of the rug."

After Cyrus had tied up the rug and sold them a pad and bade them a happy good-bye, he went back to the critical couple.

"Would you consider a Heriz?" he asked, fully aware by now that all their knowledge of Orientals was a bluff.

"Only if it's very pale," said the woman.

Cyrus unrolled a superb one, among the best in the store, just to see how far their captiousness would extend. "This has your ivory background. It also has this wonderful gray which, depending upon the way the light is that day, can go toward blue or green. It's a very subtle design, very clever. Almost reminds me of a Paul Klee," said Cyrus.

"Are all the Herizes coarse like this?" she asked.

"Excuse me?"

She rubbed her hand against the wool, making a face. "It feels so scratchy."

"I'm sorry, but you are rubbing it against the grain. See what happens when you do it the other way. Believe me, this is good old wool, the burrs are still in it after years and years, which is a sign that it is hand-spun, not chemically processed wool. And this is all hand-knotted, not just 'hand-tufted.' Last week I saw in the paper, a big department store—which shall go nameless— had run an ad that said 'hand-knotted fringe.' Certainly," he smiled. "But the rug itself was machine-made. So you have to be careful."

"Why is it so thin for this price? Are all the Herizes this thin?"

"First of all, thickness is no indicator of quality—or longevity. Second of all, the more detail in the design, the thinner it has to be sheared to give it that clarity. All the thick-sheared rugs today have blurrier designs." Cyrus noted the woman's disbelieving expression; he was beginning to lose patience. "Let me explain something to you. The reason Oriental rugs are having such thick piles today is that they are geared for the American housewife, who is so used to broadloom that she equates thickness with quality."

"That sounds sexist."

"I don't mean it to be, I am simply stating a fact. Perhaps I should have said, 'the American customer,' regardless of gender."

"Yes, I'd like that better."

"What was the name of that wug we saw at John and Fwedewika's? That was spectacularly beautiful. An Isfahan—wasn't it? I think we'd rather fancy an Isfahan. You don't have any in stock, I suppose?"

"Yes, I do." Cyrus was thinking to himself: First they ask for something geometric, then they want to see an Isfahan, which is completely floral, the opposite! "Does it need to have an ivory background, or—"

"It doesn't matter. Whatever."

"And we also wanted to see Chinese art decos," the woman called after him querulously.

Cyrus stopped in his tracks. "I have a good adaptation of a Chinese art deco rug from the thirties, which they are manufacturing now in India. It is very similar in appearance, and of course a good deal cheaper than the antique. Shall I show it to you?"

"Yes. And the Isfahans, don't forget," the man said, pointing his pipe.

Meanwhile, other customers entered the store; Cyrus gave

less of his attention to the middle-aged couple as the afternoon wore on. When they left—empty-handed, of course, after seeing practically his entire stock—he was deeply relieved; but it surprised him that, even after all these years, such people still had the power to upset him.

WITH THE PASSING OF Christmas Day, business began to decline again. Cyrus was once again able to do the crossword puzzle in the morning.

Years ago he had contracted this habit, as something to do to smooth over the tensions of waiting for the first customer of the day—like a party host whose dread is that no one will show. Ever since then, the crossword had become his reward for getting out of bed. He would make himself coffee, go downstairs and open the shop, leisurely read the front pages of the *Times*, and then, when he had teased himself long enough, turn to the puzzle. There the checkerboard of black and white squares would greet him, his personal horoscope. If he completed it (or came very close) the day would go well; if it eluded him, he took this as a warning from the gods.

His method today was to let his pen flicker here and there, amorally jumping from one corner to another, filling in the easy answers first, like a landscape artist sketching in the broad terrain. Then he settled down to tackling the obscure questions, working in the opposite way, puritanically completing one section before allowing himself to move on to the next. What he loved about crossword puzzles was finding, by going through the alphabet and so on, that he "knew" something he was sure at first he did not. After trying the latch of his unconscious several times and getting nowhere, walking away from it, pretending indifference, he would circle back and once in a while mysteriously remember—a whisper from his reading, perhaps, that had slumbered in his brain's soft underfolds.

Today the "man" was being a pest, asking about African

beetles and Danish rivers. (Cyrus always personalized the author of the crossword puzzle, seeing him as someone with his father's gentle, testing features, asking a riddle.) Sad to say, thought Cyrus, he was probably on more intimate terms with the mind of the *Times* crossword puzzle editor, Eugene T. Maleska, than with anyone else's in the universe. He knew his pet questions (*aloe*, a healing plant; *Leto*, mother of Apollo), knew his rather questionable taste in music (d'Indy, Ravel, Offenbach), knew his touching loyalty for those discarded popular writers of previous decades (James Branch Cabell, Scholem Asch, Maxwell Anderson—how often had *High Tor* been asked?), his obsession with Chinese nurses and genetic codes, even his favorite television programs ("M*A*S*H" and "The A Team"). He pictured this Maleska as a nice man with thick, black-rimmed glasses who played the clarinet, watched TV with his family and tried hard to be a regular guy and keep up with popular culture, but who was burdened by masses of Latin memorized as a young man, haunted by pedantic trivia and the urge to make bad puns, which embarrassed his wife at parties. Cyrus sometimes pretended the crossword editor would wander into his shop, and he imagined whole conversations between them, at the end of which they both confessed their loneliness in life and became good friends.

Twenty minutes later, Cyrus put away the newspaper with a bittersweet sense of accomplishment and guilt; there was one corner where he had fudged a bit, not sure about the name of Nebraska City's county or the spelling of the click beetle. But he had come close enough; he would check the answers tomorrow.

"Can I help you?" asked Cyrus of the man who had wandered in.

"No, just looking." The man had on a shabby checkered overcoat several sizes too big for him—a shoplifter's outfit. He would have to be watched.

"You don't have any wallpaper, do you?"

"No, I'm very sorry."

A few minutes later the man left. Wallpaper indeed.

Cyrus took up a small rug lying by the desk. It had a few "bites" out of the bottom, and in other places was worn down to the collar of the knots. Still usable, but not in great shape. He had promised the customer he would do what he could. First he cleared away with a grill brush the fragments left by moth damage (though the rug actually smelled of moth balls, the owner may have only thought of that precaution after the worst was done). Then he adjusted it on the desk top, pushing aside for the moment his account cards, bills, rug reference books and personal reading matter. The desk also held a knot puller, scissors, thimble, spools of thread, pliers, beeswax, Stainex bottle and professional rug color touch-up pens. Weaving was something to do when he didn't have customers. It made him feel peaceful. If the pattern had been more complicated, he would have plotted out the design first on graph paper, but it was not necessary with this piece. . . .

The doorbell tinkled. He must have dozed off; he sprang from the chair. It was Marge. The sight of his neighbor reminded him guiltily of the letter he had still not mailed to their landlord, and probably never would.

"Please, come in! How are you? You are looking very well."

"I spoke to Mrs. Jacoby. She's pulling out," said Marge, coming right to the point.

"That's sad. The Lorelei Dress Shop has been on that corner ever since I can remember."

"Yeah, well, her clientele's dying out. Mostly German refugees, elderly. She claims she's been thinking of packing it in long before she got the new notice. Maybe Florida."

"I wish her well." Cyrus paused to read Marge's latest slogans. Over a sweatshirt that said, in flowery script, PUPPY LOVE, she wore a button with the message LIFE'S A BITCH AND THEN YOU DIE. "What about—?"

"Donovan's Tavern's doing good business. He can probably

meet the increase. He says we don't have a legal leg to stand on. He sees no point in protesting." She shook her head disgustedly. "I still say we should go out on a rent strike and pay the old amount, the *fair* amount, into escrow. You know our city councilwoman, Ruth Messinger, is trying to introduce a bill that would protect shopkeepers from exorbitant rent increases. And there's a state assemblyman, I forget his name, who's also sponsoring legislation like that in Albany. If we can just hold on till either measure passes, we'll be in the clear."

"But it is my impression that Messinger is much more liberal than the rest of the city council. What are the chances of such a bill passing, when the real estate lobby in this city is so powerful?"

"You've got a point. But what else can we do? We have to fight it."

Cyrus looked away.

"Come on, Cyrus! I mean, what are you going to do when it's the first of the month?"

"I am going to go to my savings bank, transfer two thousand dollars into my checking, and write out a check to Dromgoole and Hahn."

"You're going to give in that easily to those bastards? I mean, these guys are war criminals. It would be like supporting Dow Chemical during Vietnam!"

"I can't hate them the way you do, Margie."

"Fine! Be a saint."

"It's not that. Maybe I refuse to give them the satisfaction of hating them. I don't want to let their mentality crawl into my brain long enough to hate them," Cyrus cried, and then paused, reflecting further. "Maybe I am just less optimistic about human nature than you are, and so I get less angry. It's not that I forgive; it's something else."

"I understand. All right—but could you do me one favor?"

"Certainly, my friend, if I can."

"There's a guy named Fred Corry from the Coordinating Council of Tenants Rights who's worked specifically in this problem area of retail leases, and he's supposed to be dynamite. I've got an appointment with him Thursday evening. Will you go with me? Before you write out the check—that's all I ask."

"I will go with you."

6

THE ADVISER

AS IT HAPPENED, the tenant counselor came to them. He phoned Thursday to say he would be in their neighborhood, and it would be no trouble to stop by. So, after locking up the store, Cyrus went over to Marge's to wait. Fred Corry arrived promptly at seven: he had blond hair and ruddy cheeks and an athletic build and was wearing a cobalt-blue down ski jacket. He gave the rug merchant a vigorous handshake.

The meeting took place in the backroom of the pet store. Jammed with stenciled pet-food cartons, scratching pads and a mountain of kitty litter sacks, the storeroom had a dampness and sawdust smell which Cyrus associated with open construction sites. They sat on three uncomfortable kitchen chairs with cracked, gold-speckled plastic covers. Just as one might apply for welfare in shabby chairs, so this setting had the merit of demonstrating to the outside adviser that they indeed needed help.

Cyrus and Marge took turns explaining their situation to Corry, and then asked what he thought.

"I can give you a truthful straight answer or hand you a bunch of baloney. Which would you prefer?"

"A truthful answer," said Cyrus.

"The baloney," Marge wisecracked. "No, I'm just kidding. Go ahead."

"The truth is, there are more laws on the city books protecting stray dogs or winos in the park than commercial tenants. A lawyer may try to tell you you've got this or that loophole, just to milk you. If there is something in your lease that the landlord misled you on, you can fight it. Like if he said he would redecorate and he didn't."

"I can show you the old lease. I brought it with me," said Cyrus.

"Good." Fred Corry took out his reading glasses and skimmed it. "Offhand, I don't see anything you can use. This is just a quick reading, but—"

"I don't think you will find anything."

"You never know," said Marge. "Give it a chance."

"I'm not a lawyer. All I can tell you is that if he hasn't broken any promise to you, and your lease is legitimately at an end, he can raise the rent as much as he likes. You won't win in court. Your only chance is to demonstrate, organize and lobby through the political process."

"How do we demonstrate?" Marge asked interestedly.

"Well, it depends how much you can get the neighborhood to rally 'round you. Our best successes have been in ethnic neighborhoods, where the shopkeeper who's about to be displaced is performing a unique service to that community. Like the only Jewish delicatessen in an area with a lot of Jews, or the only bodega or Spanish beauty parlor in a section that's turning Puerto Rican. When you can stir up the whole community, then you really get action. Picket lines, noise, press coverage. I've seen it up in the Bronx or in Brownsville. It's worked beautifully. The landlord was forced to back down each time."

"I am afraid there are not enough Zoroastrians in this neighborhood to support me. But maybe Marge would stand a better chance if she rallied the cats and dogs."

"Very funny."

"Let me ask you something," said Corry. "What's the status of the upper floors? Is he going to co-op the whole building?"

"For the moment, no. I am one of the upstairs tenants," offered Cyrus, "and so far none of the residents has been notified of an increase. We are protected to the extent that the apartments at least are rent-stabilized."

"He probably won't. He doesn't have to. Three or four commercial tenants can support a whole building like this. Did you know an owner can double the value of a fair-sized residential building just by tripling the rent of the few commercial tenants on the ground?"

"No, I didn't. But that's obviously what they are doing."

"Commercial space is pure profit for the landlord. He doesn't have to pay a penny on it. In a way, your landlords are not the worst by any means. At least they told you what the new rent was going to be, they gave you fair warning."

"Yeah, sure! Three weeks' worth of warning," scoffed Marge, "to come up with two thousand extra dollars a month."

"I know plenty of landlords who will go right down to the last day before offering a new lease. 'Let's renegotiate,' says the tenant. 'No, on the last day of the lease we'll talk.' The poor guy can't sleep from the suspense. If his lease comes to an end he's only got a month to do inventory and sell his goods. So he calls up the landlord again and says: 'Look I know you said the last day but just give me a hint. Are you going to allow me to survive?'" Corry had jumped up to demonstrate, and now he was acting out all the parts with gusto. "So the landlord says: 'Screw you. I don't have to tell you anything.' And he starts listing past grievances. 'You remember three years ago when the pipes flooded and you were so quick to call me? That plumbing job cost me sixty-two hundred dollars. I don't even want to *talk* to you about a new lease until I get my sixty-two hundred dollars back.' Maybe he's not serious, maybe he's just toying with the guy, but the tenant doesn't know. He can't afford to get angry, he's got to control his emotions. I keep telling this one guy up in Harlem, 'Don't lose your temper.' He's ready to go after his landlord with a gun. So anyway, the day of the appointment finally comes. Now the landlord is friendly. 'I could get more for your place, but I'm going to let you have it because you're there and you've always paid on time. What do you got, a five-year lease at a thousand dollars a month? I'm going to give you a three-year lease at three thousand a month.' 'Please, please—' 'I don't want to argue about it. If you want it, fine. If you don't, get the hell out.' So the poor guy asks for a day to think it over. He goes home and he starts totaling up figures. The most he can afford and still stay in business is seventeen hundred dollars. He calls up the landlord. 'Can I please have another meeting with you?' 'Look, I'm busy. But okay—come in tomorrow afternoon.' The tenant comes into the meeting, he's got all his facts and figures neatly on paper. 'I want you to understand my position,' he says; 'I'm selling standard-priced goods. I've got a candy store. A newspaper costs thirty cents, I can't raise it just for my customers to fifty cents. Please, I'm not making any money *now*. Please raise it to seventeen hundred instead of three thousand.' But now the landlord turns around and says, 'What three thousand? I said thirty-five hundred. Miss Brown . . . ' He calls in his secretary. She corroborates his story. She wasn't even in the room the first time, but it's their word against his. 'All right, all right,' says the landlord; 'you can have it for—three thousand.' It's a comedy. Now the poor guy's completely fouled up. He had gone in there trying to argue down the price, suddenly he's having to feel grateful that it's only three thousand. But he decides: 'What the hell, I'll sign it.' He's sunk his whole adult life into this store, he just can't walk away from it. Now the landlord starts monkeying with the security deposit. 'I'll need two months' security.' 'But you just said one month!' 'Look, some businesses are being asked six months' or a year's deposit.' It's true. It's the interest off security deposits that generates capital to acquire new property. It's all a capital game. Anyway, let me finish. I just want to go through the whole story so you'll get a clearer picture. So the very first month after the new lease, the storekeeper looks at his books and realizes, it's staring at him in black and white: he can't make it like this. He's got to do something. What is he gonna do? He can't just sit there and die. Some people at this point take what little capital they have and redecorate, figuring they'll attract new clientele. But that's a big gamble—suppose he's kicked out? Others jack up the prices. Also a gamble. You've got old established customers that expect a certain price range, you can't suddenly double everything. The longer you've been in business, the harder it is to increase your volume, percentage-wise. That's where the newly established outfit has the advantage. So what do *you* think he does?" the adviser asked.

Cyrus, who had been listening passively to the monologue, tuning out at moments while speculating about the speaker's almost manic delivery, wondered whether the question was intended rhetorically or not.

"What?" prompted Marge.

"He works harder! He puts out flyers, expands his line, he lets his help go, he fires his bookkeeper, he does everything himself. That extra money's got to come from somewhere—his labor. Now he's working not just in the store, but he moonlights. He's tired all the time. He used to make love to his wife, say, once a week? Now he's lucky if he can do it once a month. Go on, laugh, I'm serious! It takes its toll. I see these guys all day, they look at their lives like they're going backwards. They're having to hustle just the way they did when they first started out, only now they're not kids any more. They feel so angry. It's un-American. The whole basis of America is reaping what you sow. But here's a situation where you've been your own boss, you've paid your dues, the long hours—right? It's been hard, but nobody's ever bossed you. Suddenly you become a serf to the landlord, you're netting fifty cents an hour. Some of these landlords come out and say: 'You're no longer working for yourself, you're working for me. I want you to start opening on Sundays.' The day of rest, the one time to relax, to be with the family—you've always taken Sundays off! The longest day of your life is that first Sunday you stay open. You keep watching the clock, you want to scream."

"Forgive me for interrupting you," said Cyrus, "but what does happen finally?"

"People get sick, depressed. They commit suicide. I lost a client of mine just last month—an old Italian, took his life. I still haven't gotten over it. Or they throw in the sponge and walk away. 'Hey, what the hell,' you start to tell yourself, 'maybe the landlord did me a favor.' You look on the brighter side. No more shoplifters, no more whining customers. But supposing you just can't quit. I've seen guys order on credit for as long as they can, then stick their creditors for a lot of money and declare bankruptcy. But it's not nice—the storekeeper scrambling around at the last minute to liquidate as much as he can. I'm sorry to sound so negative. I just wanted to give you the full scenario."

"Then what would you advise us?" Cyrus asked patiently.

"You *could* make a motion not to be evicted, but it won't hold up. It's a way of playing for time. I spend a lot of my days in court representing people like you. Let me tell you something funny, the fastest court in the city is the one that handles landlord–commercial tenant arguments. Why? Commercial tenants have no rights; these are open-and-shut cases."

"We could always move," said Marge.

"Sure, that's a possibility," replied Corry. "The only trouble is, you'd lose a lot of your old customers. And it's getting expensive everywhere around town. See, the kicker in New York now is the short lease. In France the shortest commercial lease you can get is nine years. In England twenty-to-thirty-year leases are routine. And England has antispeculation laws: you're not allowed to do anything with a building you buy for the first five years. But over here, the landlord's role has changed. They're no longer just renting space, they're shaping and controlling businesses."

"What about the Messinger bill?" interrupted Marge.

"Forget it, that died in committee. It wasn't that well-written a bill anyway. She didn't take my advice, her approach was too rigid. What I'm proposing, my council, is an eighteen-month moratorium on commercial rent increases and evictions—and in *that* time, get it put on the ballot. If we go directly to the people with a referendum we stand a better chance than with the city council."

"Why is that?" she asked.

"Why? When you have a one-party system with a popular mayor, there's nothing you can do. Nobody on the council wants to buck him. And he's the realtors' best friend. People have to get involved in the political process," Corry said tiredly. "That's the only long-range solution. You should come to our meetings." He opened his briefcase and handed them several flyers. "Because, as it stands now, we've got a system of complete injustice. Nobody pays a fair rent in this town—everyone either has a steal or gets ripped off. Even the corporations suffer: they have to pay their junior executives seventy to eighty thousand a year, just to cover the high cost of housing. One day the corporations'll say: 'What do we need this for?' Then they'll pull out of New York and the place will collapse. The realtors don't care. They can tear it down and build it up and burn it and rebuild it and make money every time. Listen, I gotta go to my next appointment."

"I admire what you are doing," said Cyrus, "taking an active stand and helping people. Perhaps you don't want to talk about it, but how did you get involved in this kind of work?"

"One thing led to another. I was always interested in social issues."

"I shouldn't be so nosy, but how do you support yourself, if I might ask?"

"I was working in an advertising agency and I got fed up and quit. I had some money saved up, and—I fell into a little inheritance, so I decided to take a year or two off and devote myself to this." The organizer seemed uncomfortable talking about himself, or embarrassed to admit to his hard-pressed clients that he was a man of independent means.

"Very interesting," said Cyrus. "Perhaps you should run for office yourself. You are certainly articulate and well-informed."

"Not me. Listen, I gotta go." He reached for his briefcase.

"I should've been a realtor," said Marge. "Fred, thank you for taking the time to come by and talk with us."

"You have given us a great deal of food for thought," said Cyrus.

"I wish I could have been more helpful." Corry smiled affably, shaking their hands.

7

FIRE TEMPLE

THE SKY ABOVE QUEENS always seemed different somehow from the one over Manhattan. He could not put his finger on it: homier, tidier, wider, more Dutch landscape than Italian? Whatever it was, the change in atmospheric light hit Cyrus as soon as he emerged from the subway. He paused, disoriented, gazing without understanding at the corner newsstand, the H&R Block tax office, the pizza parlor, the bar, the dry cleaners, the film-developing chain, the jewelry store, and the façades above the shops, the modest one- or two-stories in brown brick with white stone trim, before the quiet Sunday streets sorted themselves out and he headed in the direction of the fire temple.

He looked at his watch: he was twenty minutes late.

Cyrus rarely attended services any more—not since his father died, for that matter. But when he had telephoned his mother to discuss "a financial problem," she had proposed that he come out to the Jashan ceremony on Sunday. She was always trying to lure him back into that world. This time he saw good reason to humor her. "We can talk afterwards, at my house," she said.

The crowd standing outside the New York Zoroastrian Center included the usual faces: his mother's cronies, some second cousins and relatives; even those he did not know looked familiar. Parsi gatherings always seemed like an extended family affair, because of the shared features—the big noses and grinning, warm smiles, the twinkling black eyes and expansive hand gestures, the worldly social poise of a mercantile people, and underneath it all something cautious, tender, skeptical, nonviolent, almost frightened, as though they were never able to forget their numerical inferiority. Making his way past a table where they were selling sandalwood offerings, Zoroastrian literature, recipe books and posters of the prophet Zarasthustra (in a style Cyrus thought of as "Bombay late-gaudy"), he nodded and bowed with respectful vagueness to those around him, suddenly feeling a knot in the pit of his stomach.

"Excuse me, Mrs. Boatwalla. Have you seen my mother yet?" he asked a gray-haired woman wearing a brown-tipped fox fur over her orange sari.

"Already inside! You know how she cannot bear the cold."

"We are off to a late start, as usual," he said. "It seems all Zoroastrian functions must start forty minutes behind schedule."

"Say Indian, and you will be correct." ·

"So it seems." Cyrus gazed up at the January sky, thick with moody, unmoving clouds behind which blue slivers struggled to find an opening. "It looks like we are in for one of those cold winter rains."

"No. The forecaster on Channel Two says it is going to be snow," asserted Mrs. Boatwalla.

"Really? Snow again?"

"I am trusting the man on Channel Two. If he says snow, you can be getting ready for a good one."

"Another snow? Thank you for the warning," he said, bowing

his head in thoughtful parting, as if deeply grateful for this difficult wisdom which he would have to digest in stages. He hurried off, taking one last look at the crowd behind him. Most of the women wore slacks and sweaters under their wraps, but a few were in traditional saris, with *mathabana* scarves on their heads to keep all their hair hidden. The men for the most part wore sport jackets and car coats, the casual attire of American businessmen on their day off.

He pulled a wine-red velvet skullcap from his pocket and placed it on his head before entering the center. From outside, the building which housed the fire temple looked no different from the other yellow brick two-family homes in the vicinity. He passed the offices and small library on the first floor, and went upstairs to the prayer room. With its metal folding chairs and pale-green cement walls, it struck Cyrus as having the air of an unused, unfinished recreation room.

He saw his mother signaling violently to him. She had twisted around in her second-row chair and was pointing theatrically to the empty chair beside her. Cyrus advanced toward her with the embarrassment of a child being summoned to perform before company. His mother stood up, presenting her cheek to be kissed: she was a robust woman in her late sixties, with a figure still quite attractive for her age. Her black mink swirled around her shoulders, and it was the fur rather than her which seemed to embrace him.

"So, Mama, I'm really delighted to see you."

"It's been a long time I haven't had the honor to see you, my dear."

He ignored the sarcasm. "How are you, Mother?"

"Chilly. This place is getting ferocious drafts. They should really redo the sheetrock. And how are you?"

"I'm fine. I have no complaints."

"Did you see my friend Bapsi out there?"

"No, but I ran into Mrs. Boatwalla."

"Oh, that woman is such a bore! She is always going on about her dental work. She thinks her mouth is a priceless national cavern."

Cyrus chuckled obligingly, feeling the stomach pain again. "Is my brother coming?"

"No, Freddy is in Baltimore. On some sort of important business deal," Mrs. Irani said with evident pride. "And his family never comes to services here unless he drags them by the nose. You know that; they are like you."

Cyrus turned enviously in his chair to watch the incoming congregation. He would have liked to sit farther back, disappearing into a more inconspicuous row in the thick of the mass.

"What is the matter? I am only sitting here because my feet get cold and it is closer to the fire," said his mother.

She had read his mind, as was her knack. His irritation gave way to fondness, and he took her hands in his, rubbing them for warmth.

"That's good. Now if you could only do that for my toes as well."

"I am not going to get down on my knees here and rub your feet, Mama!"

"Ai, what is this younger generation coming to, they do not honor their parents, how much longer must I stay alive to be forced to watch such ingratitude . . . ?" she chanted in jest, imitating an old crone. "Seriously, you know I have never demanded that you respect me just because I am your biological mother. A parent has to earn a child's respect. That is why I have always been so—so *nauseated* by this American custom of worshipping mothers, all this Mothers' Day phoniness, what that writer—I forget his name—called 'Momism.' "

"Philip Wylie," Cyrus said absently, only half-listening as she continued. He knew these views of hers by heart. And disagreed: as far as he was concerned, he did owe her respect and gratitude simply because she was his mother. He wondered what lay behind her strange, almost pathological resistance to such filial tribute. It was as though she wanted her sons to love her more "romantically," as an "individual," quite apart from her maternal function. Now he began to identify the cloudy pained bunching in his stomach. It was fear. When he hadn't seen his mother for a while, he experienced her as overwhelming or domineering, at least in the first few minutes. Was it because of her aggressive, barbed style, with its potential judgments against him, or the sudden reimmersion into the whole Zoroastrian milieu, after thinking he had left it all behind? Whichever the danger, he decided to stay calm by applying an old remedy for panic: enumerating the particulars of his surroundings.

A stone floor. That was traditional, and probably necessary for fire safety regulations. The priests milling in front in their stockinged feet, on the raised pedestal. The altar table covered with a spotless white cloth, holding the fire brazier and wine, milk, nuts and fruit (the fruit would be sliced, he knew without seeing, to make it easier for the invited spirits to sup). The priests again, looking like operating surgeons in their white cotton tunics and caps, with white mouth-flaps to prevent spittle touching the sacred fire. Checking everything to their satisfaction, then exiting. Some latecomers taking their seats. An ox-shouldered man in a green polyester suit sitting directly in front of Cyrus. The stranger turning his bullock neck to smile apologetically. . . . Why were there no rules forbidding larger people from taking the front seats? He had often had that thought in concert halls or at the ballet. In the best of all possible worlds, he mused—but who was he to complain when he was not so tiny himself? He had fallen unconsciously into that old fantasy of thinking himself invisible.

Now the priests reentered, seating themselves cross-legged on the pedestal cloth. The service was about to begin.

The rustling and talking stopped. The room was quiet. An old man began in a high mournful voice to chant the invocations, while his three assistants rocked back and forward, mumbling in unison without recourse to books. One of the servitors, a tall bony-faced man, got up and began feeding the flames with a pair of silver tongs that held several sandalwood chips. Cyrus regretted for the hundredth time that he understood neither Pahlavi nor Avestan, the ancient Sanskrit-related languages of the prayers. There were probably not more than a dozen people in the whole congregation who could follow a word of what was being said. Nevertheless, all sat attentively, straining to catch every syllable. Whether this was piety or hypocrisy or both, all he knew was that it had always been this way: ever since he was a child, they had all sat patiently through long incomprehensible services in one or another dead language. No wonder the religion was dying out, he thought. Only a hundred thousand or so Zoroastrians left in all the world. We are the dodo bird of modern religions. The eighty people in this room are just a remnant of a remnant, huddled over a fire soon to go out. It is sad, he thought. Will the world even recognize when we're gone—even sense that some spiritual force is missing?

Cyrus spied two little boys, about eight, crouching on cushions by the front in order to see better. The one facing him had large serious eyes and was holding his head up in twiglike wrists like a marionetteer. His fists were pressed into his cheeks, perhaps to keep himself awake. Cyrus's heart went out to him. The boy would soon be undergoing the *navjote* ceremony, when responsibility for his actions would transfer from his parents to himself. A ledger page would be opened in his name, supposedly, to record all his good deeds and misdeeds. Cyrus remembered his own initiation ceremony, when he was eleven. His foot had fallen asleep from sitting cross-legged so long, and when the *mobed* had raised him up to slip on the ceremonial undershirt, the *sudreh*, and tie the belt, the *kusti*, he had stumbled and couldn't stand straight. They had had to wait while a priest rubbed his leg to restore circulation. Everyone had made jokes about it afterward.

Actually, it was not so boring at that age. He remembered

that, when he was little, in Teheran and Kirman, he had liked going to the fire temple. The droning voices put him in such a dreamy state that his mind floated wherever it wished and no one could get to him. The flames had danced and capered before his eyes. He had been most religious when he was eight or nine years old.

In this section of the ritual, Cyrus remembered, they were invoking the Bounteous Immortals to descend and bring their blessings. Jashan was a thanksgiving ritual that might occur at any time in the calendar: usually someone had gotten married or had moved into a new house, or was celebrating a flush business period. Cyrus wondered which of the prosperous families to his left or right had paid for the ceremony this time.

He glanced inconspicuously at the women in the congregation, to see if there happened to be any beauties present. At first a slender, intense young woman caught his eye. She was rather flat-chested but she had a certain integrity and seriousness of demeanor. Young, perhaps still a high school girl: she wore a turquoise scarf with a flying geese pattern, perched high on her curly hair. She bit her lower lip and was leaning forward, mouthing some of the prayers by heart. Orthodox, must have arrived recently from Bombay or Karachi—she would never approve of an old unbeliever like me.

His attention wandered to a more buxom, mature beauty— a cuddly charmer, with bare dimpled midriff provocatively peeping out of her sari. She was obviously Parsi (from the Indian subcontintent), like the majority of Zoroastrians; his own people belonged to the Irani minority. In early adolescence he had lusted after just this kind of raven-haired, full-breasted, beauty-marked Parsi with large velvet eyes—still his sexual ideal. The woman he was looking at had a little boy in her lap playing with her head covering, pulling it a little at a time. Eventually it slid off. She shook her chin at him no-no, very calmly, and placidly readjusted her shawl. God would surely pardon a woman whose head comes uncovered during prayers, thought Cyrus, because her mischievous little boy wants her attention. A minute passed, and the boy seemed to be working up his courage for another experimental yank, when his mother caught him with a warning stare, just fierce enough to pin him.

In the midst of wondering how mothers went about developing effective sequences of admonitory glances, Cyrus reproached himself: Pay attention to the service. This was a good opportunity to cleanse his mind. Even if he could not follow the literal meanings of the prayers, he could still practice a sort of amateur's meditation, directing his thoughts away from the everyday worries fatiguing him. *Good thoughts, good words, good deeds—* how many times had he heard this trinity declared the essence of Zoroastrianism. It had been pounded into his head when he was small. Later he had rebelled, thinking, What could be more trite than that meaningless formula? Good thoughts. Good words. Good deeds. So what? This is not theology, this is advertising copy. *The good religion*, they call it. That's not an ethical doctrine, it's self-congratulation. And yet—how badly he wanted still to believe in it, at moments like this, surrounded by the others praying, listening to the ancient monotonal chants. He often had a yearning toward—he didn't even want to put a name on it lest it jinx him, or tempt him into the smugness of the born-again; and yet it remained inside him, an unattended calling for reverence. No, even that was going too far: just the hope for a little spiritual understanding. Over the years Cyrus had read Sufi texts and the Christian mystics and something of Buddhism; he had tried Zoroastrianism again, delving into the Gathas and the scholarly books by Mary Boyce and Zaehner. But in the end it had all seemed more of an intellectual exercise than something that really touched him and thrilled his soul.

In some ways Zoroastrianism struck him as a very strange religion, in other ways a sensible one. He preferred the Zoroastrians' forthright dualism, which pitted a good but limited god against a destructive spirit. The notion that the Creator God, Ahura Mazda, was not all-powerful, at least got around the problem of evil that had perplexed the three great semitic religions. In Zoroastrian belief there was no vantage point from which suffering and death could be seen as part of God's grand design; suffering and death were bad, pure and simple. Cyrus found this refreshing. The Zoroastrian God would never have afflicted a man like Job merely to test his faith; man was put on earth to be enlisted as an ally against the Destructive One (Ahriman) and his demon hordes. It was up to each man to choose the good path or the bad. His deeds would be tallied up at the Bridge of the Separator, and if he had been more good than bad, a beautiful maiden would lead him across the bridge; if sin had predominated, a withered old crone would take him by the hand down to hell. At the end of time a superman saviour would come and help crush the evil spirits, there would be a complete resurrection of the dead, and the good people would return to earth, in the now-perfected creation, to eat "the butter of early spring."

Zoroastrian cosmology tales had an undeniable charm. On the other hand, he did not see how a rational person could accept these myths as anything more than folklore. And many old customs seemed too clearly the remnants of a pastoral tribal religion, dating practically from the Stone Age, for Cyrus to take them seriously. Back in India and Iran, the traditionalists were still purifying themselves by drinking bulls' urine, and leaving the dead out in a tower to be picked clean by vultures. Granted, these things were no longer done by Zoroastrians in America. The health department would never have permitted a tower of silence in Queens—even in Flushing Meadows, where they dumped everything else. But there was still that comical obsession with impurity, like fussing over whether it was acceptable to throw a surgically removed appendix into the hospital wastebasket, or whether it had to have its own Zoroastrian rites of disposal.

He remained drawn to some of the old rites; he admired the

Zoroastrian gentlemanly code of charity, hospitality and toler-
ance; and he loved the idea of paying homage to the fire. But,
thought Cyrus, I cannot build my own personal religion out of
bits and pieces I find appealing, like a supermarket consumer.
As long as there is so much that remains incomprehensible or
barbaric to me, I must reject it, or at least remain a skeptic.

And yet, mightn't it all make sense if I did the practice with
simplicity and obedience? Perhaps if I had studied the religion
more deeply, my objections would go away, and another level
would open for me, much more profound and symbolically sat-
isfying. Like the carnation the old man is handing now to his
assistant: I seem to remember that seven flowers are passed back
and forth during the ceremony, each with its own special meaning. That's the trouble, everything has a meaning: the pattern of
sitting and crouching, whether it's the priest who kneels or stands
over the others. How would I ever memorize all that? No, in
any case, what I lack is not scholarship so much as faith—the
immediate, direct grasp of the gesture as truth. I wonder if my
art-history training, with its emphasis on iconographical interpretation, gets in the way of that now, or if I chose art history
because I already. . . . For instance, the *good* Zoroastrian un-
derstands that at this moment the dead spirits who were summoned by prayers are being fed—in reality, not symbolically.
But maybe if I dedicated myself to a teacher, an old priest whose
wisdom I respected; a guru. I'm afraid it may almost be too late
for that. . . .

Twisting and chafing against the old arguments, Cyrus found
he was making himself queasy with doubt. He vowed to still his
mind again and pay complete attention. The chanting had lowered to a murmur. The smoke had begun drifting to the left of
the fire. It curled in a column stopped only by the ceiling. There
were dark brown smudges above, like abstract frescoes, from the
smoke stains. Once or twice a year they would whitewash the
walls. He felt a tickling in his throat, the beginning of an urge

to cough. Usually there was a cacaphony of coughing in these services, like a concert recital when the audience registered its resistance to settling down. That made him so angry; he hated the way subscription audiences behaved at Lincoln Center. (Pay attention, Cyrus told himself. Stop thinking about concert halls.)

He was getting tired of straining his neck to see around the ox-shouldered man in front of him. His own shoulders felt stiff as a result; he decided to sit back for a while, making do with the chink of negative space left by the gap in bodies. From here he could see only the orange-red reflection of the fire, flickering against a white background which must have been the priests' robes. So be it. Perhaps this pretty, ambiguous shadow against a blur is all that God intends for me to see today. A parable of my own dim understanding, like Plato's cave parable, thought Cyrus. Oh, stop it.

But what, after all, was there to see? Would I be any closer to a religious experience if I kept straining my neck to get an unimpeded view of an old man and three younger ones positioning themselves around the fire? I can hear their droning fine, he thought as he closed his eyes.

Eventually he opened them again to stare at the stout man's suit jacket. Along that great oceanic expanse of green, an uneven spume of dandruff flakes had been churned. Cyrus had half a mind to dust off the man's jacket. What if he did? The man would probably take offense, and he would have to pretend it had been an accident, his arm accidentally skimming the material. It would be just as efficient to transform the dandruff mentally into something harmless, or calmly attractive, like snow-flakes.

Had it started snowing? He looked toward the side window. No, not yet. Perhaps the weatherman was in error this time, and Mrs. Boatwalla would lose faith in him. . . . He thought of how Bonita, his former girlfriend, used to love snow. Particularly late at night. She would crawl onto the roof ledge of the adjoining building from her window on the sixth floor. "Come on." She'd signal him to join her, but he did not trust the tar overhang. Only once did he go out there with her, and then only stayed for two minutes. The rest of the time, "I can see it just as well from inside."

That was typical of their differences. She liked to stay up half the night watching the snow dart against the lampposts like mosquitoes, while he could barely keep his eyes open after one in the morning. She always left her bedroom window open a foot, even in the coldest months. She was a great believer in the night air. He came to associate spending the night at Bonita's with shivering. They would bundle beneath her futon quilt, the mattress hard against the floor, surrounded on all sides by her stacks of books (she read everything, that was one of her most endearing traits) which stood guard during their sleep, and which sometimes the wind tumbled over with a crash in the middle of the night.

Around six in the morning, the pigeons would settle in to coo on her window ledge. It was both romantic and a nuisance, because they woke him up early. He would watch dawn light break through the window, metamorphose with infinitesimal slowness from black to deep purple to milky aubergine to skyblue. Often he would lie awake for hours next to Bonita, who liked to sleep in late. Hers resembled a drugged sleep: her flesh became very hot, as though she were running a low fever, and it developed a soft, docile texture, like a newborn's. Her skin had a scent all its own, he had never come across anything like it before or since—it reminded him uncannily of lemon chicken with raisins, a dish he had loved as a child. He once told her that and she laughed. "You're goofy," she said, tapping him indulgently on the arm. Goofy or not, he had wanted to eat her up; the tangy smell of Bonita's body had an irrepressibly aphrodisiac effect on him. As she dozed late, Sunday mornings, usually on her left side, frowning and gurgling slightly through her nose, he would lean over and kiss her lips, chapped with morning dryness and coated with the taste of sleep. Then he would cup her breasts.

"Mhmm . . . mmmhm," she would plead.

"Good morning."

"You're awake, aren't you?" she would mumble incredulously, from the depths of her dream.

"I can't sleep. I'm too aroused by your beauty."

"Gimme a break."

"It's late. It's five after ten. I promise that if we make love, I'll go back to sleep."

"Too much trouble. I'm not bothering . . . put in more goo."

"I'll get it for you. Please?"

"Still have to get out of bed . . . go down the hall . . . bathroom." Yawning, she was beginning to speak articulately, in spite of herself. "You're such a pest."

"I don't mean to be." He began rubbing his hand along her bottom, moving from there to the inside cushion of her thigh. Then he buried his face in her hip.

"You're bound and determined, aren't you? . . . Oh, all right. I feel like a Catholic housewife." She would leap out of bed, dropping an old peach flannel nightgown over her head, and give him a good-natured head-shaking smile (at least in the days when they were still getting along).

The mole she had on her inside thigh—he suddenly pictured it. It was more like a cyst, a little loose flap of ochre-colored skin. Her legs were rather bowed and fleshy, like a Japanese woman's, which excited him. With no difficulty at all he could summon now the exact dampness on her pubic curls, those pearls of moisture. He recalled how she moved sometimes in those morning trysts, half-asleep, voluptuously delayed like a somnambulist. Suddenly he was envisioning an entire lovemaking with her, from start to finish. Cyrus's throat swelled as he gave himself over to this involuntary but precise sense-memory. He felt his groin tightening and hardening, marked the constriction in his chest, held his breath and licked his lip in longing and anticipated delight. All at once he became ashamed, aware of his mother beside him and the prayer room. Supposing she *could* read his mind? He pushed the thought aside, returning with effort to the two of them in bed: Bonita's eyelids fluttering as they did when she was coming to her moment, from somewhere frighteningly far away. She seemed to be under a heavy trance (especially when she had drunk a lot); there was a demon of sluggish, morbid darkness pulling at her—the urge for oblivion. Whatever it was, he had seen that death instinct in her and felt a horror, as though he were committing necrophilia. It was upsetting, even now, to think he might have been turned on by her resemblance to a drowned woman pulled from the river.

Later, toward the end of their affair, she became depressed and would not let him touch her. She would sleep half the day, get up at noon or later with cold sores on her mouth, and sit in a chair reading a book. When she had finished the book she would toss it on a pile and pick out another, stopping only long enough to make herself some tea or bean soup. He would come home from the shop to find her still in her flannel nightgown. Sometimes she would ignore him, as though he had committed crimes too despicable to discuss; at other times she would stay up half the night analyzing his faults of character. She accused him of never understanding her, of tactlessness, of being somehow less than her idea of a man. And of course he had made stupid mistakes. He admitted them; but no matter how he tried to apologize or comfort her she would remain both desolate and hysterical, curled up in an inconsolable ball, insisting that he was trying to drive her crazy with "simulated reasonableness."

I must stop thinking of Bonita, he told himself, groaning aloud. That was five years ago!

Large scraps of flaming ash had begun rising into the air. Some drifted outward over toward their seats. The smoke was making his eyes water. (At least she didn't kill herself, thank God for that.) Cyrus panicked suddenly, having the sensation of being trapped at the bottom of a well filling with smoke and remorse. An urge had been building inside him to move from the second row to somewhere farther back, and now he could no longer put it off. Cyrus whispered to his mother that he needed to move. She nodded.

He crept toward the back where the latecomers were standing. They smiled at him in camaraderie as he joined them. How beautiful the fire looked from here. He was glad to have a more detached perspective, a view of the whole. Perhaps because he was nearer the door, he also felt a greater sense of choice, as at the railing behind the parterre in a movie house where outgoing patrons linger to rewatch a scene, while newcomers pause momentarily, unwilling as yet to commit themselves to a seat and be lost in the story.

The old priest was making circular motions with his tongs over the water pot. Cyrus envied him; he wished sometimes he were old like that and had outlived the burden of his sexuality. This was not the same priest who had officiated at his father's funeral. That was Mr. Modi; as children they used to laugh at him behind his back, calling him "Mr. Moto." Modi would sometimes accept invitations to their home on holidays, saying very little but grinning piously and eating enormous amounts. Cyrus's family was not very devout, yet his father was the first to offer his house for any Zoroastrian social gatherings. It had been quite enough for his father to see himself as a good religionist by identifying with the social and cultural—one might even say the ethnic—aspects of Zoroastrianism. Cyrus remembered how feelingly his father would speak about the persecution they had suffered under Moslem rule at the turn of the century, when he was a boy in Kirman: "The worst was the *jizya,* that terrible poll tax we had to pay as non-Moslems. But we were also forced to wear dark, dreary clothing, we were forbidden to wear stockings or ride horses. If a Zoroastrian riding a donkey should happen to pass a Moslem, he was forced to dismount. We were not even permitted to carry umbrellas—don't ask me why! And yet, our quarter was the cleanest, the most orderly. We had a council of leaders who handled all disputes. We lived almost apart from the Moslems and we governed ourselves. We were poor, yet we always had a water supply, even when everyone else's had run out."

Cyrus would ask him about violence. "Yes, certainly. There were times when mounted horsemen would attack our people, especially those that went outside the gates. But Riza Shah—the old shah—was a friend to us. He favored Zoroastrians. Through us he could feel connected to the glories of the ancient Persian empire. Whatever the reasons, we were happy. Then, when he abdicated in 1941, some of the limitations on Zoroastrians got reimposed. After a long while of putting up with it I saw there was no future for us there. So I brought you to the U.S. And I am very glad I did. This country is the best on earth."

Cyrus smiled, remembering his father's unshakable patriotic affection for America. He was not one to be disenchanted easily by a breach of idealism. He always gave wonderfully moderate advice, like: "If you make an enemy, we don't say it is necessary to turn the other cheek, just stay away from the person."

Dear Father, thought Cyrus. Even on his deathbed he was trying to teach me. That time when I visited him in the hospital, and he said to me out of nowhere something like, "Contentment is our highest wisdom." What was it? "The first duty of a Zoroastrian is to enjoy himself in life. We are not ascetics, Cyrus." He was worried about me. At the time I thought he was looking through rose-colored glasses, to deny the reality of his own physical agony. . . . Now I understand; I have committed the cardinal Zoroastrian sin: pessimism. If only I had had the sense to inherit my father's zest for living. If he had only stayed around longer to teach me.

Cyrus let out another groan. He was embarrassed to see the

man beside him take note of this involuntary confession. In another minute, he realized, he would be unable to stop his thoughts from approaching that slope of grief which represented a danger for him in any reverie. Cyrus blinked his eyes several times (the smoke, he might have explained) and, a moment later, succumbed. His heart opened to receive the comforting pain.

In the hospital room the light was blue. There was a strong smell of Lysol; they always mopped the floors around dusk. The place was overheated—or felt that way because he had always just come in from outside. He tiptoed to his father's bed, where there was a glass and water pitcher on the night table, and a brown instrument box like a radio with a set of dials to call the nurse or someone else; he'd never inquired. His father's arm was hooked to an intravenous bottle; the liquid went *glub-glub*, little bubbles traveling up and down the glass spine. He always thought of how a person can die from having an air bubble injected into him. Already he would want to go, to have the visit over, to be taking the elevator down. His father opened his eyes, looking dour, cross with him, but Cyrus knew this expression was caused only by his not wearing his glasses. Or maybe the bed needed adjusting; he was tempted to play with the buttons and send his father up or down chaotically, as if that sudden animation might clear the air. A pale green curtain divided his father's from the next man's bed. "Mind if I . . . ?" Cyrus said, half to his father and half to the roommate, while pulling the curtain for privacy. The other man, an old Latvian dying of cancer, gave him a look of paranoid loathing. Cyrus hated this monkey sharing the room with his father. He rarely had violent thoughts but he would have liked to take a crowbar to this other patient's skull, or strangle him with his bare hands.

"Sit, sit," his father said. He'd lost a shocking amount of weight. Without the dark-rimmed glasses that held his face together, his father's usually wry, collected features looked undefended and diffuse. "Father, don't you want to wear these?" asked

Cyrus, offering him the bifocals on the night table. His father swallowed hard (Cyrus had never appreciated until that moment what an act of endurance and will power swallowing might take), and managed to get out: "Not now. I don't need them." This last sentence made Cyrus want to burst into tears; he kept pressing his father to put on his glasses, as if that would cure everything. His father's skin had turned sallow and his head was curved and beaked. His arm attached to the intravenous looked pathetic, like a boiled chicken wing. It did not seem possible for a human being or any creature to live longer than a few days in that condition. The nurse entered the room, and his father's eyes reached for his. It was unnerving and yet fascinating to stare into the expression of a person slipping over the edge. A privileged glimpse of death. As his father's eyes, those of an anxious setter, clung to him, he responded with the most foolish, the most self-conscious of smiles. . . .

Cut it out. That's enough. Cyrus shuddered.

There was one part he liked in the funeral, in that whole nightmare. That was when he and the other corpse-bearers, his brother and his uncle and the priest Mr. Modi, were all tied collectively by one sacred sash, according to custom. Roped together so that they had to choreograph their movements as they rested the body on three stone slabs, they reminded Cyrus of astronauts in space sharing a companionship of weightlessness made possible only by death. He wished for that moment that he could stay tied indefinitely to the other men, without ever having to return to solitude and decision.

He hadn't cried. He was exonerated by the Zoroastrian belief that sorrow and grieving were bad, and that tears should be kept to a minimum, lest they impede the soul's progress. His mother, however, had cried copiously. Cyrus remembered with fresh bitterness how she had turned only to his older brother that day for comfort, practically ignoring him. Something had gone wrong between his mother and him around that time, a shared mistrust had developed which they had never put right. But why am I so petty? thought Cyrus. Why can't I just forgive her for the way she treated me all those years ago?

"Would you like to look at my prayer book?" asked the man standing beside him.

"Thank you," said Cyrus, wiping at his tears. "It's this smoke, I can never get used to it." The man nodded kindly. Cyrus began turning pages in the Avesta, glancing at the right side which held English translations, grateful to have the distraction of a book in his hands. He was not really sure what he was looking for; but just as people open the Bible or the I Ching at random, hoping for guidance, so he wished he might come upon a relevant passage by chance. He stopped at a prayer of contrition. Reading it slowly, word for word, so that the words might sound in his mind as his own thoughts, he suppressed for once the urge to question problematic passages. He sensed that only if he read it all with equal reverence, solemnity and sincerity, only in this way could the prayer offer any comfort.

> . . . *I repent, am sorry, and do penance for any sin I may have committed against my superiors, the religious judges and rectors, or the leaders of the Magians. I repent, am sorry, and do penance for any sin I may have committed against my father and mother, sisters and brothers, wife and children, kith and kin, dwellers in my house, my friends, and all others closely connected with me.*
>
> *I do penance for having talked while eating or drinking. I do penance for having walked with unshod feet. I do penance for having made water on my feet. I do penance for having been false, spoken calumny or slander, or for having lied. I do penance for the sins of sodomy, of having intercourse with a woman in her menses, or with a harlot, or with a beast. I do penance for having been guilty of any kind of unlawful intercourse. I do penance*

for having been proud or overweening, for mockery and vengefulness and lust.

I repent, am sorry, and do penance for all that I ought to have thought and did not think, for all that I ought to have said and did not say, and for all that I ought to have done and did not do. I repent, am sorry, and do penance for all that I ought not to have thought but did think, for all that I ought not to have said but did say, and for all that I ought not to have done but did do.

I repent, am sorry, and do penance for every kind of sin which I have committed against my fellow men, and for those they have committed against me.

I do penance for any sin for which I may have been responsible—sins which the accursed Destructive Spirit fashioned forth in his enmity to the creatures of Ohrmazd, and which Ohrmazd has declared to be sinful and through which men become sinners and by which they must go to hell.

I have no doubts concerning the truth and purity of the Good Religion of the worshippers of Ohrmazd, none concerning the Creator, Ohrmazd, and the Amahraspands, the three nights' reckoning, or the reality of the Resurrection and the Final Body. In this religion do I stand, in it I believe without doubting, even as Ohrmazd taught it to Zoroaster, and Zoroaster taught it to Frashoshtar, and Jamasp, and Adhurbadh, son of Mahraspand, after submitting to the ordeal and emerging from it victorious, transmitted it in due succession to the righteous religious rectors from whom it came to us. I believe in whatever this religion says or thinks. . . .

This penance have I performed in order to wipe out my sins, in order to obtain my share of reward for good deeds done, and for the comfort of my soul. I have performed it so that the way to hell may be barred and the

way to Heaven opened, resolved from now on to sin no
more, but to do good works. I have performed it in order
to expiate my sins in so far as they need to be expiated
and out of love for all that is holy. I dissent from sin and
assent to virtue. I am thankful for good fortune and con-
tent with whatever adversity or misfortune may befall
me. . . .

In thought, word or deed I repent, am sorry, and do
penance for all the sins for which men can be responsible
and for which I have been responsible and the number of
which I do not know because they are so numerous.

When Cyrus had finished reading the prayer to himself, he
felt emptied. He listened to the peaceful breathing in his chest,
detected there a remnant of pain or simply feeling. The chatter
of self-reproach had stilled long enough for him to experience a
blank repose, and for the present to take its rightful place. He
watched with patient interest the conclusion of the ceremony.

AFTER THE SERVICE had ended a line of congregants formed by
the altar, removing their shoes and presenting offerings of sandalwood to the fire. Everyone else milled around, accosting one
another with voluble ordinary greetings. One would never have
guessed that they had just been engaged in solemn prayer (but
that was a form of Parsi tact, thought Cyrus). He accepted a small
morsel, from a dish being passed around, which contained delicious honeyed nuts and apples, and waited calmly in the back
for his mother, who was making her many good-byes.

"Wait!" she called to him. "I want you to meet a friend of
mine—Bapsi's niece." She waved vehemently to a young woman
to join them. It was the girl of the turquoise scarf.

"Hello, Auntie!" the girl greeted Mrs. Irani gaily, her black
eyes sparkling.

"Are we relatives then?" asked Cyrus.

The girl lowered her eyes without replying.

"Scherezade, this is my younger son, Cyrus—you know, the one I told you about in the rug business?"

"A pleasure to meet you, Scherezade, even if we are not related. In fact, more so."

Still no reply. He saw that teasing would not make a dent in her demeanor, that of the traditionally raised modest girl who does not talk to strange men. But she did manage a blushing, dimpled smile.

"Scherezade came from Karachi a few months ago. She and I are great friends, we talk on the phone all the time. She is going to school here."

"Ah, very good," he said warmly. "What are you studying?"

This was too direct a question not to answer, yet she obviously would have preferred to avoid it. "Hotel management," she brought out finally, with a curious defiance.

Too bad, thought Cyrus. But he was still interested.

"She is going to Queensborough Community College," his mother put in. "She takes the bus, it's not far from here."

"That must be convenient for you," said Cyrus, regretting the patronizing avuncular tone which had crept into his voice. "I hope you are enjoying your studies."

"Well . . . ," she said reluctantly, with a shrug. "Yes and no."

"She is leaving out the most important part!" interjected Mrs. Irani. "Scherezade is a very distinguished classical Indian dancer."

"Is that so?" Cyrus asked encouragingly, getting no answer.

"I tell you she lives for dance. She chews my ear off about it by the hour, she gets so excited she demonstrates all her new steps for me—"

"Not so, Auntie!" the girl said laughing, and gave his mother a pinch. He was struck by how lively and spontaneous she was

with another woman, and how bashfully stiff with him—or probably any man. He wished he could see a little of that laughter
gravitate in his direction.

A tall man in his early thirties had come beside them, waiting
for an opportunity to enter the conversation. Cyrus recognized
him as one of the priest's assistants from his white robes, though
he looked rather different with brown loafers over his stockings
and without his white mask. He was grinning a shy toothy smile;
he had a long, pitted, horsey face with a fringe of beard along
the chinbone, though his upper lip was clean-shaven. Cyrus
jumped to the conclusion that he was the young woman's fiancé
from the doting way he looked at Scherezade, and immediately
he himself gave up all hope for her.

"Meher, this is my son Cyrus—one of my sons. He is a very
distinguished scholar of art history—"

"Formerly," Cyrus put in, "and undistinguished."

"—and now he is a respected dealer in rugs."

"I am very honored to meet you," said the young priest,
bowing and placing his hands together.

"Please, it is entirely my pleasure, I am unworthy—"

"And Meher is a very celebrated engineer and the brother of
Scherezade—and, as you can see, a very accomplished *mobed*."

"I was very impressed watching you," said Cyrus, suddenly
liking the man immensely. "I think you did a beautiful job with
this morning's Jashan service."

"Are you interested in Zoroastrian practice?" asked the other
man, with a searching expression.

"I am, of course, but I'm quite ignorant, I'm afraid."

"He knows, he knows vast amounts! He just won't admit it,"
cried Mrs. Irani.

"I assure you, I am a total ignoramus in these matters. How
I wish I *were* versed like you. You ought to be very proud to
speak Avestan and Pahlevi so well. I would do anything to have
your skill."

"If you would like to learn more about the sacred texts," said Scherezade's brother, inclining his head, "there is a study group, the Gatha Society, which meets here once a month on Sunday evenings. A small group—and we would love to have you join us."

"Thank you, I am deeply honored. I will have to consider if I can do it just now. At the moment business matters are consuming me."

"Whenever you have the time, we would be honored to have you as a member."

"By all means. . . . Well, it was so nice meeting you, Scherezade, I hope to have the pleasure again, and an honor to meet you, Meher . . ." Cyrus bowed to the sister and brother, offered his mother his arm, and the two left the fire temple together.

8

MOTHER
AND SON

THEY BEGAN WALKING toward his mother's house on 168th street.
Neither spoke for the first block. A gentle, pesky snow had started,
with the wind blowing the flakes every which way, so that none
seemed to land on the ground.

"Well, what did you think? She's a nice girl, isn't she?"

"Yes, very nice."

"And to my eye she is pretty. Of course I am not a man, but
. . . you agree?"

"Yes, very pretty."

"So what is wrong with her?" Cyrus's mother asked curtly.

"There is nothing wrong with the girl. The girl is perfect.
Only what makes you think I have anything to offer her? She
seems so young, so pure and innocent; I would feel like a worn-
out, degenerate old man next to her."

"Oh, you are never satisfied!"

"Suit yourself: it is *my* fault, I am never satisfied. In any

event, I think I made a poor impression on her. She only spoke
two words to me the whole time."

"Let me be the one to find out. I will call her tomorrow."

"Please, don't!" he shouted, then immediately toned himself
down. "I need more time to think. To get used to the idea."

"Don't be so nervous. No one is signing any papers. I can
still phone her just to gather her impressions."

"Mother, I forbid you to call her up for such a purpose,"
Cyrus said, adding a mournful smile to take the edge off the
command. "Let me handle my own romantic affairs."

"Very well." She looked amused, as she always did when he
suddenly asserted his temper. They both knew she would make
the call anyway. "Here, we are home." She opened the front
door with her keys. "Just a moment, while I turn off the alarm."

Cyrus's mother pivoted in the hallway, a subtle movement
of her neck and shoulders telling him to remove her fur coat.
Well-trained, he immediately complied. "You can put it in the
hall closet, please, if it's not too much trouble."

Having found a coat hanger, he followed her into the kitchen.
His mother took an already prepared Saran-wrapped lunch from
the refrigerator and turned on the microwave. "I have lamb ke-
bab. Is lamb all right for you?"

"By all means, please. You know I am not vegetarian." His
mother had moved into this house seven years ago and he was
still not used to it. He looked around at the kitchen, with its
olive microwave oven, tan double refrigerator, washer-dryer,
stainless steel electric range, food processor, coffee machine,
icemaker—all shiny, easy to clean, and impersonal. A far cry
from the old country. He knew what his mother would say: We
had enough of those antique-filled houses back in Iran. Here I
want everything modern.

"So. What have you been doing with yourself?" asked Cyrus.

"I am sure the life of a woman my age has very little interest
to you."

"Of course I'm interested. You are my mother. What have you been up to?"

"Let's see . . . I get up in the morning, have my little breakfast. I read the morning paper. I do the crossword occasionally. Still interested?"

"I also do the crossword puzzle. Go on."

"Sometimes I go into town to see a matinee with a friend. Not very often. You know I am still volunteering as a docent at the Queens Museum. I am showing visitors around and giving talks about the exhibits to small groups. Next month they are doing a show on Japanese calligraphy, and so I am having to take a crash course which is offered to the volunteer staff. When they are short-handed they put me in the bookstore. Or at the information booth. I prefer working a cash register. Oh, yes: I have also started a little volunteering at the new burn center at Jamaica Hospital. Polly roped me into that. You can't imagine what it is like there. Last week a little girl came in with second-degree burns all over her body. It was horrible to look at. But I have the feeling I am needed, whereas at the museum, the volunteers mostly are a bunch of silly rich women with white gloves. Snobs, and you know I cannot bear snobbism. There's an old Farsi proverb, 'We all wipe ourselves at the same place'—or at least I hope so. Anyway, I'm not sure what to fill you in on because it's been so long since we've seen each other. Did I tell you about my experience a few months ago on jury duty?"

"I don't think so."

"Well, it was fascinating, but some other time. Let's get to the point. You know I don't like shilly-shally. What is the problem you mentioned on the phone?"

"My landlord is tripling my rent to three thousand dollars a month. I need a loan to manage for the coming year. Perhaps as much as twenty thousand dollars."

"And then in a year's time you will come back and ask for another twenty thousand?" His mother stood up and checked the dish in the microwave. "It's ready."

"No, by that time I should have figured out a way to improve my sales so that I can meet the increase by myself. All I need is time. I am asking you to help me buy some breathing room while I work things out."

"It sounds to me like just throwing good money into a bottomless pit. How are you going to squeeze double or triple the sales you are presently getting from that hole in a wall?"

"I don't know yet. Maybe I can advertise. Or appeal more to private collectors. There are a number of possibilities I am considering."

"My poor boy, you are a dreamer. I don't see what you find so attractive in the first place about a broken-down shop like that. You don't care any more about the rug business, you are just in love with your own inertia. You will do anything to avoid rocking the boat."

"There is a good deal of truth in that."

"Change is life. Look at me, I am still learning new skills, taking on new challenges. You don't see me standing still; nor did your father. Inertia has never run in this family. Why are you so afraid to start something new?"

"I don't know. But even if I were to change, I would need time to put things in order."

"Well, I have to think about it. What makes you think I have so much extra money lying around to loan people? I have my fur coat, this house, my car—and that's it. A little pension to live on. Some stocks and bonds. But Freddy takes care of them. I would have to ask Freddy's permission first in any case, I cannot just write out a check for twenty thousand dollars!"

"No, Mother, I understand that."

"Do you? . . . Why don't you buy your own place? You keep throwing your savings away to some thief of a landlord. That way you will always be in a monetary hole."

"Mother, it costs half a million dollars to buy a building in New York. If I don't have the money to meet my rent, I certainly don't have enough to buy a building."

"But you don't need half a million at once. You could take out a mortgage. You see, *if* you had come to me like a man and said, 'Mother, I want to buy out my landlord,' that would be one thing. But you are so—so long-suffering, so passive, you accept whatever misfortune comes your way. You just try to survive. You don't seem to know how to assert yourself."

"There is truth in that. You're right."

"And it won't do you any good to keep agreeing with me! That is just another form of your obstinacy. I know you very well. Can I get you something to drink?"

"Just some water, please."

"Seriously, you should think about buying your own property. Maybe not in Manhattan but in Brooklyn or Queens. What about New Jersey? Or upstate New York, like the Kermanis. They did very well in Schenectady with their rug business."

"I admit that would be the sensible thing to do. But I prefer to continue to rent."

"Why? Because you are lazy. You have no incentive."

"No. I admit I am lazy in certain ways, but it's not only laziness." Cyrus considered his words carefully. "It's this way: I have chosen a life with minimal financial rewards. All right, I accept that I am not much of a success. But in return for being a failure I ask the freedom to think my own thoughts, and not to have my mind cluttered up constantly with questions of money, property taxes, tax shelters, maximizing the profits on a piece of real estate. That is not me. I am not a landowner and never will be one."

"Very clever. Begin. What are you waiting for?"

"I am waiting for you to sit down."

"Begin, I will be there in a moment. I have to get some relishes out of the refrigerator. What was I saying?"

" 'Very clever,' " quoted Cyrus.

"Yes. Very clever. You would like to portray your motive for not owning property as somehow idealistic, noncapitalistic, intellectual. But the real reason is that you are selfish. The same reason that you don't consider buying a building has made you unwilling to get married and settle down. You live only for yourself. You are terrified of any commitment. Not only that, you have become alienated from your own people. In time of need nobody is going to be there. If you had a wife or somebody it would be different. But this way, nobody is going to help you, nobody is going to rescue you when you are in trouble."

"But what about you, Mother? I am turning to you now."

"I, I will not always be around. Also, I have to look after myself. Because if something happens to me I don't think you are going to be able to provide for me, isn't it so?"

"Don't assume so."

"Why not? Just as you have no feelings for the community, so you have no feelings for me."

"A non sequitur if ever I heard one. I can have feelings for my mother without having them for the whole Zoroastrian community."

"But you don't. You are cut off from everyone. You are a hermit. And it is all because you are afraid of the risks of getting involved."

"I am not a hermit. I see people every day," Cyrus said mildly.

"Nevertheless, can you deny that you lead the life of a semi-recluse? It used to be that a hermit would seek out a mountain hut to get away from people, but nowadays one can retire from life in the busiest cities. Even more so. What are you laughing at?"

"I am just appreciating your turn of phrase, your perspective. Go on."

"I doubt you are going to appreciate what I say next. I will tell you what your real problem is, Kurush. You are a coward."

Cyrus shrugged. He was prepared to take any number of insults if it would put his mother into a more generous mood.

"You are afraid of life. And that makes you a coward."

"I am not the bravest person, Mother, true. I wish you would accept that about me, after all these years."

"No, I *don't* accept it," she said, "and you want to know why? Because you are not cowardly by nature. It is only that you have become so passive. Everything is fate, Kismet! You won't take your fate in your own hands."

"You keep saying that. But fate is what cannot be conquered, what is meant to be. That is the meaning of the word."

"You know what I mean, don't quibble about definitions. What I am getting at is that you don't *act* to better your life. You drift. Deep down you are afraid of something. That is why you never got married, Kurush. You are afraid that if you lived with one woman, she would bore you. Certainly there are boring moments in marriage, I don't say not. But so are there in living alone. We both know that now, from experience. However, you are too wrapped up in yourself to permit anyone to get close. Probably what you are is a narcissist. Don't smirk. I read a magazine article recently about the narcissistic personality. The author was a Swiss woman; she attributed it to the mother's treatment of the child in the early years. I don't know what terrible mistakes I made, but I must have done something wrong with you. Because somehow I did not give you the courage to face life."

"It's not your fault if I am not courageous," Cyrus said. "For that I have only myself to blame."

"But if a child is frightened of life, a mother must take responsibility."

"No, Mother, this time you're wrong."

"How, wrong?"she demanded, half irritably, half pleased to be contradicted.

"I certainly have my faults. And I repent, do penance and am sorry for all of them, believe me. But I am also kind to people, I am tender to the best of my ability, I am able to give love and to receive it. And I thank you for teaching me to be that way." He smiled at her.

"Maybe so. But then how do you explain that you have no wife to look after you?"

"I often wonder that myself. The way I explain it is the same way I explain poverty, homelessness, suffering, all human want. There are those who have and those who don't have. The ones unfortunate enough not to have must not blame themselves for their own deprivation. That only makes things worse. Especially if it is not in their power to correct it. Unless I am completely deceiving myself, I am a fairly ordinary man, not so good, not so bad—and not so narcissistic. It happens I have not had the luck to meet a woman I could love, who would love me too. I am not saying I have not made romantic mistakes, I have made plenty. But it would be arrogant to blame myself entirely, as if I had *contrived* not to find the right person, just out of sheer perversity on my part. I assure you, it is not."

"But you do have the power to get married. Even if you aren't sure it will make you happy a hundred percent."

"A *hundred* percent? You know, Mother—I have never felt happy."

"Am I to blame for that too?"

"Certainly you are not. I don't blame anyone, not *even* myself. That is what I have been trying to tell you. . . . If I look back, I can't remember a single day when I was joyful for more than—say, ten minutes, before returning to my old melancholy. Oh, forgive me, there was sometimes a whole hour of pleasure, occasionally in the company of women, or looking at certain paintings, or listening to a beautiful piece of music, or reading a wonderful book. Sometimes a rug can still give me that pleasure when I hold it in my hands. I have a fondness for antiquarian things, for exquisite handiwork, I can get lost in the details, the history. But as for what one normally means by *happiness*, no, I don't think I have had any true experience of it. I am just trying to be honest, not self-pitying. I will go so far as to say that perhaps there are people, myself among them, who lack the biological capacity for sustained happiness."

"Oh, I don't believe that!" his mother said impatiently. "Are you finished with this? Would you like seconds?"

"No, thank you. I'm full. It was very good."

"Is it all right then if we go into the living room? It's warmer there, and I can turn up the thermostat."

Cyrus got up and moved into the living room, where he sank into the old familiar couch, recently re-covered with nubby Egyptian cotton. He watched his mother pull the heavy burgundy drapes.

"Do you mind if I shut these? The snow gets in my eyes and distracts me."

"Please go ahead."

When she had finished, she sat in an easy chair diagonally across from him. "Please listen very carefully to what I have to say."

"I am listening carefully," Cyrus said with a smile.

"All right. . . . Don't mock me though."

"I wouldn't think of it."

"Let me see if I can find the right words. . . . You are evading the responsibility of doing something constructive with your life with the excuse that you have not the capacity for happiness. Everyone has that capacity. It is an organic reflex, like breathing. Like skin sensitivity. When you were a child you often fell into delight. Your eyes would sparkle so, when you played with your toys or sand castles. Do you remember those summers we spent in Kirman at Grandma's house? I thought of you then as a very happy child. Playing in the sand, do you remember?"

"The sand, yes, but not the sensation of contentment. All I recall is getting sinus headaches. But that is beside the point. I was really speaking of my adult life."

"Also, when you were little, you were very brave. You climbed trees and whatnot like a monkey. It was Farokh who was the frightened one."

"Freddy? I find that hard to believe."

"Why, because he always bullied you? In his own circle of boys he was very timid, he let them order him about and do whatever they pleased. He was so passive I had to intervene at times to protect him. Whereas you, Kurush, you were always the leader. You used to organize treasure hunts among all the neighborhood kids. Do you remember that?"

"Vaguely. Well, what do you suppose happened to me?" Cyrus asked in a good-natured, speculative tone, as though he were inquiring after a distant cousin.

"I don't know." His mother's face clouded over. She seemed to be struggling with a dark memory, unsure whether to share it with him. She glanced contemptuously at her thick fingers with their manicured fingernails, and began flicking them. They sat in silence for a long moment.

"What were you going to say?" Cyrus prodded.

"All I know is that, when you were a teenager you became reserved. You pulled back from everyone. Including me. You always had your nose in a book."

"That's true, I fell in love with reading."

"You were in your own private world. And you had no further use for your mother. You pushed me away, again and again you pushed me away. It was quite brutal."

Cyrus was about to defend himself, but he sensed from her tone of voice that she was telling him something too important to dispute just then. "Is that . . . why you think there came to be a barrier between us?"

"When you went away to the university, Cyrus—you became a snob. I was not smart enough for you any more. You would turn up your nose at my opinions. You made me feel that you did not need a mother any more. In simple terms you rejected me. And it hurt. Like a knife in my stomach."

He was surprised to see her eyes wet. "But don't you think— don't you think it was normal for a boy my age to have pulled away from his mother, in order to become his own man?"

"Maybe. But it hurt me deeply all the same. I am not one to go where I'm not wanted. If a person doesn't like to talk to me, fine. I don't like to talk to him."

"I am not only a 'person,' I'm your son. I would hope that a mother's love would be strong enough to withstand any number of temporary adolescent rebuffs from her child."

"Love you I always did, and continue to do so. But the hurt remains. I am the kind of person who is unable to disguise her feelings. I cannot fake feeling fine on the outside when inside I am crying. What can I say more?"

"I am glad you told me this. Maybe now we can begin to clear the air. For my part, I remember, around the time of Papa's funeral, it seemed to me that you turned only to Freddy for support. You were the one who ignored *me* then. You acted as though you had only one son. You even made him sole financial adviser. That hurt my feelings deeply too."

"I can appreciate that. But you see, Freddy had stayed closer all along. He would call me nearly every day, to see how I was doing. But if I heard from you once every four months I counted myself fortunate. And you are still like that. Even before your father died, Freddy would call me every day or every other day and tell me his troubles at home or in the office. You never confided in me. I never knew if you were 'seeing' someone. You kept your whole life separate from me, isn't it so? I felt completely shut out. That is no way for a mother to feel."

"I am honestly sorry to have been so secretive," said Cyrus. "It's never been easy for me to confess my troubles to other people. I am coming to you now, though."

"Yes, because you want twenty thousand dollars."

"Well, we are talking. That in itself is good, even if you don't give me a penny."

"I wish I could believe that you mean that."

"You may as well. I am usually honest."

"Yes, you are not a liar, I will give you that."

"Thank you, madam."

"There is one more thing we never discussed, while we are clearing the air. That time you were in the hospital when you—lost your mind for a while. The first day I came to the clinic they wouldn't permit me to visit you! Do you know how unhappy and guilty that made me feel?"

"But Mother, I was having a nervous breakdown. I was sedated. I was asleep the first twenty-four hours anyway. Are you saying it was my fault that they wouldn't admit you?"

"No, no. I know it wasn't your fault. But everyone at the clinic seemed to be accusing me, by their way of—and the psychiatrist who interviewed me was a terribly rude man! You know, to them it's always the mother's fault."

"I don't blame you at all. It was my own foolishness."

"But you see, when they finally let me in to see you, what I felt from you underneath is that you *did* blame me. If you want to know why there is this 'barrier' between us, that is the reason. It's because I always feel you are judging me."

Cyrus fell silent.

"Perhaps it's my manner," he said at last. "I don't mean to appear judgmental. Often I am just listening neutrally and, from the blank expression on my face, you may think I'm having all sorts of stern thoughts. It's not so."

"Ha! I am insulted even that you listen to me neutrally. I am your mother, I want you to listen with love and sympathy, not neutrally as you would a perfect stranger. You see, that's what I mean. You are entirely too detached, Cyrus. You lack the spark of family feeling."

"Sometimes I get the sense that whatever I say to you, you will find a way to make it be an insult and turn it against me. I was sincerely apologizing just now. . . . All right, I confess I have no clear idea what you mean by this phrase *family feeling*."

"If you had children, perhaps you would understand what family feeling is."

"It is not too late for that."

"Listen, I would love you to give me a grandchild. Seriously," said his mother, with a keen look, "what did you think about the girl I introduced you to today?"

"She is very sweet. But very young and innocent, and Orthodox. I don't think she would approve of me in the long run."

"She is not as innocent as you think."

"You mean she is not a virgin?"

His mother threw her hands up mischievously: "I don't want to say one way or the other. But she is not as young as you think. How old did you guess she was?"

"Nineteen?"

"Ha! Twenty-four, soon to be twenty-five."

"Really? . . . Still, I am on the verge of forty-five, she probably sees me as an old man. My hair is graying, I am in debt, or about to be, on top of that a coward, as you say—believe me, I am no bargain."

"Just leave it to me. I will take care of everything."

"Please, Mother, this is America in the late twentieth century. We don't believe in arranged marriages any more."

"That's what you think. Besides, someone *must* intervene. If your father were alive it would be different, I could sit back and let him take care of it. But you are so stubborn and frightened, I must lead you by the hand."

'I am perfectly capable of calling her up myself."

"Fine, I will give you her number and you can call her now."

"All right, give me her number."

"You will never call. You are too much of a hermit."

"Can we change the subject please?"

"What would you like to talk about? I cannot arrange that loan by myself. You will have to speak to your brother, who is co-signatory. But I must tell you from where I stand that I would be inclined to oppose such a loan as a bad business proposition."

"Fine, then I will go to a bank."

"And pay thirteen and a half percent? You're crazy. That is what interest rates are up to now, you know that, don't you? Close to fourteen percent."

"You do keep up, Mother. I never knew you were such a shrewd financier."

"We all have to be financiers these days. I am not so weathy that I can afford to ignore such things. Would you like some dessert? I have some cookies and honey cake. Will you have some tea?"

"Just a piece of honey cake, thanks."

"Please have tea, you must have tea."

"All right, I will be happy to. Then I must be going."

"So soon? You just got here a minute ago. Well, come into the kitchen with me while I put up the water. We can continue to talk there." They rose and went back to the kitchen. "Listen, I was serious a minute ago. I would love a grandchild."

"You already have one: Eddie."

"Yes, Eddie. He is a very disturbed boy. Freddy is at the end of his rope with him."

"Disturbed? I am not sure I would go that far," said Cyrus.

"I am telling you, there is something wrong with Eddie, I don't know if it is physical, mental, emotional or environmental. Something."

"I have the feeling, on the other hand, that he is being made the scapegoat for all the problems in that household."

"You think so? What sort of problems?" she asked with avid interest.

"In the marriage. I don't know, it's not for me to say," he added cautiously. "I am an 'outsider,' as you put it."

"I never used the word *outsider*. But go on, tell me, I am interested in your viewpoint."

"Well, I just get the impression sometimes, watching the two of them together, that . . . they are not entirely happy with each other."

"That Ruttee, she is such a zero, there is nothing to her. How could Freddy put up with her all these years?"

"You think so? I find her a sweet-natured person," Cyrus said tactfully.

"*Sweet*! Ha! What you don't know about that woman underneath the veneer. . . ." So they fell to dissecting the problems of Freddy, Ruttee and their son, Eddie. Cyrus was enjoying this cozy tête-à-tête with his mother. At the same time, he held back from putting too much stock in their having achieved a durable understanding, partly because he remembered a number of similar tête-à-têtes. When it was over, she would probably go back to being suspicious of him and nurturing old wounds, while he would return to not letting his mother become a regular witness to his life. She might never speak to Freddy with quite the same vulnerable edge in her voice as she did to him—or with the same honesty—but she would always trust her older son more, as long as the phone calls went back and forth about weekly annoyances of head colds and plumbing. It was almost as if she saved Cyrus for special occasions, where her heart needed the theatrical romance of rejection, confrontation and reconciliation; and he, being the good boy he was, did exactly what she wanted, by staying away and not calling until such time as he was needed.

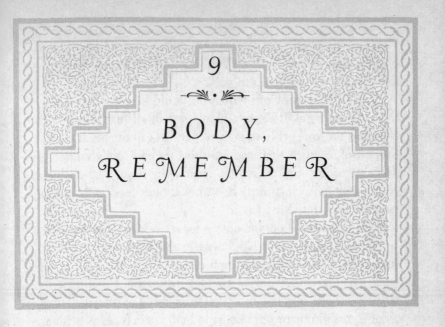

9

BODY, REMEMBER

"You know, Uncle Cy, I think you should get rid of all these bullshit racks. They suck!" said Eddie. Cyrus raised his eyebrows at his nephew's language. "Do it like those shops in the Village, with all the rugs rolled up."

"You think so?"

"I know so! When you go through all that hassle of rolling out each fucking rug, they feel like they—they got to buy. You have to make the customer feel guilty, like Pop always says."

"Your father—" Cyrus stopped himself from making a cutting remark, surprised to hear the teenager cite this authority. For years, Eddie had not gotten along with his father. Cyrus, who had experienced Farokh's overbearingness in his youth, could sympathize. But if the boy suddenly felt allegiance to his father's point of view, that was a good sign; he would not be the one to undercut it. "Your father may be right. But some customers prefer to browse by themselves. I am that way myself."

"You can't sell shit that way. People come in, they check it out and they're out of there. You've got to trash these racks, so the customers'll need you more."

Cyrus could think of nothing he would like less. "You may have a good point. The only problem with all that rolling is it is bad on the knees. I have known men back in the bazaars, still in their fifties, with such bad arthritis they can barely walk."

"But people want *at*-mosphere in a rug store. The Arabian Nights routine, you know, a hookah and bunches of pillows and hassocks and shit."

"If I had a few thousand dollars for remodeling, maybe . . . "

"Deck the place out like Persia in the old days. People are suckers for that corny Disneyland junk."

Such glib business advice sounded incongruous coming from a new skinhead who had just been thrown out of school. It took all of Cyrus's humanist principles to look squarely at his nephew in the boy's new, foolish baldness. Poor Eddie, he had wanted to come across as a nihilistic hooligan, while somehow his fuzzy dented skull made him look like a battered child.

The shaven head had been the latest of Eddie's minor confrontations with high school authorities, leading to this one-month suspension. It was decided that he should be apprenticed to Cyrus for the month, since Eddie had once let drop that the only relative of his he liked was his Uncle Cy. At first Cyrus resisted the idea; he did not relish having a noisy assistant around who would force him to keep inventing chores. But in the end he accepted, thinking it might be a way of helping Eddie. Farokh sweetened the deal by offering to pay his son's wages; and Cyrus secretly hoped that by doing his brother this favor, he might stand a better chance of appealing to him for a loan.

Most of all, Cyrus was flattered to learn of his nephew's partiality. Since the rest of the family tended to treat him as a dreamy failure, he looked forward at least to redeeming himself in his nephew's eyes. But as it turned out—perhaps because the advance word had made them both a little self-conscious—when they began working together Cyrus saw no evidence of this famous affection on his nephew's part. The boy talked to him readily enough, but his tone was sullenly belligerent, bordering on contemptuous. Cyrus did not know whether to blame Eddie's parents' influence, or accept the boy's rudeness as universally directed. In either case he could not help feeling hurt, which made him retreat into characteristically formal manners.

"I am going out for a while," he said to Eddie. "Would you please take over the ship's command? I leave my life's work in your care; I am counting on you to dispose of it. If customers have questions, please refer them to the price tags. May your kindness never diminish. . . . I thank you with all my heart, my speech and my thoughts." He raised his fingers teasingly to his lips and forehead, hoping at least to win a smile from his sullen nephew with these old-fashioned formulas.

The best thing about having the boy around, he had discovered, was that he could now take an hour off in the middle of the afternoon. Sometimes he walked over to the Museum of Natural History and watched the rendezvous of couples and friends on the stone steps in front, or the Egyptian hot dog vendor at the entrance to Central Park. If the weather was good, he would pass a half hour in bench-sitting reverie, distracted only by the occasional flare of a skirt and an interesting pair of legs.

Today, however, he had an itch to visit the used bookstore around the corner, in the middle of the West Eighty-eighth Street block between Amsterdam and Broadway, run by his friend MacCourt. Strictly speaking, MacCourt was not a friend—Cyrus had never yet been to the bookseller's house; but they shared, along with a passion for reading, the outlook of withdrawn marginal shopkeepers in an otherwise booming neighborhood. MacCourt's indifference to customers was so fabulous it reached misanthropic proportions, and made Cyrus seem a high-pressure salesman by comparison.

When you entered MacCourt's bookstore, which was not easy to do because of the roped-together sets of Carlyle and James Russell Lowell barring the way, the owner would not even look up from his page. Barricaded behind two desks which met at right angles, and which were piled high with *National Geographics* stratified like the Grand Canyon in layers of crumbling sedimentation, MacCourt himself might have passed as a sample of taxidermist's art, so fixed was the hawklike profile he gave to the world. When a customer approached the desk to pay, clearing his throat in hopes of getting the owner's attention, MacCourt would turn his neck alone, fixing his hard hazel eyes behind smudged horn-rimmed glasses on the intruder. If that were not enough intimidation, sometimes he smiled, revealing a bottom row of horribly twisted brown teeth. A man in his late sixties, he seemed stitched to a pea-green cardigan sweater, dust-laden like everything else in the store, and a faded flannel shirt buttoned to the top. His one youthful feature was a vital, glossy mane of iron-gray hair, which tumbled forward in slicks like James Dean's.

Cyrus was one of the few customers he seemed willing to recognize, grunting an occasional "How're you today?" on seeing him come in. More than that Cyrus himself would not have liked. When he entered a bookstore, he preferred not to strike up a conversation with the proprietor until he had surveyed the stock.

Turning his back pointedly to the cash register, Cyrus began working his way through MacCourt's shelves, which ran from biography to history to religion, then to art, fiction, poetry and the natural sciences. He was already steeping himself in that timeless, pressureless, monastic atmosphere of good used bookstores everywhere. The experience reminded him oddly of moving through the moist environment of a greenhouse; here as there he felt cut off from everyday practicalities.

Eventually, he knew, he would settle on one of several possible purchases, since the only fitting conclusion to this adventure was an acquisition. Cyrus's book-buying urge was like others' compulsion to gamble—a head-swimming hunch and the sudden need to lighten his wallet. He had his eye on a lovely edition of Morier's *Hajji Baba of Ispahan* with plates, but at seventy-five dollars it was too expensive. Lately he had been stockpiling bargain finds which he did not really feel the energy or desire to read when he got home: dutiful cultural gap-closings, like Cardinal Newman's *Essays* or Foucault's book on punishment. Reminding himself of this tendency, he put down the first volume of Heidegger's study of Nietzsche he had been holding in his hand.

Like a dreamy child sent on an errand who forgets what he was supposed to fetch, Cyrus stared up at the spines on the poetry shelves without comprehension. Finally he pulled down a slender volume of Cavafy, enjoying the way it fit trimly in his hands. Then he read where the book had a mind to open itself, at a poem called "Body, Remember":

> *Body, remember, not only all the times you have been*
> *   loved,*
> *Not only the beds where you have lain down.*
> *But also those desires which for you*
> *Shone clearly in the eyes,*
> *And trembled in the voice—and some*
> *Chance obstacle brought them to nothing.*
> *And now, when all that is in the past,*
> *They seem very like those desires*
> *To which you gave yourself—how they shone,*
> *Remember, in the eyes that looked at you,*
> *How they trembled in the voice, for you, body, remember*

Cyrus read the poem slowly, absorbing it into himself. As sometimes happens when one stumbles without defenses upon a work of art, he was extraordinarily moved. At the ending his throat swelled with the constriction that goes before tears. He pictured the wings of a woman's back turned against him. He had always loved their backs. Shadows of former lovers turning in bed, stretching their arms and shoulders, rose over MacCourt's grubby bookshelves, and all the while he repeated like a mantra, *Body remember, body remember.* The very cells of his skin, the nerve endings, retained the imprint of sensual memory, Cavafy was saying, and even those unconsummated desires of long ago could be summoned, the poet promised, with visionary distinctness. What a consoling idea.

Cyrus started to read a few other poems, which he saw were also good, but he was too inspired by this one to take in very much. He decided to buy the book, and to keep it on his night table to reread "Body, Remember" before closing his eyes. Turning to the inside cover, he experienced a shock: in his familiar rounded hand MacCourt had penciled O.P. $25.00. Steep for a sixty-four-page used book. With all the one-dollar bargains in this place, none of the real finds had escaped the bookseller's practiced eye.

"This little Cavafy . . . " Cyrus approached the desk. The other customers had gone; he had the owner alone.

"You found something you like?" MacCourt asked, laying down his own book.

"Yes. But it seems expensive for such a little *translated* selection."

The bookseller examined the volume. "It's out of print. First edition. Twenty-five dollars is reasonable."

"It's not as though I mean to haggle."

"No, I understand."

"I'm sure you're right, the price is fair. It's just that . . . " Cyrus gave an eloquent shrug, meant as testimony to his lack of wealth.

"Tell you what, we'll waive the sales tax. How's that?"

"Perfect!" Cyrus lightened his wallet by two tens and a five.

MacCourt handed him the book in a paper bag and smiled his crooked-toothed grin.

Now Cyrus was suddenly eager for a chat. "I have been meaning to ask you, how is your business these days?"

"Business is rotten. Nobody reads any more," said MacCourt. "I'm thinking of selling this place and retiring. The only thing stopping me is that I don't want to give it to those idiots who would turn it into another goddamn clothing store or wine-and-cheese bar."

"You should be glad you are on a side street and not on the avenue, like me."

"This neighborhood, I don't know—it's getting to be only for the rich and muggers. Nothing in between any more. You know, I almost got held up the other day?"

"Really? What happened?"

"A spic came in, looking the place over. Kid didn't strike me as a literature lover, if you get my drift. I brought out my gun and started cleaning it. He disappeared."

"I didn't know you even had a gun."

"Sure, ever since I was goddamn held up a few years back. Don't you?"

"No . . . because I would never want to use it. For some reason I have not been robbed yet," said Cyrus.

"You're bucking the odds."

"But even if I were, let them take the money. I am strictly nonviolent."

"Oh, I'm not," said MacCourt, grinning evilly. "My right of self-defense. If they want to start something, I'll be happy to blow 'em away. Ever read Trotsky's *Terrorism and Revolution?*"

"No. But what were you reading before, may I ask?" said Cyrus, peering over the counter.

"John Dos Passos's memoirs."

"And are you enjoying it?"

"Well, he became a Goldwater reactionary in his old age,

and that goddamn side of him bugs the hell out of me. But he has some interesting things to say about people I knew—"

"You knew Dos Passos?"

"Not him, no. But the rest of that old *Partisan Review* literary crowd. I knew—let's see, I knew Jimmy Farrell, Mary McCarthy, Paul Goodman, Dwight MacDonald, Delmore and his wife, Fred Dupee, Rahv, Trilling, Wilson, Barrett, that whole gang. And I'll tell you something. Every single one of them was a deceitful sonofabitch and a cold-blooded egomaniac," MacCourt said with debunker's relish. Seeing some resistance to his statement on his auditor's face, he qualified: "Well, Dupee and MacDonald were all-right guys, and Farrell could be human—on occasion. But the rest of them, a bunch of cold fish."

"I'm surprised to hear that about Paul Goodman. I've only read one or two books of his, but I would have thought from his democratic views—"

"Goodman was the biggest ass of the lot!" roared MacCourt. "You want to hear about Paul Goodman?"

Cyrus was not sure he did, but he said yes.

In nearly every taciturn person lurks a rampant monologuist. Out of MacCourt now came tales of political betrayals in the forties and fifties. They were all cowards in the pinch, or closet Stalinists, or more often just artsy opportunists preferring cultural celebrity to disciplined organizing work. MacCourt acted like the last faithful Trotskyist. Much of what he indicted the others for did not sound particularly awful to Cyrus, who detected an un-expected strain of Victorian sentimentality running beneath the anecdotes: the bookseller's harshest contempt was reserved for family transgressions, like the literary lion who had made himself unavailable when his brother-in-law needed an expensive eye operation. Cyrus began to feel depressed and claustrophobic lis-tening to all these bottled-up animosities.

At a momentary pause in the recounting, Cyrus said: "I must go."

"I may as well close up for the day. Everybody's probably—

out of town. Why don't we just pull down the blinds, put our feet up and listen to some lieder? I've got boxes of seventy-eights here. Elizabeth Schwartzkopf, Kathleen Ferrier, Elisabeth Schumann with Toscanini . . . "

"That sounds wonderful. I would like nothing better—but I have to get back to my store. I left my teenage nephew in charge."

"Too bad. Care for a parting nip, then?" MacCourt asked amiably, bringing out his whiskey bottle.

"With the greatest of pleasure."

The bookseller found two dusty shot glasses and filled them.

"To your health." Cyrus drained his glass. "Well, it's a pity but I must be going. If you will give me a raincheck on the lieder . . . "

"I've got boxes and boxes of old records in the basement here. Operas, symphonies, you name it. Come by some time around closing, we'll lock up and put our feet on the desk and have a drink and spin some records."

"With the greatest of pleasure. Truly I would like nothing better. Thank you for the good whiskey and talk; you have been very gracious."

"No big deal."

"Well, I will not take up any more of your time. With your permission I will leave."

"So long. And buy a gun. You'll feel better all around."

Cyrus drew the door behind him. Once out in the street, he felt relieved but sluggish. He was not used to drinking in the middle of the afternoon, and the whiskey had gone straight to his head. Still, it was touching and flattering that MacCourt had chosen to talk to him for so long. Sad, in a way, to learn that what lay behind the bookman's silent mask turned out to be mostly bitter grudges. That often seemed to be the case. Perhaps he is only an alcoholic looking for drinking company. Still, I should take him up on his invitation soon. He must have some musical gems—

Cyrus stopped dead in his tracks. A crowd had gathered in

front of his rug store. They were laughing and jeering, he realized in horror, while Eddie harangued them like a carnival barker. It was all taking place with a nightmarish viscosity.

"These are fuckin' heirlooms, dude, smuggled out of Iran by the old merchants. The revolution is costing those guys a bundle, see, they're hard up for bucks. The ayatollah would have a spaz if he knew these carpets had been snuck out of the country. National fucking treasures, right? He would have my poor unc totaled. We're taking a big chance here, Khomeini's death squad could be after us and we be smeared all over the place. Are you trying to say you're not going to buy when we're risking our asses for you—"

"That's enough." Cyrus had pushed his way through the crowd, and now took his nephew roughly by the arm. "Get inside!"

"See you later," Eddie said, waving pleasantly as he stumbled into the store.

Cyrus locked the door and twisted the printed sign to the side which read SORRY WE'RE CLOSED. Then he turned out the lights. His voice, unused to expressing anger, started shaking. "Sit down. You must be crazy. Tell me, what made you do such a thing?"

"I got bored."

"Oh, you got bored!" Cyrus noticed his voice was trembling. He had the urge to smack the boy across the face.

"No one was coming in the shop, so I figured I'd go out and get you some customers. You told me to get rid of this junk." Eddie smirked, but his blush contradicted the attempt at nonchalance: the top of his shaven head had turned beet-red.

"And do you think you will attract customers with such foul language? All you have done is bring shame down on me. You have made us a laughingstock!"

"Oh, *shame*, gimme a break, that's such bull."

"You don't think there's such a thing as shame? I feel sorry for you." Cyrus sat down, still feeling violent. "I have to face these people every day. What will they say about me and my shop now?"

"Oh, come on. This is New York. No one gives a shit."

"Is that why you shaved your hair off? To be a clown? You think if people laugh at you they will like you more and become your friend?"

"You don't know nothin' about it," Eddie muttered, turning his head away.

"What did you say? I didn't hear you."

"I feel sorry for guys your age, you get so freaked by what people will say about you. At least my friends are honest. We know like the end is gonna come. It's all going to blow up anyway. So what's the point of all this puke? This salaam junk?"

Cyrus was so miffed he began to smile. "I will have to speak to your father."

"Oh, Jesus. The world's about to blow, and you're going to send me to the principal's office."

"No, that's not what I meant to say. I am sorry I mentioned your father. Whether or not I tell him about this is another issue." Cyrus got hold of himself, growing thoughtful. He paused to select his words. "You and I must come to an agreement by ourselves. Just now we are both speaking in angry clichés. First of all I am not a generation, I am a person, your Uncle Cyrus—remember? I had understood . . . that you liked me. If you still do . . . you must treat me with respect. Please realize that it is of no importance to me if the world blows up tomorrow or not. I can do nothing to stop that. But in the meantime you show courtesy here. Or get out." Cyrus glanced at the boy. "Is that clear?"

"Y' know, I'm not stupid!"

"No, you're *not* stupid. That is why I don't think you should hide behind stupid excuses, like blaming the evil of the world for your foolish irresponsible behavior. Now I will tell you what I would like you to do. I would like you to take those rugs over there—take them into the back room and beat them, please, by the window."

He led his nephew over to the pile, placing his arm around Eddie's shoulder in a gesture combining directional firmness and tenderness. All his rage was gone; he felt nothing but pity for the boy.

The rest of the afternoon Cyrus worked on bills, giving his nephew a wide berth. Once the front door was unlocked, a few customers wandered in. One even bought an Indian dhurrie. At around six-fifteen, Cyrus was getting ready to close up for the night when the last customer of the day entered and stood in the middle of the shop. With her Capezio drawstring bag and gray sweatpants under a sheepskin coat, she looked as though she had just come from a dance rehearsal. A mass of stylish brown curls framed her pretty but pinched face, with its sharp nose and morose eyes.

"Can I be of any service?" asked Cyrus.

"I'm not sure. . . . I didn't bring any money with me. Is it all right if I just look?"

"Certainly, by all means." He led her over to the most inexpensive rugs first. She turned the racks with a preoccupied frown, as though looking through a wallpaper sample book. He stood at a tactful distance, like a waiter available to be summoned. Finally he cleared his throat, prompting her to speak.

"How much is this one?"

"That is a prayer rug. Do you know anything about Oriental rugs?"

"No, but I'd be happy to learn."

Cyrus unhooked the rug from its clippers and laid it on the floor. "The 'feet' at the bottom mark the places to stand or kneel. The rug is always pointed toward Mecca. You put your hands on the top when you are praying, on those two niches. I will not demonstrate but you get the idea. The lamp signifies: 'Allah is light.' " He noticed the woman's color change. She looked Jewish; perhaps he had touched a sensitive spot. "Prayer rugs are not only for religious purposes, they are also a mark of social prestige. And they are for everyday use. Some are even reputed to have magic powers."

"What magic powers?" she demanded.

"For instance: there is a story told of a Sufi dervish, a holy man, who was refused passage by the captain of a ferry. So he spread his prayer rug on the water and—just like that!—the rug turned into a raft and took him across." Cyrus shrugged with a mixture of skepticism and open-mindedness.

"I like that." The woman gave a delayed chuckle, and her manner relaxed. Her eyes shone. Cyrus imagined a spark of attraction pass between them. "What about these?" She pointed, sauntering coquettishly over toward the higher-quality rugs.

"Please do me the honor of looking. Do you want to see more prayer rugs?"

"All right. Anything." Cyrus followed in back of her, making the after-you gesture. She had peeled off her sheepskin coat and she seemed lighthearted, almost flirtatious now, a different person from when she had entered the store. He noticed with appreciation how the girlish top of her body blossomed into voluptuous roundness beneath her sweatpants.

"Can you tell me anything about this blue one?" she asked.

"That is good quality. In unusually fine condition for its age. You know, people don't walk on rugs with shoes so much in the Middle East. That preserves them better. . . . This particular rug has a very interesting *boteh* design."

"What's that?"

"The fig symbol. This," he pointed, then patiently refolded his hands.

"Why do you say it's good quality? What makes this one good quality?"

"It can be a number of things. The wool, the weave, the color, the design. Here the overall design has good balance. The details are specific and clear, yet delicate. The colors are vivid but not crude. You can also see how tightly knotted it is," Cyrus said, turning over the edge. "All fine handiwork—like *petit-point*."

"Is that the main indication of quality, the tightness of knotting?"

"That is what conventional wisdom says. But it depends to some extent on the material. There are rugs with large loose weaves that have an appealing boldness. Just as you cannot say that a painting with tiny brushstrokes is necessarily always better than one with looser," he added with a smile, letting her know that he possessed some culture beyond this narrow realm.

"And how much is it?" she asked, returning the smile.

"Five hundred and fifty dollars. I might be able to give it to you for less. . . . "

The woman looked at her watch and said, "I have to run! Maybe I'll bring my, uh, roommate in later in the week. He has to approve."

"By all means," said Cyrus, suddenly chagrined. "But if you were to go over to Madison Avenue in the Seventies, you will find that this rug would cost you five hundred more. The identical rug."

"Thank you for your lesson. And for all your time."

"It was my pleasure," Cyrus returned, starting to make a half-bow, then catching himself, remembering Eddie's earlier sarcasm.

A nice-looking woman, he thought as she vanished down the street. Too bad they always have a roommate.

Night had descended on Amsterdam Avenue; all the neon signs were lit. "You can go now," he went back to tell Eddie. He began locking up.

His nephew seemed to be lingering around, finding excuses not to leave. As they brought down the grille over the front window, Eddie found his powers of speech.

"Look, Uncle Cy, I'm sorry about the scene before, making a total fool of myself in public."

"We all make fools of ourselves from morning till night. Myself, I do it regularly. Forget it. I will see you tomorrow."

"Don't tell my father, okay?" Eddie pleaded in an undertone.

Cyrus went upstairs to his flat and fixed himself an eggplant pilaf. He read the evening paper. After dinner, he considered phoning his brother and telling him what had happened, for the sake of honesty, and maybe even asking for Eddie to be taken off his hands. But he was too weary tonight to listen to Farokh's blustering. He would wait and see if the boy's behavior improved. In any case, it was only for a few weeks.

He turned on the television and watched a detective program, but his attention kept straying. He felt exhausted. Eddie, MacCourt, the customers, the lack of customers, had all taken it out of him. Or was it something else entirely? Why was he so much more tired than usual? He reviewed the events of the day, particularly the argument with Eddie. But it seemed to him that he had acted correctly. No, some other mistake, or something left undone, he could not put his finger on what, must have drained him, leaving him with this sense of defeat. He decided to go to bed early.

As Cyrus got under the bedcovers, he remembered his Cavafy book. He turned on the night-table lamp, fetched the little volume which felt so good in his hands, slid into bed again and opened it to the table of contents. He found the page and turned to it slowly, with suspenseful leisure, as if offering himself an aperitif. "Body, remember," he read out loud to himself, "not only all the times you have been loved. . . . " But this time the poem struck him as threadbare and banal; its magic had fled, and in its place was the embarrassing sound of his voice practicing a sanctimonious sermon to an empty church. Was it Cavafy's fault, or his? It must be his. Another time, perhaps; he turned off the light and closed his eyes.

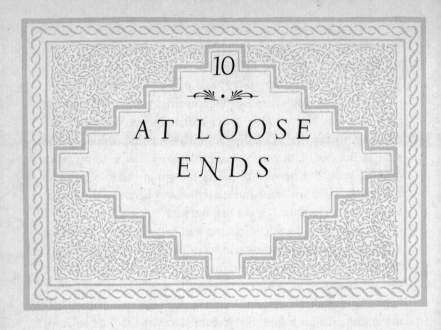

10

AT LOOSE ENDS

THE MONTH'S SUSPENSION ENDED, and Eddie was allowed to return to school. Cyrus had almost grown used to having the boy around. He thought that if business ever picked up, it might be nice to hire an assistant—someone better-mannered and more stable than Eddie, of course—to help with the heavy work and provide some companionship.

Meanwhile, on February first, he had gone to his bank and withdrawn another two thousand dollars. At this rate he would be broke in four more months. What's going to become of me? he thought. Somehow the danger didn't seem real. After he had gone to his mother to ask for a loan, and she had put him off, his energy to deal with the crisis had been used up. He would simply have to wait for enough anxiety to build inside him again before taking other measures. Cyrus understood full well that his objective financial troubles did not depend on his interior readiness to face them; time was running out, regardless of his mystifying lack of concern. It was as though he were waiting like a child for some outside force, some deus ex machina, to rescue him.

The problem was that he disliked even having to think about financial matters. He resisted this train of thought just as he might have an intellectual blowhard who insisted on dominating every conversation. Whenever, in fact, supposedly refined people talked at length about stock-market tips or tax strategies, he felt embarrassed for them, as though they had unintentionally expressed some repellent attitude, like racial prejudice. And now he too was having to give his mind over to this tripe.

What will become of me, what next? he asked himself, yawning from the sense of quandary. I probably should just shut down the business. But what will I do instead? I'm too young to retire. I could return to school and complete my doctorate. But how would I support myself meanwhile? I could try to teach a pickup course here and there on Oriental rugs, like at NYU or the New School. I could drive a cab; but I'm not a very good driver. I could travel through Asia or Latin America, living by my wits. What wits? I could try to devote myself to humanity, join Mother Teresa in Bombay, work in a hospice or a famine program . . .

What do I really want? To be crushed, once and for all? But if I am thrown out of here I will simply have to pick myself up off the ground and start all over again, from a worse position than I am in now. It's not enough to declare oneself a failure, a nobody. I still have to fight the struggle for existence. And failure is such an arrogant self-description. Why should I be any different from most of humanity? My mistake was in clinging to the notion that there was more in me that needed to come out; that I had not yet "realized" my potential. Why? Because I used to score high on IQ tests or graduate entrance exams? That was twenty-five years ago. Off with these lendings. I don't even have the right to call myself a failure. I am performing at exactly the level I was always destined to achieve.

What I really want is to stay in this rug shop. Not because I've been so happy here—on the contrary, it's been a bleak, bare life for me. The paradox is that now I have to move heaven and earth just to stay in a situation where I'm suffering and unfulfilled. But at least it's a suffering I'm familiar with.

I think I would like to die. The more one learns, the more one wants to die, wrote Leopardi. (I must try to find a complete edition of his *Notebooks*, if it exists in translation; I'll ask MacCourt to keep an eye out.) I would really like to die. I would not like to die. Put it this way: If it happened, I would have no serious regrets about leaving this life. I am ready to go. I am more prepared to die than to live, probably. Lately, all these thoughts of suicide, almost every day. . . . Somehow it's easier to imagine putting a noose around my head and kicking the chair away than transforming myself into a dynamic businessman. I don't really want to kill myself, then why do I keep thinking suicide? It's because I'm lazy. Imagining my corpse provides me with a burst of self-pity without requiring that I act. I tell myself, Look, I'm doing all I can just by staying alive another day, by resisting the temptation to kill myself. Nonsense. I should be wary of the danger of calling my own bluff. One day I may turn a cold ear to my own excuses and simply go through with it. No, no, what I have to do is think of some solution to the problem in front of me. I should call my brother and ask for a loan. I know just what his reaction will be. . . . Well, what if I ran a big sale? In retail a sale always has messianic potential. My window is already filled with bargains, throwaway rugs for $59, those big Pakistani monsters for $150. How much cheaper can I make my prices? Maybe I should go in the other direction. Throw out every rug but the twelve best, and hang each with austere space surrounding it, like a posh painting gallery. And double my prices. But that's so pretentious. It reminds me of the way Parisian greengrocers isolate the pears and wrap each individually, charging an arm and a leg. No, I can't do that, it's not me. Besides, I don't have the money to redecorate and pull off that kind of chic. . . . I could hire a hobo to walk back and forth with a sandwich board. Or skywriting: AMSTERDAM CARPETS. With that slogan I once saw somebody use; what was it? "A Room Without a Rug Is Like a Kiss Without a Hug." That might exceed the word limit for skywriting messages. I could hire a blimp with an electrical sign that keeps revolving, or . . .

It was four-thirty. Night seemed to fall earlier than usual this winter. Cyrus lay down on the couch, tired of his thoughts that kept circling like the blimp's electrical message. He was tempted to read a few pages; at least an author's thoughts always went somewhere, taking him along for a free ride. Cyrus leafed through his old copy of Plutarch, trying to find a favorite passage: Why didn't modern books use this pretty gilt edge on the sides any more? Money, of course, he yawned, putting down the book and listening to the sound of the rain. The steam heat was making him sleepy.

The girl at the fire temple drifted into his thoughts: her wide dark startled eyes and shy neck. He pictured making love to her, but it was not easy to see it clearly. He thought of the woman customer in the sheepskin coat who had never returned. Then Bonita. In the end, his imagination rested on a woman he had never met, a mysterious worldly woman who understood him and even laughed at him, who refused to take his moroseness seriously, and who brought him again and again to the peak of sexual happiness.

WHEN THE DOORBELL TINKLED, Cyrus opened his eyes. Realizing he had been dozing, he sought to hide the fact from Marge by energetically leaping up to greet her. "Come in! You're looking very well today. Please, would you like some tea? I was just about to put some on."

"No thanks." Marge brushed her hair away from her eyes. "It's dark in here. You ought to put on some more lights."

"You sure no tea? I beg you not to disappoint me, it will only take a minute. No? . . . Very well. Please sit down, make yourself comfortable."

"I can't stay. I just came by to give you this flyer about a city-wide retail tenants' meeting. Fred Corry wanted you to have it."

Cyrus took the paper and read it over. "Thank you. Are you going?"

"I'm not sure, I may be out of town. But you go. Corry told me you made quite an impression on him."

"I said nothing at all. He did all the talking."

"True enough," said Marge. "Well, what you been up to?"

"I was just sitting here thinking of ways to lure more customers into the store. I could try stenciling messages on the sidewalk. Ridiculous, isn't it? Every day I see full-page ads in the paper for rug sales. The big companies like Einstein Moomjy can get an eight-and-a-half-percent discount because they make hundred-thousand-dollar orders and pay cash, whereas I can only pay thirty-to-sixty days. . . . Even so, I hear that Macy's carpet operation is losing a lot of money. And they are not the only department store like that. How can I compete with these major dealers for a shrinking market? I am at the end of my rope. I may as well just hang myself."

"Don't let it get to you."

"Of course not, it is just a manner of speaking."

"Well, I've got to get back to the store."

"When are we going to have our dinner?" Cyrus asked.

"Soon, soon."

"How about tomorrow night?"

"Tomorrow's no good. I'll have to call you when I've got my calendar. We'll figure out a time."

"You always say that," he answered with a playfully mournful smile.

"No, I have to go out of town for a few days, but as soon as I get back."

"All right. You promised, remember now."

"I may have some new developments to report when I come back."

"What developments?"

"Bye-bye," she said, wiggling her fingers mysteriously, and was out the door.

Cyrus had gone back to thinking Marge was a lesbian. Certain cues, gestures, and most of all, blank spots in her conversations, ellipses and pronoun evasions, suggested someone practiced in leading a double life. He no longer flattered himself that she was after him. If anything, over the last few weeks she had been keeping her distance. Perhaps she was disappointed in him for not having supported her organizing attempts more. Well, she was bound to be disappointed in me sooner or later, thought Cyrus. In spite of the fact that he had dreaded getting romantically involved with her, now that Marge seemed gone as an amorous possibility he felt a letdown. He missed the lift of flirting, and the power of withholding himself from someone he had fantasized at least desired him. In its place was an older curiosity about gay women. He respected them, in both their disenchantment with men and their election of woman as their erotic ideal. It would be nice to have a frank chat about it with Marge over dinner— that dinner which he had so wanted to avoid when it was first proposed, then had resigned himself to submit to, and now felt cheated out of.

The steam heat must have been giving him a headache. He forced himself to step outside by the doorway and get some air. From there he could see people running stiff-legged in the heavy rain; it cheered him considerably. The pink-orange vapor lamps sliced through the black downpour. A man was darting with a newspaper over his head from doorway to doorway. The Korean grocer across the street was hurriedly dropping plastic covers over his fruit crates and dragging them inside. Awnings flapped and slammed, threatening to sail off in the wind. It was moments like these that Cyrus liked being a shopkeeper: standing under his bit of protection, enjoying the passing parade, arms folded across his chest. Presently the man running with the newspaper dashed into his entrance. Just to escape the rain for a few minutes he went inside and began inspecting the merchandise. Cyrus managed to sell him an Afghan saddlebag cover by the time the storm had stopped.

I MUST CALL MY BROTHER, he thought. He stared at the phone without moving. Six o'clock, perhaps this wasn't a good time to ask for a favor. Everybody would be going home for the day. . . . Oh, why not?

"Yes, please, I would like to speak to Farokh Irani. . . . Yes, Freddy Irani, that's right. Tell him it is his brother calling."

Cyrus waited patiently, wiping his mind clear of any practice phrases so that the request might have a more sincere spontaneity.

"Hello, Irani here. Cyrus? It's very noisy, let me close the door. . . . Thank you for taking care of Eddie."

"It was my pleasure."

"Mother told me something about you wanting money. Is that why you are calling?"

"Yes."

"Excuse me, I can't hear very well. Speak up! You are mumbling as usual."

"Yes! I am calling in regard to a loan." Cyrus tried to sound the words sharply and clearly, but in no way could he compete with the piercing vocals of his older brother. In fact, he had originally fallen into the habit of soft-spokenness as a protest against Farokh's buzz-saw voice, and even now he felt like holding the receiver away so that his inner ear would stop tingling. "Did Mother tell you my landlords had more than tripled my rent?"

"She told me, she told me. Why don't you drop that dead-end store and come work with me? I need help. *I need help.* I can't rely on anybody but my own people. These others are swindling me right and left. At least if you are swindling me the money stays in the family."

Cyrus wondered if these shouted words were for his benefit or for the employees outside the door. "Thank you for the generous offer."

"But?"

"No, Freddy, I don't want to work under you. It would be a disaster for both of us."

"Not under, *with* me! I could handle the finance end and you could do the public relations: take people out to lunch, write letters, handle foreign correspondence. This was our father's firm, so it belongs to both of us. You can come in as partner. You're good at writing and being polite, things I am not so good at. Your only problem is that you have no head for business."

"You know me very well."

"So how will you ever make a success in this rug nonsense if you are no good at business?"

"I don't need to make a success, I just need to get by."

"In the business world there is no such thing as getting by," roared Farokh. "You either make it or you sink like a stone. When will you ever learn that, my poor little brother? For all your university education, you know nothing about the real world. Book learning will never teach you how to put food in your stomach. People with their noses in a book, what do they earn? Nothing. Most of them become schoolmasters. They earn less than I pay my cleaning woman. You are acting like a sissy. You may as well wear bangles on your wrists!"

"When you have finished with this ritual abuse, please let me know if I can have my loan."

"I am not against giving you a loan in general, but I don't think it would help you. It will only get you into bad habits. And I don't want to lead you down the wrong path. Tell me, what would such a loan be? A bridge to nowhere. Six months later you'd be back where you started, and then you would not only have to pay that *mader-chode* of a landlord, but you would have to pay *me* back. And I am not in the business of offering loans that can't be made good on time."

"Then the answer is no?"

"Why are you so quick to accept defeat? You give up without a fight. This is a conversation, a back-and-forth. I want to hear reasons. Pretend I am a banker. You come to me, you want me to part with some of my hard-earned dollars. I must be convinced, talk me into it. Let's go, I am a busy man."

"What is this, a role-playing lesson?" said Cyrus. "Forget I even asked."

"Don't get so offended! You are so quick to take offense. I am only trying to toughen you up, to get you to present your case effectively as you *must* in this dog-eat-dog world of ours. You have to come to the point, communicate. The modern business world is all about this one word: *communications*."

"All right, I will come to the point. I need twenty thousand dollars to carry me for a year. I will pay it back to you in four installments, five thousand dollars each year, starting one year after. You can use my stock as collateral. I am asking you this as a family favor, a one-time emergency request."

"Okay. I'll see what I can do about it."

There was a silence. Cyrus recognized the formula by which, in Parsi-Zoroastrian circles, someone asking for money was routinely put off. After several months of hearing these words, the petitioner usually gave up of his own accord.

"You'll see what you can do about it?" Cyrus repeated tensely.

"Yes, I said I would. What's so strange about that? I have to check with my accountants. We have been having cash-flow problems of our own recently."

"All right. I understand."

"Meanwhile, please reconsider about coming to work with me."

"Thank you, I will give it serious thought." Cyrus could not forgo adding: "Although I don't know why you would want to hire a 'sissy' who has no business sense."

"As always, you take me much too seriously! I was just joking."

"Sorry. Forgive me, it is nerves. And thank you for listening so patiently to me. Give my love to Ruttee and to Eddie. By the way, how is Eddie doing?"

"The worst. We are just now thinking of placing him in a drug rehabilitation center for marijuana addiction." Farokh had lowered his voice. "I can't go into it now, I'm in my office and these people outside are trying to swindle me. But will you be home later? I will call you later."

CYRUS WENT UP THE BLOCK for dinner to his favorite coffee shop, the Parthenon. The waiter serving him tonight was also his favorite, Yannos: this man had a way of holding his head upright that was classically dignified. When he looked through the plate-glass window toward Columbus Avenue he was like a sailor on deck staring ruefully at the ocean. Just now Yannos had a five-o'clock shadow, but otherwise, with that wonderful distinguished profile of his, he reminded Cyrus of a middle-aged European matinee idol. With any luck he might have been Rosanno Brazzi instead of a waiter at the Parthenon.

"What will you have?" Yannos asked.

"The moussaka. And a glass of retsina, if you have it."

"I'll check."

Cyrus stared indirectly at the couple a few booths down from him, trying to eavesdrop. The man and the woman were having some sort of painful discussion. The woman would say something and the man would mutter a reply, and then there would be a long silence. They both seemed in their mid-twenties; the man, whose back was to Cyrus, was very skinny, with long straggly hair that ended in a wispy tail; the woman, facing Cyrus, had dark kohl eye makeup and hennaed hair, unwashed. She looked as though she was not getting enough sleep.

When Yannos returned with his food and wine, Cyrus thanked him warmly. The waiter started to leave, then hesitated. "I will not be here after next week," he said in his thick accent which it took Cyrus a moment to decipher.

"Oh, why? They didn't fire you, did they?"

"No. But I'm going back to Greece. I can't take this place any more. New York is too crazy for me."

"I am sorry to hear it."

"You are not from this country either?"

"No, from Iran originally. I came over when I was still a boy."

"Ah, so you are used to it."

"Not exactly," said Cyrus. "I will always feel like a non-American. But I like New York. And anyway, it is too late for me to go back to Iran, especially with what is going on there now."

The waiter nodded gravely, then added in a lower voice: "I think they are closing this coffee shop down."

"What, the Parthenon? They can't!"

"I hear talk all the time that the people who own the building are asking . . . ," and Yannos made the universal gesture of two fingers rubbed together, then moved off discreetly.

When he had finished his meal, Cyrus left a large tip. He went up to Yannos, who was taking a plate into the kitchen: "If I don't see you again, good luck. I will miss you. I mean that sincerely."

"Take good care of yourself," said Yannos. The waiter gave him a sad, fraternal smile; at that moment they were two copies of the same man.

BACK IN HIS APARTMENT, Cyrus examined the antique rugs hanging on the walls. It had been a long time since he had taken a

careful look at them; yet each of these pieces in his private collection had made him as excited as a passionate lover when he
had first acquired it. He remembered sleeping with the light on
all night when he had first hung the Yomud, in case he might
awaken and want to look at it. Now he scrutinized it dispassion-
ately, pretending to be a bored connoisseur at an auction house
late in the day. If he were someone with a lot of money, would
his heart leap at this? What had seemed at first so daring—the
clash of greens and blacks (actually deep blue, read as black)—
now struck him as a vulgar trick. But what about the Malatya?
Its pattern of interesting triangles was classical and yet savage,
and the strong oranges and browns still thrilled him. It was true
that, since he had bought it, a slew of this Malatya prayer-rug
type had been appearing on the art market; it was almost a cliché.
Fifty percent of the Turkish rugs at American auctions, he had
read recently, never sold. Still, this one had a sort of ferocious
authenticity, to his eyes—such an incredible sense of conviction
that surely it would overcome the American prejudice. . . . And
yet, he wasn't sure about the Malatya either any more. It disappointed him. He looked at the Senneh kilim with the Herati
design, a nice piece. There was a very subtle color play of rose
and olive with black outlines on an ivory ground. A little fey and
self-satisfied, perhaps.

In this way he went up to each in turn, finding fault, until
he came to the Tabriz picture rug that his uncle had left him.
This rug had nothing to apologize for: it might fetch anywhere
between seven thousand and twenty-five thousand dollars, depending on the briskness of the bidding. He smiled in admiration
at the pear tree in a vase, the animals and birds against a deep
magenta ground, the brick reds and lively blues, the meander of
leaves and blossoms. It was rare, discreet, joyous, playful, everything you could ask of a rug. No, he could never sell the Tabriz,
it was a present from his uncle. He would sell everything else,
and even then, maybe hold back the Malatya and. . . .

What a stupid investment artworks were. Quite apart from

their cursed illiquidity, one became attached to them and hated to give them up. At the time he had thought he was clever, putting his then-surplus capital into beautiful rugs he would enjoy looking at, rather than bond certificates. But now he saw the folly of having made these objets d'art his one hedge against bankruptcy.

He hated to hand these loved ones over to the cold machinery of the auction houses—not only that, but they took as much as forty percent commission right off the top! Cyrus suddenly had an idea. He could call Aberjinnian and ask his advice. The man knew all sorts of interior decorators and collectors, some quite respectable. He would want his cut, too, of course, although he might be willing to locate a buyer out of the sheer goodness of his heart. You never knew with Aberjinnian. He was a strange man, obnoxious, competitive, yet intelligent, shrewd. He liked to exaggerate his coarseness, thought Cyrus, but underneath it all there was a certain generosity and even a—civility. . . . If I explain the situation to him, he might very well decide to do it as a favor.

11

BROKEN CITY

Every other Sunday Aberjinnian conducted a short-notice auction in one of the hotels in the metropolitan area. He would rent a public room, and place an ad in the newspaper saying something like: a shipment of Oriental carpets had been refused by an importer who had over-ordered, with the result that twenty-five bales of carpets were to be auctioned off piece by piece at bargain prices. The truth was, the auctioneer owned the rugs and had no intention of selling them at a sacrifice. Aberjinnian's auctions were not intended for the *cognoscenti*, but for Sunday strollers out for a little excitement.

At the Sheraton Center, Cyrus took the escalator to the second floor and wandered around the corridors until he found the Imperial Room. Already a small crowd of people were bending their heads like penguins over the carpets, which had been laid atop the red hotel broadloom. Zack, Aberjinnian's assistant, a burly Israeli with mustache and muscular arms, moved through the crowd asking if anyone would like a particular rug to be brought up front. This was a way of baiting customers into bidding later, since in the end all the rugs, regardless of expressed interest, were carted to the front for auctioning.

Cyrus could have arrived at the end of the auction to discuss his business proposal, but he had never seen Aberjinnian "perform." He had first met the Armenian in the showrooms of lower Fifth Avenue, as a middleman, not an auctioneer meeting the general public. "Please be seated everyone. Please take a seat. The auction is about to begin," Zack announced, circulating. Eventually the audience was seated in folding chairs and waiting. A low murmur went through the crowd: Where is he? Where's the auctioneer?

A side door suddenly opened, and Aberjinnian shambled on, positioning himself between two clamp floodlights. As always he wore brown, a color that took dirt well. His polyester suit shone with cocoa embossed squares, and he wore a mud-colored sweater over a tan shirt and wide brown tie. He squinted with his hand shadowing his brow, seeming to be bothered by the floodlights.

"I am not used to having the audience so spread out. If you will please move from the sides to the middle more, and come closer up, you will all see better and I can save my voice." Only two people obliged. "Suit yourself." He cleared his throat tentatively. "I am going to say first a little about Oriental rugs, though I am sure you do not need to be told about them. In fact you probably know more than I do!" A few chuckles. "But just in case there are some out there who are not experts in the field, I will explain that these carpets are all handmade. Their value is going always up and up, because you cannot get handwoven goods like these any more, they are all becoming machine-made. Smart investors know that they are one of the wisest investments you can make. You can pass them on from generation to generation as heirlooms; you can even sell them to the museum. Any questions so far? Yes?"

"Where do they come from?" asked an elderly man with beautiful white hair.

"Most of them come from—a country in the Middle East I cannot tell you the name of, because I would get into trouble. This much I can say: they come from a country where labor is still very cheap. But it is rapidly becoming industrialized, so in the very near future these rugs will be a thing of the past. Are there any further questions? Please, don't be afraid to ask."

"Are they used?"

He winced, as though insulted. "They are all new carpets. These are not secondhand goods, believe me, you can take my word for it. These are the antiques of the future." He paused, pleased with his verbal formulation. "No further questions? I must tell you that I went recently to Iran and I came back empty-handed. Because they are asking such high prices that it is impossible to pay. Here is a commodity where you know the value can only increase. And they don't need elaborate care. If you want to clean them, just use ordinary soap and water. Any last questions?"

"What kinds of dyes are used?"

"The dyes are all natural. You people ask such suspicious questions, you are very tough. I feel like I am in a roomful of police inspectors! We could go on with this delightful conversation for hours, but some of you would like the auction to begin. Please, what do you say? Let's start. Zack, will you hold up the first item?"

The initial bids were cautious and low, invoking the auctioneer's disgust. "I thought this was New York City. This is not very fast. Is this New York City, Zack?"

"It looks that way outside."

"I have my doubts. Continue."

A few rugs later, Aberjinnian broke off the bidding again to demand of his assistant: "Why did you drag me all the way here for this? I am never coming back to this town. This is—this is a broken city. Excuse me, but you will read about this auction in the paper tomorrow. I had heard that New York City was in trouble, but not this much! Have we no more bids? Do I hear two hundred? Excuse me, does anyone here even have two hundred dollars?" A few nervous titters. One man slowly raised his hand. "Finally! Two hundred, two hundred twenty-five? . . . Ladies and gentlemen, you want bargains, all right. I can understand that. But this way you will drive me bankrupt! This is not fair, that is not the American way. I am entitled to make a living too. Do I hear two hundred *ten* dollars? You want me to lose my shirt, I understand. I am waiting. . . . All right, I see a hand, now how about two hundred fifty? No one. Two hundred ten once, twice—take it away, Zack, they can have it. It breaks my heart, but what can I do? . . . This hunting rug is one of the handsomest in the show. We must have a minimum reserve of six hundred dollars and at least two bids."

"Three hundred!" yelled out a man.

"No, this is not a Chinese auction, this is an American auction, the price goes *up*. Maybe the gentleman does not understand the meaning of the word *minimum*. The lowest bid we can accept is six hundred dollars. This is a Shah Abbas carpet, the only carpet to be named after an individual."

"Three hundred fifty!"

"The man is a comedian. Three hundred *fifty*? You see this design of the hunting scene? You would pay three hundred fifty if an artist gave you that on cardboard! Here you would be getting it handwoven. It took two people one and a half *years* to make this. And no vacations. No Christmas, no Labor Day. Show them the back. You can tell the quality of a rug by how tight the weave is. Feel it." He instructed Zack to take it over to the audience; some leaned over to feel, but most were reluctant to touch the wool. "You don't have to buy, just feel it! That way you can go home and at least you will have learned something."

"Five hundred dollars."

"I am glad to see someone appreciates quality. That is still very low. Six hundred, six hundred and fifty? Yes? . . . That is too low. Put it away, Zack. Tonight you people will dream about this hunting scene, and for the rest of your life you will kick yourself for not buying it. I feel sad for you. Take it down." His assistant started to fold the rug away. "No, wait," the auctioneer detained him. "One moment, I just want to ascertain something for myself." Aberjinnian faced the audience with hands on his hips, like a cross teacher scolding a classroom of children. "Why are you people here? What *do* you like? Do you prefer Chinese rugs? Indian? Moroccan? Russian? We have a carpet for every taste. I want each of you to leave with something of your own today. This beautiful young lady, why didn't you bid? Don't you want to go home with anything? I know. You are waiting for the door prize! We have no door prizes here. Show them the next rug.

"Does anybody like this rug? . . . I am *sure* that no one likes this rug at all, that's why you are not speaking up! Look—you don't have to bid if you say you like it. I want to know just for my own information. How many people think this is a nice rug?" Over a third of the audience raised their hands. "Well, then bid! Why are you here? Are you all relatives of each other? You are ganging up on me! You are all in league, I can feel it. I want to hear a bid of five hundred dollars for this rug. There's one! Five hundred from the woman with the feather hat—how about five hundred fifty? . . . No? You are purposely tormenting me. All right, miss, the rug is yours, I give up, you can pick it up afterward. Highway robbery. *Next!* All right. This time I am not setting a minimum. We will all play a little game. You like games, don't you? I want to find out what you in New York *think* this rug is worth."

"One hundred fifty!"

"One hundred fifty *dollars* or pounds sterling? You are insulting me now. If this is all you think such a fine rug is worth, what will you say when I show you the magnificent silk Kashan I have in store? . . . Fine, we will take a two-minute break so people can come up to the front and request individual rugs. I'm not going to auction off rugs that no one is interested in! Please, people, this is taking up my time, it is taking up your time. It will go much faster if you participate."

At intermission, the crowd milled around, smoking cigarettes and chatting. Some went up guiltily to the front to do their homework. When the second half began, the auctioneer continued flogging the audience and expressing astonished disenchantment, though from Cyrus's viewpoint he was getting quite good prices for the merchandise. Aberjinnian had structured his auction in such a way that, toward the very end, when he introduced the large Indo-Kashan he had been promising all along, this fairly undistinguished rug sold for an inflated three thousand dollars.

Cyrus waited until the crowd placing orders at the front table had thinned out, before approaching his friend.

"You are a master. I stand in awe."

"Junk, all junk," Aberjinnian said in an undertone. "Imagine if I had had quality stuff. Why didn't you bid, Irani? I saw you out there."

"I was tempted. The adrenaline starts flowing in an auction—you have the itch to raise your hand, even when you know better."

"Come, we'll sit in the corner and talk. I would buy you a drink downstairs but I have to stay and keep an eye on things here. . . . Shall I send out for tea?"

"No, please don't bother."

"All right. Zack, I'll be in the corner talking with this gentleman. Please finish wrapping up here." He led Cyrus to the end of the long ballroom, where two folding chairs waited for them.

"So. I am surprised to see you. After you did not attend the last time I invited you—to the good auction—I thought you might be angry at me."

"Not at all. I was just very busy."

"I understand. Still, it's a pity you did not make the last one because I had some really decent pieces there to sell."

"Unfortunately, I already have too much stock. I need to get rid of what I have first."

"The way to make money in rugs is at the buying end, not the selling end. I'd have given you a much better price than these fools paid today. But that's your affair. You have your own suppliers."

"I am glad I finally saw you in action. It was a fascinating performance," said Cyrus.

"All psychology. I manipulate their hostility, because they are all essentially racists who hate people from our part of the world. I get them to think they are putting me through an auctioneer's nightmare. They want me to suffer, so I suffer in front of them—but not too much, because they are also essentially good kind Americans."

"Amazing. But why did you tell them the dyes in the rugs were vegetable when they are chemical?"

"Tell them anything, so long as they buy. Besides, I told them the dyes were *natural*. One man's natural is another man's artificial. In the Middle East there is nothing more natural at present than using aniline dyes. I know, you think that makes me a con artist. I am—but a con artist with substance. I like that," he grinned. "Maybe I will have cards printed up: 'Aberjinnian, Con Artist with Substance.' "

"You could do worse."

"But you didn't come by to hear me boast. That you can do any time. What is it, my friend?"

"I am in—an embarrassing financial situation." Cyrus lowered his voice, although no one was around. "My landlord has tripled my rent and I cannot make enough to pay. But I want to stay where I am."

"Naturally."

Why "naturally"? Cyrus wondered, annoyed, but he was in

no position to challenge Aberjinnian's air of shrewd omniscience. "I have a few good rugs that I have been holding onto, my private collection, so to speak. I have a nineteenth-century Malatya prayer rug that is very high quality, and I mean it. And a beautiful Yomud piece, excellent wool. I also have an unusual Senneh kilim with a Herati design, fairly old and in perfect condition. I have a Daghestan, mid-nineteenth century. . . ." Cyrus was starting to lose heart. "A very simple Talish Caucasian which has a dark blue center with strips of *abrash*."

Aberjinnian was silent. He shrugged. "What do you want me to do about it?"

"I was hoping you could help me find buyers. I don't have the time to go through a big auction house or a gallery—"

"You mean, to go to a reputable dealer. So you came to me."

"That's not it; but however you want to put it, I am asking for your help."

"Go on. What else do you have besides this Daghestan and the Yomud and the Talish Caucasian? No Persians?" demanded Aberjinnian. "Are you one of those Iranian reverse snobs who turns up his nose at his own people's culture? Persian rugs have always been considered the finest."

"Yes, that's right, I don't disagree. But I collected Caucasus rugs because they were more geometric and abstract, so they were more like the modern paintings I was drawn to in graduate school. Anyway, what difference does it make? If you want to know the truth, I am not crazy about many Persian rugs. All that fussy ornamentation is too sweet for my taste."

"Also easier to sell. I am just inquiring. So you really have no Persians?"

Cyrus hesitated. "I have an old Tabriz picture rug, a tree of life with birds and animals—"

"I remember the Tabriz. I saw it when I came to your house, remember?"

"That's right. So you know all these rugs. Anyway, the Tabriz was a gift from my uncle and—I would rather not sell it."

"How much do you want for the others?"

"I need about thirty thousand dollars. They're all good."

"You don't have to keep saying that, I believe you. Still, I don't think you would get anywhere near thirty thousand dollars in today's market. Ten years ago, maybe. The great boom of the seventies is over, my friend. Rugs are undervalued now, I don't have to tell *you* that. Everyone has been burned, the collectors have gotten very cautious and conservative. . . . I don't understand how you didn't make a pile of money in the seventies, when even the greatest idiot could have gotten rich selling rugs."

"It is one of the mysteries of life, I suppose."

"In any event, how do you hope to stay in business the next few years if the rent is so high?"

"I will try more aggressive merchandising."

"Why don't you try that *now?* That way you won't have to break up your 'priceless collection.' It seems to me you haven't thought this out, my good friend." Aberjinnian turned his moon face to see what Zack was up to. Cyrus felt a hot flash of exasperation at the man's tone. By the time Aberjinnian returned his attention, Cyrus had regained his composure.

"You're right, I haven't thought it out sufficiently. You have much more experience in these matters than I. Still, whatever I do, I need to raise capital for it. I can give you a few good rugs to sell, if you think you can do something with them. I know you are in contact with private collectors and interior decorators who might . . . be willing to go outside the usual channels for quality and a bargain."

"What would I get out of it? It's a good deal of work, and it may come to nothing."

"What would you think is fair?"

"Fair is not the issue here. This is business, my friend. In the first place, I am only interested in handling the Tabriz. The rest is a waste of time. In the second, I would want, oh, forty percent."

"But that's what a fancy gallery or auction house charges!"

"Of course. Am I less worthy than a gallery?"

"No, certainly not, but I thought you would understand that I am in a financial trap. I need as much money as I can realize from this sale, and so I came to you, as a friend. . . ."

Aberjinnian smiled; he chuckled to himself softly.

"What's so funny?"

"Thirty percent. For friendship's sake."

"Thank you."

"But we are only talking about the Tabriz, right?"

"I will have to think about it," said Cyrus. "Give me a week or two to mull it over."

"Do you have slides of all the rugs?"

"No, not all, but I thought I could leave them with you. Or else anyone interested can see them at my place. I am always around the shop, or I could leave you the key."

"Cyrus. Have slides made."

"All right."

"I guarantee nothing. But for a start, there is an odd group of collectors I know who meet once a month. The Rug Fanciers Club. Have you come across them yet?"

"No, I don't think so. Is it like the old Hajii Baba Club?"

"Not quite. The Hajii Baba people were old society types, wealthy shipping magnates and scholarly millionaires. These are not so much millionaires as mystics," said Aberjinnian, "although some of them do have money. More than one of them came to rugs via drugs. They were smuggling hashish on the road from Marrakech to Kathmandu, and they got tired of it, of the risk maybe. So they sat at the feet of various swamis in India. They got all involved with Sufis and Tibetan monks. Now they have this funny idea that rugs possess some spiritual significance. I don't understand it; in America they always want the rug to be something sacred. A magic carpet. To us, a rug is a utility object: we store things in it, we use it as a valise, we take it on picnics, make it into a mattress, or a blanket if it's cold. Look, I was 'conceived' on a rug like those over there. So much for spiritual significance."

Cyrus smiled. "I'm not sure I agree."

"Why not?" demanded Aberjinnian.

"I agree up to a point." Cyrus rubbed a finger over his mustache, thinking it over. "Americans are a young people. They yearn for objects that have been in the family for centuries. It's precisely because craft objects like rugs have been 'sanctified' by worn daily use that they still have their aura."

"Their what? I did not hear the last word."

"*Aura*, like the light around a saint's head in medieval paintings, the halo. I am using the word in the way the critic Walter Benjamin did, in his famous essay, 'The Work of Art in the Age of Mechanical Reproduction.' But let's not go into all that here," he broke off, suddenly feeling pretentious invoking this lofty intellectual name in the Imperial Room of the Sheraton Center.

"Why not go into it? Do you think I am too stupid to understand? I am a man who likes to learn new things. Tell me about this Benjamin's essay."

"Well, I'm not sure I understand it fully myself—it's very dense, and it's an atypical piece in the context of Benjamin's canon. The gist of it is that works of art formerly had a cultic significance that came from their being used in rituals and religious practice. Like a magician's mask, or medieval church altarpieces. And from that special use an 'aura' developed around an art object, which placed it at a distance from ordinary life. But with photography and film, with the technological means to mass-produce identical images as well as products, the aura began to decline. If there are a million reproductions of the Mona Lisa, the original no longer seems so unique, so authoritative. It has lost some of its distance and magic. . . . But because Benjamin was a Marxist, he tried very hard to take a dialectical position which foresees positive as well as negative possibilities in this breakdown. He claims, for instance, that the decline of the so-called 'bourgeois elitist' aura around art may open new ground for a radical political culture. But underneath, you sense he is still ambivalent and saturated with nostalgia for the old aesthetic mystery. It's all left very unresolved. . . . There is a famous disagreement among Brecht, Benjamin and Adorno about this question. . . . In any case," Cyrus pulled up short, "when it comes to rugs you can see the attraction they might have for people in an assembly-line society. As you said before, the weavers work very hard. They are working for months on end, resigned to the task at hand. And the focus gets very concentrated and the choices are simple and humble. Even the creative part is logical, not arbitrary but methodical, patient, obedient to the tradition. And finally one begins to sense the spell of the rug emerging, like a beautiful aura. It is the monotony of the work, the loneliness of the work, sitting on some rock in the middle of Turkey, just making this thing, that is the—prayer, if you will."

"You are a poet, my friend."

"Please, don't make fun of me."

"I'm not. I admire you. You know so many things that your head must be filled with ideas. Auras, eh?" Aberjinnian looked at him appraisingly. "You are so learned, Cyrus."

"On the contrary, I am very ignorant."

"How, ignorant? You read so many books."

"I read books, and a little bit sticks to me. But I know nothing deeply. My intelligence is extremely limited."

"Don't tell me, I can distinguish intelligence. I am a man of the world, and I tell you that you are very bright, but you are lacking in confidence."

"Well, thank you for saying that."

"I have no wish to flatter you, I mean it." Aberjinnian patted Cyrus's knee. "I must go. Just to change the subject, did you take my advice?"

"What advice are you referring to?"

"Did you go to a swing club and meet a lovely lady?"

Cyrus smiled vaguely. "No I haven't."

"Ah, you see, that is the root of your problem. You are sexually starved. No wonder you have been going through such a bad time. By the way, what became of your neighbor, the one who had her eye on you?"

"Who? . . . Marge?"

"The one with the problem with her leg. Did you fuck her at least? You told me you would give me the whole story the next time you saw me."

"There is nothing to tell. She moved to Rochester."

12

A DINNER PARTY

OVER THE PHONE, his mother began stiffly: "I have a favor to ask of you." Cyrus waited. "Very rarely I ask you to do something for me, isn't it? Please humor me this once."

"Certainly, if I can. What is it?"

"My friends the Jessawallas are in town from London. I am having a few people over next Sunday night for a dinner party in their honor."

"You know I don't like dinner parties, but—very well, sure."

"You are saying you'd rather not come?"

"I will, for your sake. The only part that disturbs me is why you always make such a fuss over Jessawalla. Just because he's rich. I mean, would he ever think of throwing a dinner party for you?"

"That has nothing to do with it. His wife, Veera, is the daughter of my old classmate from Teheran. And the fact that he is rich, you know, could help you in your present problems."

"I am not sure I understand," said Cyrus. "What could I ask him to do for me? Become a silent partner in my little shop?"

"That is up to you: use your imagination. It could be a very important opportunity if you play your cards right."

"Must I?" he asked, only half jesting.

"You always used to say that when you were little," his mother noted. "If I called you in from play, you'd cry 'Mommy, must I?' If we were about to leave to call on relatives, it was always 'Must I go too?' That was when I used to call you 'Mr. Must-I,' remember?"

"Just tell me when I am to report."

"Come at seven. Earlier, if you like. We can have a little visit first."

DISLIKING THE AWKWARD first minutes of parties, Cyrus arrived at his mother's house at a quarter to eight. When his mother opened the door, it was a shock to see, just past her shoulder, the girl she had introduced him to at the Jashan service.

"Mother, what are you up to?" he whispered. "You could have at least prepared me!"

"You might never have come." He dubiously inspected his old gray sweater and navy blue coat with toggle buttons. "You look fine. Come, this way." She steered him toward the kitchen. "Scherezade, you remember my younger son, Kurush?"

"A pleasure to see you again." Cyrus offered his hand. There was something very fresh-looking about her small features and curly black hair.

"I am glad to see you again," she managed to say. "Can I get you something to drink? Whiskey, beer or wine?"

"A glass of wine, please. . . . I hope my mother is not exploiting you as foreign labor."

"Not at all. I don't mind helping Auntie," she said, retreating rapidly into the recesses of the kitchen like a frightened mouse.

From the living room came sounds of a typical Zoroastrian social gathering—boisterous, jovial, every other statement peppered with oaths or laughter. He heard his brother's voice let out an *"MCBC!,"* Parsi shorthand for a standard curse involving incest with one's mother and sister, and the company's laughter. It seemed to Cyrus that Freddy, in marrying a Parsi, had adopted not only Parsi slang but even the accent at times.

"I will tell you another. This one is cleaner! A psychiatrist tells his patient: 'You're stupid.' The patient says: 'I'd like a second opinion.' The psychiatrist replies: 'Okay—you're ugly!'—Wait, my brother has just arrived. Everyone be quiet! I am going to salute my brother's arrival." Freddy held out both hands for silence. He had grown fat recently, but Cyrus could see his gestures were still those of a manic youth intent on being the life of the party. "Quick, quick, pull my finger!"

"He is going to fart," his wife, Ruttee, warned placidly. She was a jaundiced-skinned woman with thick glasses in pointy black frames.

Sure enough, a rumble of gas issued from Freddy's bottom, and Ruttee held her nose and ran to the other side of the room.

"Thank you, Farokh. I appreciate the fanfare."

"No problem, brother. Any time."

"That reminds me, what Freddy just did," said Veera Jessawalla, "of the time I was working as a stewardess for Air India. This was in the days when Air India was still a Parsi airline. On long flights the stewards used to do motion picture charades to entertain the customers. So this one fellow Jimmy, he was so funny, he got up and put a white napkin on his head for a cap and he dropped his pants down to his undershorts. Then he started going up and down the aisles and he was letting out an *awful* smell. No one could guess what he was doing, so he said, 'You give up? You give up?' What do you think it was? *Gan with the Wind!*"

When the laughter had subsided, Cyrus's mother said to him: "You remember Meher, Scherezade's brother?"

"I certainly do."

The tall priest, again in white ceremonial jacket, bow tie, trousers and skullcap, rose enthusiastically and offered Cyrus a firm handshake, towering over him like a basketball player. He had not remembered her brother being so tall. There was something reassuring about this man's serious, horsey face with pockmarked skin and gentle smile; Cyrus was pleasantly surprised to see him here.

Cyrus went over to the guest of honor, who made a half-hearted attempt to get up. "Ooh, forgive me, I am too comfortable to stand," said Darius Jessawalla, extending his hand crosswise over his shoulder. Cyrus nodded, staring down at the man the Zoroastrian community called the Mogul: he ran a large international construction company, sold steel, owned an advertising agency and who knew what else. The Mogul's blue silk shirt was open at the neck, allowing a generous view of his silver chest hairs and powerful physique. He had a trim gray mustache and alert calculating eyes that roamed frequently and impatiently around the room. Although bald (except for an encircling fringe around the ears), he was the kind of man who could turn any trait to advantage: Jessawalla's baldness connoted virility. "How are you, old fellow? You look well," he said to Cyrus.

"Appearances are deceiving. . . ."

Jessawalla's wife Veera, a strikingly good-looking woman in her early forties, with full regal black hair and the ripe figure of an ex–beauty queen, stood in her elegant cerise sari, her arms out to embrace Cyrus. She kissed him more warmly than he had expected (he had not even been certain she would remember him), on both cheeks, and he inhaled her sweet but subtle perfume. Veera had on enough jewelry to start a new life in exile should her home assets ever be seized: masses of gold and silver bracelets that caused her arms to jangle when she spoke, a diamond necklace and matching earrings and rings—all of which was proper current upper-class style (the older generation of Zoroastrians had tended to hide their wealth).

Cyrus sat in an easy chair some distance from the others. Scherezade had returned with his wine on a coaster and was taking everyone's refill orders. When she left the room, Cyrus's eyes trailed absentmindedly after her slender schoolgirl figure in black velvet skirt and white blouse, noticing her bra strap through the back of her blouse.

"So, Darius, you are in from London?" Cyrus asked Jessawalla politely.

"Not London—Austin! Before that we were in Toronto, Geneva, Dubai, Paris, London, Istanbul. You name it, we have been there on business all in the last six months."

"That must be tiring for you." Cyrus turned to Veera.

"Yes, one gets travel-weary. But one gets used to it."

"Somehow she always manages to find a second wind when there's a chance of a trip to Paris."

"I live for Paris," agreed Veera, her eyes shining from the mere sounding of the word. "In Paris, there I feel *alive*." Alongside her pleasure at the thought of Paris might be read her contempt for and dissatisfaction with everything which was not Paris— including, Cyrus thought, his mother's prosaically middle-class living room in Queens.

"Why don't you ever take *me* to Paris?" Freddy's wife, Ruttee, demanded, squinting behind her thick glasses.

"So you can run up bills at all the shops?" Freddy said. He turned to the Jessawallas with the zestful expression of beginning a joke. "You may not know this, but my wife cannot be trusted in a shopping center. She writes out a check and doesn't bother to record the amount after. I tell her, *please*, from time to time call the bank and ask what your balance is. If it is too low I can throw a few thousand dollars in. No—that's too rational. She says, 'Why you can't get your secretary to call the bank?' How can my secretary check the balance of someone else's account? I have come to the conclusion you cannot win with women. Let me tell you, Cyrus, about Parsi wives, before you get married to one. Parsi women do not feel secure unless they have one thing. Can you guess what it is?"

"What is it?" Cyrus asked patiently.

"One million dollars in a CD account. No stocks, no securities, it must be cash or gold."

"Since when?" Ruttee objected. "You're lying."

"Don't contradict me, woman!" Freddy roared with relish. He had a way of bullying that was comical and endearing, but bullying nevertheless. "She keeps telling me, my wife, that she is worried we don't have enough money. She hears on the radio—1010 WINS no less!—that the economy is bad, so she fancies herself an economist. Now I don't mind a woman speaking up, but at least take the trouble to find out what you are talking about. 'The economy is bad' doesn't mean a thing. Bad for whom? Bad for me may be good for you. Am I right?" he asked Jessawalla.

"I will stay out of this one," the guest of honor laughed.

"Oh, he is twisting things, the way he always does," cried Ruttee. "It gets me so frustrated!"

"How am I twisting things?"

"I am not going to go into it in front of all these people!"

"Why? I want you to go into it! Go into it! I'm not afraid."

"Ruttee," said Cyrus placatingly, "you know what the Persian poet wrote: 'If, in the middle of the day, the king says that night has come, then tell him you can see the moon and stars."

"Whatever you say, Great King, Great Master," she salaamed her husband, "Royal Highness . . ."

"Quite right. I'm glad you are finally catching on." Freddy winked, and took a gulp of Scotch.

"Freddy, you wouldn't like Ruttee to treat you like her master," Mrs. Irani waggled her finger. "It's better for you that this lady has a mind of her own."

Cyrus winced inwardly, knowing that his mother thought the opposite about her daughter-in-law. Just then Scherezade reentered the room, watching the scene with a quiet, amused smile.

"She *should* have a mind of her own, *and* agree with me. Because I am always right. No one can dispute that. Except for women's libbers! The worst mistake today is this women's lib," Freddy said, looking around provocatively.

"Bad for whom?" quoted Veera.

"Ah, MCBC—you are all ganging up on me!" Freddy threw up his hands, and everyone roared. "Come, sit down here next to your brother and me, Scherezade." He patted the sofa cushion.

She looked at Cyrus's mother uncertainly, to see if anything else needed to be done, then crossed the room and sat down between them.

"Now you are like a flower between two earths," remarked Jessawalla.

"That's very pretty. Did you make it up?" asked Ruttee.

"Of course not."

"Where is Eddie?" asked Cyrus. "He couldn't come?"

"He is grounded for the week," said Freddy, with a dark look that discouraged further inquiry.

"Darius, did you get a chance to talk to Meher? He is just arrived from Pakistan," said Mrs. Irani, hoping to draw out her silent guest.

"Really? Is that so? Are you taking a doctorate in religion here?"

Meher paused: he always considered his words first, even when asked a simple factual question. "No, computer engineering at NYU. I study religion on the side for myself."

"Very commendable. We certainly need new blood to carry on the ministry," said Jessawalla. "What part of Pakistan are you from?"

Meher seemed to deliberate. "From Quetta, a small city high up, north of Karachi."

"Of course I know Quetta," Jessawalla said smoothly. "You know, there used to be a sort of rivalry between Karachi and Bombay when I was growing up."

"Sibling rivalry," put in Freddy.

"Yes. We in Bombay would consider our co-religionists to be 'country bumpkins,' and the Karachi Parsis thought of us as godless 'city-slickers.' "

"In Karachi," said Meher slowly, "we say that . . . after building our town, Spenta Mainyu molded the form of Bombay from the debris that was left over. That is why the climate of Bombay is so inferior to Karachi's."

"Very good. You have me there!" Jessawalla laughed appreciatively.

"On the other hand," said Cyrus's mother, "people speak of Bombay the Beautiful, but not Karachi the Beautiful."

"They were talking about the old days," sniffed Veera. "Now I find Bombay dirty and overcrowded."

"Oh, but Bombay still has lovely places, hasn't it?"

"Yes, a few. But the housing problem is awful, there are too many people; it is just getting too depressing," said Veera.

"How sad. Still, I would love to go back there sometime," said Mrs. Irani. "After all, it's the center of Zoroastrian life, isn't it?"

"You must remember," said Veera, arching an eyebrow, "I am not from Bombay but from Iran, like you. We are the real thing. These other Zoroastrians, these Parsis from India and Pakistan, I call half-and-half, you know? *Dobras.*"

"Half of what? I am a hundred-percent Zoroastrian and proud!" insisted Jessawalla.

"Now Veera, I can't allow you to run our guests down. You are sounding like such a snob," Mrs. Irani said teasingly.

"And besides, everyone knows that the Zoroastrians who stayed behind in Iran were mostly illiterate farmers—*Irun junglee.*" Jessawalla dropped this bombshell, then sat back, his eyes twinkling with anticipation at his wife's haughty outrage.

"Since when? *Ha!* Who told you that? We are the real aristocrats. We are the originators of the faith. . . . Well, anyway, I married a Parsi so now I am Parsi too. No complaints."

"I am very glad to hear it," said her husband.

"I was just telling my friend the other day—"

"Which friend? Boyfriend or girlfriend?" prodded Jessawalla.

"Girlfriend. But if you keep pushing me it will be boyfriend," countered Veera. Everyone laughed, and she added with a wink, "Just make sure I am not too old before you give me permission for a boyfriend. I want to be able to enjoy it still."

"Who is holding you back?"

"Never mind. Just remember how lucky you are to have a faithful wife like me."

"How did you two meet?" asked Cyrus.

"I was working as a stewardess on Air India. And this man here started talking freshly to me. By the time the plane landed we were engaged."

"She is simplifying."

"Not by much," said Veera. "In those days, to get a job on Air India was considered being part of an elite. All the steward-esses were either Parsi girls from good families or Anglo-Indian girls. Plus a few Irani Zoroastrians like me. We were all very pretty. I remember this one stewardess particularly, she was a *beautiful* girl, smashing looks, but she couldn't speak English well. Jasmine was her name. We were on a long flight where we had to serve one thing after another on a very tight schedule. She was always lagging behind. I said to her, 'Jasmine, we must start on the dinners.' 'But I am still serving horvy-dory.' " Veera imitated the girl's singsong South Indian accent, driving Freddy into hysterics. "I tried to teach her: hors d'oeuvres, 'or derv-re.' She would say, 'hory-dory.' Just never could get it right. One time she said, 'Man over there wants crumpled eggs.' 'Don't you mean *scrambled* eggs?' I asked. 'What is difference? You have to crumple eggs all up. Same thing.' "

Everyone laughed, and Veera was encouraged to continue. "Oh, we had such good times. Especially when Jimmy was work-ing as flight steward. One time I had a man on board who was a real pest. He had fingeritis. Every few minutes he would ring

for me: 'Just a little coffee' or 'Just a little glass of orange juice.'
This went on for hours. Finally I got tired of it and didn't respond.
My passenger grabbed Jimmy from the aisle: 'I ring stewardess.
Why she no come?' Jimmy said, 'Well it's because you are wearing the poor girl out. Asking for this and that.' 'I can't help it.
I have headache.' 'Why didn't you say so? I'll bring you an
aspirin.' So he gets the man an aspirin, and the man turns it
over suspiciously. Finally he says, 'But—this is Indian
aspirin!' Jimmy said, 'What's the matter, you have a foreign
headache?' "

"That is Parsi wit," Jessawalla said appreciatively.

"That Jimmy was a riot. He would stand by the door as the
English passengers were leaving, and tilt his head ever so politely
and say, '*Mader-chode . . . mader-chode . . .*' " The gathering
burst into laughter. "And they had no idea it meant 'mother-
fuckers.' Poor Jimmy," Veera sighed. "I was so sad when I learned
that he died recently." The room fell silent.

"How come you are sitting way over there?" Freddy asked
his brother. "What, are you sitting far?" The company burst into
laughter again; even Cyrus grinned at the old pun at his expense.
Sitting far referred to the Zoroastrian custom of women being
segregated from the household during menstruation. Cyrus played
out the joke, crossing his legs mincingly like a woman with
cramps.

"Seriously, come closer, *mader-chode*. Join the party."

Cyrus moved his chair closer to the coffee table, which was
filled with cheeses, honey cakes, fruit, spring onions, pistachios
and mixed nuts.

"We were kidding just now, but I have often wondered if
there isn't some truth, some scientific basis to our belief," said
Jessawalla, "that the touch or the glance of a woman in her
'menses,' so to speak, can be harmful."

"Certainly there is truth," Cyrus's mother responded readily.
"I can tell you from my own experience. If I happened to go

near flowers when I was in my period they would wilt faster. If I passed by a plate of pickles, they would spoil."

"How do you mean, 'spoil'?" Cyrus objected. "That's only superstition."

"They develop a layer of fungus on top. You don't believe? It has been scientifically proven, Mr. Know-All. I'll tell you something else you may find hard to believe. There is such a thing as sympathetic menstruation. When I was, say, only in my twenty-first day, and another woman was staying in the same house—this happened with my cousin—and she started menstruating, I would start also."

"You don't say!" Jessawalla sat up excitedly. "That is what I was getting at. Who knows if it is biological or psychic forces at work, but there is something behind it all."

"Certainly. Don't you agree, Scherezade?" Mrs. Irani asked.

The girl nodded with strange calm eyes. It gave Cyrus a disturbing thrill to think of this slightly built young woman across from him menstruating.

"But what about the idea," said Cyrus, "that menstruation is the 'devil's kiss'? And that a woman cannot therefore go into a prayer hall during her time? Don't you find that offensive, Mother?"

"That is just custom," she shrugged.

"It's a custom," Ruttee chimed in. "You do it and you don't think about it."

"My brother has become a big feminist," Freddy remarked.

"Only on my best days am I a feminist. I wish it could always be the case."

"If you are such a feminist, then you need to consider," said his mother, "that our women are worked very hard. Sitting far at least gives the woman a little rest each month, a little privacy for a few days."

"I see what you mean. Still, it sounds unjust when the worst man, the foulest evildoer, may go into a house of worship with no one objecting, while the most innocent maiden who has just entered puberty must be kept away, out of some idiotic fear that she will 'harm' the holy books." Here Cyrus looked directly at Meher, as though challenging him to make a learned scriptural defense, but the *mobed* only smiled enigmatically and said nothing.

The cooking timer sounded; Scherezade leaped up.

"I think we are ready to sit down at table," said Mrs. Irani.

Cyrus started to rise, and found Darius Jessawalla in his path. "Please, after you."

"I wouldn't think of it. You go first."

"May I be sacrificed for you."

"I am nothing, I am your slave."

"You are too gracious. I cannot accept this honor."

"The food will grow cold if we keep this up much longer," said Jessawalla. They both laughed.

"You sit here, Darius," said Mrs. Irani, "at the head of the table. And you, Veera, over here, next to Meher. That way we have boy-girl, boy-girl."

When everyone had been assigned a place, Cyrus realized that his mother had maneuvered it so that he and Scherezade were sitting next to each other. This whole dinner party, he thought, might be nothing but an elaborate chaperoning device.

Properly speaking, there was no dining room in his mother's house. She had squeezed the old family table, with all its leaves added for tonight, into an oval alcove between kitchen and living room. The long table was covered with a bewildering variety of food, hot and cold, Iranian and Parsi. There were kebabs of chicken, lamb and beef, rice with sauce, curried shrimp, cucumber salad and spicy salad, Bombay duck, dal and vegetable leaves; wine, beer and large plastic bottles of Sprite and Pepsi-Cola.

"You have really prepared a feast for us like I've never seen!" Jessawalla told Mrs. Irani.

"Oh, it's nothing. Scherezade helped me with it, and she made the dal herself. Good, isn't it?"

All the young woman's best points were being put on display.

"It's delicious," Cyrus complimented her. "So . . . how are you finding New York?"

"I love it!" said Scherezade. "I come home exhausted just from looking. All the beautiful things in the shop windows. And the people in the street, they are all so interesting to watch. You know, like they are in a dance? . . ."

"I understand exactly what you mean. That's right, you are a dancer."

"Oh, no. I am just beginning. I take aerobics and Indian folk dance, that's all. Just for fun."

"What else do you do for fun?"

"I go to happy hours!" she said gaily, lowering her voice so her brother would not hear. "Sometimes my girlfriend and I meet in Trader Vic's after an exam and we drink daiquiris. They have such delicious frozen daiquiris, and a wonderful spread during happy hour."

Cyrus was at a loss for a suitable response. This young woman had expressed so much vivacity about something that mattered not at all to him. Finally he said, "How are your classes going?"

She wrinkled up her nose. "American History is boring. The professor—he tries to make it interesting, when he sees you are falling asleep. Sometimes he's so funny to watch, pacing up and down, I have to keep myself from laughing."

Cyrus instantly identified with the boring professor. "So history does not excite you."

"I like ancient history. But this is too recent—too many dates to memorize. The Louisiana Purchase, the Spanish-American War . . ."

"Why must you take American History, if your field is hotel management?"

"It is part of the degree."

"Have you begun your hotel studies yet?"

"Just one course: Major Figures in Hotel Management History."

They laughed. "It seems you cannot escape history." Cyrus sensed the others watching them. "What else will you study to prepare for hotel work?"

"I don't know," Scherezade said, looking a little sad, and added in a lowered voice: "I am only taking hotel management because I can't think of anything else to do with myself."

"I know the feeling," said Cyrus, touched by this confession. "How will you use it after you graduate?"

"*If* I graduate."

"Don't be so modest, of course you will."

"I am thinking to go back to Karachi and manage a hotel, if I am lucky enough to find a position."

"So you are only in the States for a little while," Cyrus asked, feeling a pang of disappointment which surprised him.

"That depends on many things. . . ." She looked toward her brother by way of explanation. A silence fell between them, and Cyrus thought it best to return to the larger conversation.

"In Paris," Veera was saying, "we went to a dinner at the ambassador's house, after Zubin's concert. It was a gorgeous mansion with high ceilings and flowing marble staircases. The ambassador had invited all these other famous conductors, and when we sat down to dinner, Zubin said, 'I want our Parsi onion and tamarind salad—*kachubar* and *patril*.' So they had to bring it to him. And all the other conductors were eating this hot spicy salad soaked in tamarind sauce and swallowing gallons of water!"

Everyone roared, holding their sides. Cyrus pretended to join in, but it was the sort of joke whose humor he could never fathom.

"Did you catch that profile they did on him on '20/20'?" Ruttee asked. "When people ask me what is my religion, I say, 'You know the famous conductor Zubin Mehta? Well, I am Zoroastrian, like him.' So now they tell me every time he is on the television. 'You must watch tonight, Ruttee, Zubin Mehta's going to be on!' they say."

"What I like about Zubin Mehta, he has a real feeling for

the community," Cyrus's mother said. "In every interview he mentions he is a Zoroastrian. I hear that when he comes into a new city, he always asks to sit down to dinner with the local Parsis—"

"And to sleep with their wives!" quipped Freddy.

"That's not true and you know it. He is very happily married."

"Although he was something of a womanizer," said Veera.

"How do you know?" demanded her husband.

"Never mind!"

"He has such a wonderful feeling for music. Don't you agree, Cyrus? My son is an expert on classical music."

"Please, I am nothing of the sort." He silently glared at his mother for dragging him into this potentially dangerous discussion.

"But you *are* fond of music, yes? So tell us your opinion of my friend Zubin's conducting. I am sure we have much to learn from you," said Jessawalla expansively.

"It depends on the piece of music. Sometimes he is excellent—especially in his specialty, the nineteenth-century Romantic repertoire. He can get a full lush sound out of an orchestra." Cyrus paused, wondering whether it was worth it to cross the Rubicon. "But . . . to be honest, his conducting seems to me a little coarse, vulgar, sentimental, a little 'extroverted' for my taste. With baroque composers or with the moderns, he lacks some introspective, spiritual quality."

"Well, no one is good at everything. You can't fault a man for that."

"Yes, but to me he doesn't take quite as much care with the musical structure as he should. In that respect I preferred his predecessor at the Philharmonic, Pierre Boulez."

"But Boulez is so dry, isn't it?" said Cyrus's mother.

"Yes, some people complained that Boulez was 'cerebral.' But I found him to have a much better musicological, scholarly grasp of the score than Mehta."

"I don't pretend to be an expert on music," said Jessawalla. "I'm only a businessman, maybe my tastes *are* 'coarse,' but I always thought that music should have a touch of sentiment. Isn't the whole purpose of music to stir us, to move our hearts?"

"Certainly. I don't disagree."

"Well, then! Zubin goes around the world and is acclaimed everywhere he plays. China, Israel, Japan, Brazil. Are all these people so easily fooled? You talk about music as if it were a game of chess. A game of chess is a game of chess!" With that angry *bon mot*, the discussion ended. Cyrus saw no point in arguing against everyone. He had obviously deeply offended Jessawalla, and now he would never get a loan out of him.

The conversation turned elsewhere; Cyrus withdrew into himself, only half listening. It was dinner party chitchat, Zoroastrian style. He had heard it many times before. The people here, he was thinking, were decent, fun-loving, humane, but they had no use for the life of the mind, for the things he valued or might have contributed to the discussion. That was why he always felt alienated at these social functions, even while he envied the others their Rabelaisian jokes and high spirits.

Cyrus began studying people's mouths as they spoke. What was the meaning of that ambiguously discontented, almost bitter expression on Veera's lips? What had she expected from life and not gotten—she who would seem to have so much? He liked her full mouth, with that dark, rather morbid brown lipstick shade— in fact, he was extremely attracted to her. Wouldn't a mature, sexy woman like Veera make a better wife for him than Scherezade? he wondered. But women like Veera cost money.

Freddy's lips he had always liked. The bottom one had a way of dangling in three sections, with a wet infectious grin that could start people laughing before they were even sure what he was going to say. But sometimes Cyrus would notice a trembling in that lower lip, just as his brother was getting ready to seize the spotlight. Freddy tried so hard, Cyrus could not help feeling pity for him at times. And love: it surprised Cyrus how much he loved Freddy when he saw him in person, although when they were separated he was not often moved by affection for his older brother.

He stole a sideways look at Scherezade's lips, which were a little thin and virginal. Odd to think of a twenty-four-year-old still being a virgin in this world. Perhaps she wasn't, perhaps she had more experience than he suspected. He pictured biting her lower lip, till she cried out—till a drop of blood pooled on the bottom. He pictured that mouth of hers closing slowly over his penis, and moving up and down. She did have small, lovely teeth. Yet his body, sitting next to her body, experienced none of the desire he felt toward Veera—experienced no outward movement, in fact, which was a dangerous sign, unless it was simply fear. . . .

Cyrus focused on the clean-shaven upper lip of Meher. For a second he wanted to kiss it. Sometimes, in the past, when he had respected a man's character or words, he had had the sudden urge to kiss the talking man full on the lips. Did this mean he was underneath everything a homosexual? Latent, perhaps—and since he was not the most sexually adventurous person, he doubted he would ever test it in this lifetime.

His sister-in-law's lips. No, there was nothing enticing there. He might manage to kiss her eyelids, perhaps, or the top of her head. . . . And the Mogul? A handsome man, no doubt about it, with that clipped gray mustache, but no, it might tickle. His mother? How often he had kissed her on the mouth as a boy, and then there came a time in adolescence when he would do anything to avoid it. At the thought of kissing his mother on the lips again, he felt a faint disgust: the game was getting tiresome.

"Have you seen the latest figures? We are down to a hundred ten thousand in all the world," his mother was saying. "The *Wall Street Journal* article says we are dying out."

"Don't buy Zoroastrian stocks!" joked Freddy. "We are becoming an endangered species. We must get the Environmental Protection Agency to put us on their list."

"Why do we keep losing population?" Ruttee asked crossly.

"Why? Because we don't screw enough!" said her husband.

"No, it's because the Zoroastrian boys keep marrying out," said Veera. "And the girls too. All our customs are too difficult and complicated to maintain, that is the root of the problem. Our religion has failed to adapt to the modern age."

"There is still plenty more," said the hostess, gesturing toward the dishes of lamb, eggplant, chicken and salad. "After all, we must keep up our strength, we last survivors."

Meher cleared his throat. "I would say, on the contrary, that we have assimilated too much to the modern age. Today we only pay lip service to Zarathustra's ideals. Our younger people are educated in the Western rationalist tradition, which unfortunately denigrates religion and the emotional, religious part of a person."

"But in a way you are supporting Mrs. Jessawalla's contention," said Cyrus. "Isn't the decline partly because our religious leaders have failed to build a synthesis between the old faith and the demands of a modern technological age based on Western rationalist traditions?"

"First of all, we have had many liberal reformers in the priesthood, a whole progressive movement, and all it accomplished was watering down so much of the rituals and dogma that if we kept listening to them, we would have no doctrine left. Secondly," said Meher, "the Gathas of Zarathustra are as sound a guide for the modern age as for any other. Have you read them?"

"Only in translation, I'm afraid," said Cyrus.

"You must study them—all the way to the depths, because they go very deep. You strike me as a man of learning. What is keeping you?" Meher looked at him piercingly.

"I don't know," murmured Cyrus. "Maybe someday I will. But just now we were discussing the other question of demographic decline. Extinction, if you will."

"As long as it doesn't happen in my lifetime, I don't care," said Freddy.

"We are dwindling away, and unless we get new blood we will disappear entirely," cut in Veera, suddenly very intense. "It seems to me the real problem is intolerance. I have never understood this insane prohibition against mixed marriages or conversions. If a Zoroastrian marries out, at least give the spouse and the children a chance to convert. My friend Zarin was cut off, *ostracized* in Bombay, for marrying an Arab. Her own family were unbelievably cruel to her. This I saw with my own eyes!"

"Calm down, woman," Jessawalla said smiling, "you will upset your blood pressure."

"Don't muzzle me, Darius, you know I don't like that. You think the same as I, only you are too much of a diplomat to say it out loud."

"I am perfectly willing to. I only want to see that you don't lose your temper, and that you give others a chance to speak." He gestured toward Meher, who had been sitting upright in his chair.

"I believe we do not have to recruit new blood," said Meher, pausing to stroke his cropped beard. "We pay too much attention to numbers. What matters is what is in our hearts. That we stay close to Lord Zarathusht's teachings. To struggle throughout our lives to serve the good, to be of service to humanity, to be unselfish and kind, to tell the truth—this is what is important. If we obey the laws of our religion, it doesn't matter if we are a hundred thousand souls, two hundred thousand, a million, or only ten, Zoroastrianism will live on."

"Look, we have lasted for thirty-five hundred years, and we will last thirty-five hundred more," said Jessawalla. "That I am sure of."

"I wish I could agree with you," said Cyrus. "It seems to me—and I believe Zaehner pointed this out, too—that Zoroastrianism in its purest form is a religion dependent on protection by a throne. It doesn't recognize a true separation between church and state. Since the Arabs conquered Iran in the seventh century and kicked most of us out, the whole enterprise has been hanging by a hair. Our people have had nothing else to look forward to but the end of the world and the resurrection, if one can believe in such things as resurrections. Even so, the traditional religion did all right as long as it was embedded in rural society. What is killing it is not population decline *per se*—that is just a symptom—nor the refusal to allow conversions, which would scarcely affect the overall picture: I mean, how many Christians or Moslems or Jews would want to become Zoroastrians in the modern age, even if we let them? No, the real culprit is urbanization, and that is irreversible."

"You sound so—cynical," said Scherezade.

Cyrus was taken aback. "I hope not cynical; I'm trying to be realistic."

"Then defeatist, maybe," she countered.

Again he was surprised by Scherezade's boldness in criticizing him. He realized he had underestimated her. "I am sometimes defeatist, I admit. Then how do you see the problem of our declining numbers?"

All eyes were on Scherezade, the youngest and most earnest member of the group, as though she were suddenly delegated youth's spokesman.

"Well, this is only my simple way of looking at it, but—it used to be that our people married young and had lots of children. Now everyone acts so choosy, and unless everything is perfect about the other person they turn up their noses. I have some girlfriends that are so spoiled they are only thinking of themselves. They don't want to get married because it will end their fun, and they don't want children because it will ruin their figures. This I don't understand; it shows no feeling for the good of the family or the good of the community."

"She's right," said Jessawalla. "It's also partly that we are victims of our own economic success. The Zoroastrian community is affluent, and as a rule people who are affluent have children who stay in school longer, marry later and have fewer children themselves. The same thing's happening to the Jews—"

"Yes, and something else," Scherezade went on. "In the past there were more arranged marriages. Now everyone looks for love, and they don't know how to find it, they can't make up their minds. The burden is too much for the individual."

"Maybe that was the best way, arranged marriages," Cyrus murmured.

"You! You would never sit still for it. For you, marriage is crossing the Bridge of Doom," his mother said, pouncing.

"We are dying out because of bachelors like my brother here, with no strength in their pajamas, no virility," roared Freddy. "Or maybe his pajama only gets strength for boys."

"Seriously, Cyrus, don't you feel guilty sometimes for failing to do your part? We need every able father we can get, you know," said Veera, with a flirtatious smile.

"You all make my being a bachelor sound like genocide. Flattering as it is, I cannot accept that the survival of the whole Zoroastrian race rests on my inadequate loins. But yes, I would like to marry and raise a family someday." A silence fell.

"Would anyone like more wine? We have plenty."

"This eggplant sauce is very good."

"Yes, it is the most delicious eggplant sauce I have had in all my life."

"Bravo! Bravo! Mrs. Irani, you are truly a masterful cook," said Jessawalla, standing up. The others took this as permission to rise and start moving away from the table. "It was all excellent, excellent."

"Please, you must forgive me for having only these few morsels . . ."

"Everything was wonderful. Superb!"

"No, it was nothing special, I'm afraid . . ."

"Mother, you have outdone yourself this time. This is the

best meal I have ever had in my life. . . . No offense to you, Ruttee, but the truth is the truth," said Freddy.

"Nothing to worry. I agree, I could never equal it."

"Please, you are being too gracious, it was just a few scraps I threw together at the last minute. Next time you come I hope I will do better. . . ."

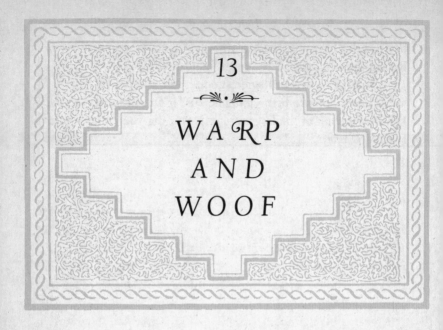

13

WARP
AND
WOOF

MARCH HAD ARRIVED, and still the winter clung. The snow, which usually stopped by the end of February, continued to fall, long after its last poetic possibilities had been exhausted. Traffic had slowed to a crawl, even along Amsterdam Avenue, a route favored by taxicabs because of its staggered lights. Only the buses (when they finally arrived) seemed the proper size for a snowstorm: they were dignified and their tilting blue frames stuck out in the white swirl, as they plodded along with the unhurried manner of a civil servant.

On the side streets, the snow lay banked before the cellar yards of brownstones, looking sooty and yellowed, with the texture of a Styrofoam coffee cup used for cigarette ashes. In front of the houses the uncollected aluminum garbage cans, bursting with Sunday newspaper sections, sported white crusted mustaches around their lids, a frozen foaming at the mouth.

Going around the corner to the used bookstore one Monday,

Cyrus saw a CLOSED sign on MacCourt's door. He wondered what could be the matter. He would have to wait a little longer for that copy of Morier's *Adventures of Hajji Baba of Ispahan*. A week later, a handwritten note was tacked up: *Closed on Account of Illness*. The carmine set of James Fenimore Cooper, the burly military histories and the Shaw letters in the window all looked uneasy, with the store darkened at midday. Cyrus thought of calling the owner at home and offering his wishes for a speedy convalescence. But he realized he did not have MacCourt's home address, and hesitated to call the whole column of MacCourts listed in the Manhattan phone book. In the end he sent a get-well card to the bookstore, hoping it would be forwarded.

The slides Cyrus sent to Aberjinnian had so far elicited no response. Not that he expected much from that quarter. He had only four thousand dollars left in his bank account, and now he felt the panic. It struck Cyrus that everything he had done up to this point had been a matter of going through the motions. He had acted in such a way as to be able to tell himself afterward that he had done all he could, that he had made an honorable attempt—but for whom, or what, was this dumb show being performed? Underneath every gesture to save himself lay the same obstinate passivity. He would continue to ask for loans and call up rug collectors, but he wondered whether he even wanted to succeed. The urge was growing stronger merely to drift into some downward fate, like a rowboat drawing ever closer to the water-fall's lip.

CYRUS HAD BEEN STANDING for some time in his doorway, watching the mailman tromp through the chunked snow. What will I do? What *should* I do? he asked himself, but his brain refused to supply the formula. Instead he was transfixed by the crystal clarity of the midday sunlight, which brought out the true color in everything. How sweet and blue the sky looked between buildings, when it finally stopped snowing! He remembered walking across the frozen lake in Central Park last Sunday—there was that same crystalline exactitude. He had felt almost ecstatic. A frail little boy with mountains of wrappings around his head had come skating toward him yelling: "Beep! beep! I'm picking up speed, you better get out of my way!" He had been charmed by the boy's fantasies of omnipotence, then made a little sad. Now, as he watched the street, he thought: What lies behind this awful paralysis of mine? Rage and terror? But those are only words. Is there really so much fear inside me? There must be, although it feels more like numbness at the moment. I am not allowing myself to experience the full brunt of the terror. All I know is that there seems to be some connection between my paralysis and my perfectionist anger at myself; that's what drove me out of graduate school. Why couldn't I have permitted myself to do inferior art scholarship? I might have gotten better with time. Well, too late now. . . .

Cyrus went back inside. It did not look good for a shopkeeper to stand in the doorway too long, advertising his lack of customers. He opened the accounts-receivable ledger. Arnie was due to make an appearance that afternoon. If everyone who owed him money paid the full amount in thirty days, he would have a grand total of—he pulled out his pocket calculator—$2,716. Enough for one month's stay of execution. The phone rang and he picked it up absentmindedly, while trying to think of a way to prod these unpaying customers. It was his mother.

"I meant to call to thank you for that lovely dinner party. I even thought of writing you a note," said Cyrus.

"Please, I hope we are past the thank-you-note stage," his mother said curtly. "I know you have more important things on your mind."

"What can I do for you?"

"I saw you speaking with Scherezade at the party."

"Yes, we had a brief conversation."

"Well? Did she pass?"

"It is not a question of an examination, Mother."

"Of course it is. Don't play innocent. You cannot trifle with a person's feelings like that."

"Who is the 'person' we are talking about, you or her? Your own matchmaking pride may be offended, but as for Scherezade, no one has trifled with her feelings. I still scarcely know her."

"Then why does she call me up every other day and ask if I have heard from you? Do you know that girl is crazy about you? She is night and day dreaming of you, she thinks you are Prince Charming, she is totally living in a merry-go-round of love."

"First of all, I don't believe you. I thought she found me cynical and defeatist."

"Think what you please. I am telling the truth."

"Second of all . . . look, Mother, this is a young girl from a small town in Pakistan. Probably she has been around very few men in her life. She has lived a very sheltered life. She could certainly not have met many unmarried Zoroastrian men in a place that size, so she is inclined to 'fall in love' with the first available man she sees. You know what I am talking about."

"So what? You are lucky that a nice young girl is smitten with you, for whatever reasons. If she is ready to be a loving wife, so much the better. Would you prefer that she be contemptuous?"

"The point is that she doesn't even see me. She sees a romantic abstraction."

"And if you were not such a sissy you would know how to take advantage of it."

"Thank you, Mother. I am going to hang up now."

"Don't you dare! Don't you dare hang up! I am not going to be breaking that girl's heart. I cannot face her on the phone without at least taking some word back."

Silence on Cyrus's part.

"Well? Just tell me. Do you think she is pretty?"

"I do think she is pretty, but—"

"Very good. That is all I wanted to know." His mother cackled on the other end. "I will tell her you said so."

"Please! You are only going to hurt her more in the end, I'm afraid, by creating false hopes."

"Not at all. The truth is always welcome. I am merely reporting what you yourself said."

ALL THROUGH THE AFTERNOON, while one part of his mind managed to serve customers, another part wondered if his mother was exaggerating, as was her wont, getting worked up over nothing, or whether there was some reality to this story of the girl's infatuation with him. If only he could take her out a few times and find out what his true feelings were. At least he would see if they could communicate. Unfortunately, he could not make a single move toward Scherezade without her brother and the whole community treating it as a betrothal. He would have to proceed very carefully. Behind these considerations was another: Could he really go back to that dense little world of Zoroastrianism, which he had escaped in his youth and partially regretted leaving ever since?

The next day his own brother telephoned. It seemed to be a conspiracy.

"I see that Mother has picked out a wonderful young woman for you. You dirty old man, what fun you are going to have."

"Please, all this is impossibly premature," Cyrus began.

Freddy brushed aside his objections. "You understand that in spite of my cash-flow problems, if there was a wedding that would be another story . . ."

"Are you saying that if I got married, you would loan me the money?"

"I would not put it so crudely." Freddy cleared his throat. "But certainly if you were getting married you would have extra expenses, and the family would come to your aid, as a matter of course."

"But I've been telling you I have extra expenses now!" cried Cyrus.

"Yes—but must it all be your way? You always do whatever

you want, you are such an egoist," retorted Freddy, suddenly getting angry. "Think of Mother's feelings for once. She is afraid she will never live to see your bride's face."

"Leave 'brides' out of this. In what way am I more of an egoist than you?"

"You are selfish. You almost never go to your mother's house, you aren't on speaking terms half the time with me, you will have nothing to do with any of your other relatives—"

"What do you mean, I'm not on speaking terms with you? You had no difficulty ringing me up just now."

"But I never see you for six months at a time. I even get the feeling you are ashamed of me," said Freddy. "Don't shut me out of your life, brother. We are all alone, you are the only brother I have in the world."

"I am sorry you felt that way," Cyrus said mildly, taken aback. "That wasn't my intention."

"For instance, when I asked you to come to work with me, you treated it like an insult. I meant it seriously. Please give the matter some thought. And the girl as well. Anyway, I have to go now. The messenger is banging on my door."

Cyrus put down the phone receiver feeling both exasperated and guilty. So, they would let him go bankrupt unless he did exactly what they wanted. That was their definition of family feeling! Very well, maybe that was what he should do. He would simply marry Scherezade, take care of his financial problems and his loneliness all in one stroke. What difference did it make if he felt no real desire for her? Maybe that would develop later. In any case, what difference would it make if he did not find happiness in love? He had never been happy; she would probably never understand him; he would be lonely, but in a different, changed way. I must stop protecting myself, Cyrus thought; I must simply take the plunge. To act in any direction, good or bad, would be an improvement. Maybe Aberjinnian is right. I need a woman. I have been poisoning myself with the fetor of my celibacy.

14

SWING CLUB

ON A FRIDAY NIGHT, Cyrus made up his mind to go to a swing club. He had a few drinks to steady his nerves, but his heart still pounded as he neared the address on the ad.

He had chosen this one for the simple reason that it was located on West Fifty-fifth Street, across the street from City Center and near Carnegie Hall. It was a district he trusted, certainly more than the Times Square area, and he hoped that a facility on this block would be cleaner, if not clean.

Strange that this neighborhood, with its elegant Old World apartment buildings and hotels, its traditional cigar stores and grand-piano showrooms, should also have housed porno moviehouses and massage parlors. These blocks gave off mixed signals of seediness and prestige.

Cyrus stared at the placard: THE NEW THING ONE FLIGHT UP. He opened the door and looked up a narrow flight of stairs, at the top of which was a red lightbulb. This trite symbol of sin reassured him, as would three balls outside a pawn shop. When he had climbed the stairs, he rang a bell and was buzzed in. He entered a reception room with blond imitation-wood paneling. The Dynel carpet caught his professional eye. Behind the desk a young receptionist with dark hair in a ponytail, wearing glasses and a yellow sweater, was talking on the phone. Cyrus, taking off his fedora and waiting to be noticed, was able to make out from a few words the tone of the conversation. "But if you don't love him what difference does it makes?" he heard, before she put her friend on hold and asked matter-of-factly if she could help him.

"I called before. Irani."

She looked down the list on her clipboard. He sensed that her efficient business manner was a way of distancing herself from the purposes of the club. Perhaps she was a college student working here on weekends, with a textbook hidden under the desk.

"First time?"

"Yes."

"You pay eighty dollars as a membership fee the first time. And after that it's fifty dollars each time you visit. You change in the locker room to your right." He gave her the money. She handed him a brown towel. "The management insists you take a shower before going into the main lounge. And here's a locker key, it's for your own protection. Make sure you lock up all valuables."

"Thank you."

"Have fun," she added. He started to thank her again, but she had already turned back to the phone. With some reluctance he left the reception room and made toward the lockers.

Cyrus slipped off his overcoat and rested it on the bench. Having dressed carefully, almost nattily, with a powder-blue vest that went well with his tie and his good cinnamon wool suit, he digested the irony that no one would see it. The women he had sought to impress with his outfit would have no other basis for selecting him than his pale, flabby body, of which he was not proud.

The room seemed underheated, potentially drafty. He thought of the cold winter night outside, and began getting goosebumps. Maybe I'm too old for this sort of adventure, he thought. In the past, in his travels, he had gone once or twice to prostitutes. These experiences had not provoked him to disgust, but neither had they thrilled him; they had in fact been almost thoroughly neutral. However, a swing club was different from prostitutes, his friend Aberjinnian had assured him, because all were equally amateur and chose each other. He took off his glasses and lay them on the bench. The room went slightly blurry. The atmosphere around him became more amniotic.

As he undid his knitted tie, a naked woman with curly red hair entered the locker room. He murmured hello. What etiquette prevailed? Was he supposed to start up a conversation? After all, he *was* here to meet women. He sensed her shyness equaled his own, and turned his eyes away to undress in silence.

Her body had moved him. Cyrus had expected to meet only homely, desperate women in such a place. Hers was the sort of figure he appreciated most: a graceful back, slender legs, not too tall (about five foot four), with ample round ass and high breasts, fairly full. The breasts he had seen only for an instant before she put on a camisole. Her skin was almost sepulchrally white, with pale carrot-colored freckles here and there.

He looked up again as the redhead brushed by. There was a moment's accidental contact of her thigh against his as she left the room; the whiteness of her back lingered in his mind, reminding him of a doe hopping into the trees.

With his clothes folded neatly in the locker, Cyrus felt calm. His new equanimity surprised him, but he did not dare to question it. It was based on a simple trick: telling himself that he need not do anything, he could merely watch the first time. He tucked a prophylactic into his towel and latched the locker. Sliding the elastic key ring over his ankle, he was reminded of municipal swimming pools he had gone to as a boy, when he had first arrived in America.

If I don't want to engage in sex, I won't. I will do nothing that is a violation of my character, thought Cyrus, smiling a moment at the pompous sound of this vow. He showered in one of the stalls. Then, having dried himself so as not to catch cold, he tiptoed, brown towel around him, into the large communal room.

It was bare except for judo mats and stereo speakers. Red lights dimly lit the darkness. Cyrus had to squint to make out the arrangements of people. In one corner was a couch, with a man gently, dreamily stroking a woman who sat on the floor between his legs. Against the far back walls there seemed to be makeshift plywood doors leading to cubicle-sized bedrooms. A black woman was simply resting in a ball on a saucer chair. Near the middle of the long loft, against the wall, a clump of three men and two women were reclining on mats. Cyrus, uncertain, decided to join this larger group. His first thought was: there are not enough women for men. He wondered if this were always the case in swing clubs, or if it was just momentary circumstance. He counted ten people in the room. It would be funny if, with his characteristic instincts, he had chosen a failing, unpopular club.

Taking a spot against the wall, near the group but at a sufficient distance away so that he would not seem to be intruding, Cyrus sat down. He wanted them to get used to him first as a peripheral shadow, and he wanted to take his time watching them. The wall against his spine seemed an absolutely essential support; without it, he would be adrift.

Of the two women, one had straight blond hair and pointy shoulders, a slender figure, and a face of pleasing if conventional American good looks. From time to time her features would wince in an angry or doubtful grimace, however, which interested Cyrus. The blond woman kept fixing her towel around what looked like small breasts. The other woman, obviously her friend, was short and plump with voluptuous bosoms which she proudly left uncovered. She had a mane of black frizzy hair, a zany, clownish, expressive face and a loud Brooklyn Italian accent, and was doing most of the talking. No one in the group looked older than twenty-five. Cyrus felt out of place with his iron-gray hair and lined features, but he also told himself he was more mature than the other men. They were young, puppyish, and seemed like ordinary good boys from the boroughs who had come into Manhattan for an exciting night. One of them had warm brown eyes and a beard, and fatty deposits that hung from his chest like breasts: he looked Orthodox Jewish. He was not the sort that Cyrus had expected to find here. Next to him was a muscular young man, with perfectly trimmed mustache, regular features and purple-tinted aviator glasses. These glasses struck Cyrus as an unfair fashion advantage in the otherwise democratic context of anonymous towelry. The third man got up and left before Cyrus had had a chance to take him in. Cyrus was more concerned with watching the man with the aviator glasses stroking the blond's ankle, as though establishing territorial rights. The roly-poly bearded man played footsie with the loud brunette. Cyrus preferred the blond, but feared he was already too late. He wondered about the interesting redheaded woman who was now nowhere to be seen. Had she left already? Just his luck.

The conversation among the group was the sort of small talk one might hear at a city beach on a slow Sunday afternoon. Food preferences, favorite music groups, the pluses and minuses of different discos. He was amazed that he had paid eighty dollars of his dwindling savings for the privilege of eavesdropping on this banal palaver. Cyrus's mind drifted, letting itself be occupied by the loud music. He remembered taking out a pretty Italian girl in high school, when he was still too innocent to know what to do with a woman. She had insisted on going to the beach with her group of friends, and they had sat around talking just this way for hours, and Cyrus, already too serious and intense, had not known how to participate; when the sun went down and the other couples pulled their blankets over their heads to make out, she was so annoyed at him for being "antisocial" that she would not let him touch her.

Presently he became aware that the blond was looking at him. "You want to join us?" she asked.

"Sure, I would love to." Cyrus left the wall and sat down beside her. She took out a canister of marijuana and some rolling papers.

"Who wants to start?" she asked, offering the first cigarette around.

"Let him go first," her brunette girlfriend shrieked, nodding at the fellow with aviator glasses. "He ate me good an hour ago. He deserves it."

"You want to roll?" The blond offered Cyrus the canister.

"Please, go ahead."

"Are you from Guatemala?" the bearded man asked him.

"No, that guy left," said aviator glasses.

"You Italian too?"

"I am Iranian. At least I was born there. My parents came to America when I was ten."

"What part of Irania?"

"Teheran, mostly."

"Have you ever seen Mykonos?"

"I've never been to Greece," Cyrus confessed.

"It's supposed to be beautiful, Mykonos," the bearded man said respectfully.

Cyrus accepted the joint, thinking he had rarely heard such aimless conversation. Perhaps if he smoked this the evening would begin to fall into place. On the other hand, grass sometimes made him moody and silent and "tragic," which was why he had stayed away from it for years.

The bearded man was bending over the chubby girl and

whispering in her ear. At first they were giggling, then she pushed him away and said in her shrill, croaking voice: "No thanks! I've already been in a coupla orgies. That's enough orgies for now. I don't know about you but I care about my body! I'm only twenty-two, what's gonna happen to me when I'm forty if I keep doing orgies? Sure, you want to play orgy with me. You want a piece, and *you* want a piece, everybody wants a piece. But what's going to be left of me?" she said angrily. "You're always thinking only of yourself." She brushed his hand away from her leg. "No, don't touch me! I don't want to be touched."

"Sorry."

"Know what I want? I wanna go roller skating! And when I get everybody lookin', I wanna take off my skirt and have hot pink panties underneath." She broke into a big grin, and everybody laughed with relief that she was not really angry, just playfully growling. As if to reinforce the point, the round little brunette placed the bearded man's hand back on her leg.

It was going to be as hard to pick up a woman here as at a singles bar, thought Cyrus. The reason he did not go to such places was precisely that he could not manufacture the necessary "pickup" chatter. He took another drag of the offered joint and listened to the rock music, trying to distinguish the instrumental threads. Though a bit bored, he was not anxious: he had already decided he would leave in twenty minutes if nothing further happened. The grass made the inside of his cranium warm. The more he withdrew, the more he sensed an eerie gentle manliness emanating from him, as from a Buddha.

Just as he was thinking he might get up and leave, the blond girl leaned forward from her shoulders. "You want to join us?" she said.

Cyrus sensed the question meant something different than it had before. "Yes. This is my first time here. What happens?"

"It depends," she winced. "Sometimes nothing happens. Sometimes you go off and make it. Depends what you like."

"What do you like?" he asked quietly.

"I usually go with my girlfriend and a guy."

She stood up and moved toward one of the doors near the locker-room end. Cyrus rose, too, thinking of excusing himself from the company, but repressed the impulse, which might be taken as gloating over the other men. It was a pleasant surprise to have been singled out, though perhaps it was only because he was the newcomer. . . .

He followed the blond girl into a small dark room with two mattresses. She seemed nervous as she hunted in her pocketbook for cigarettes. A wave of hair fell over her green eyes. He noticed now that she had the perfect, smooth skin of a billboard model. Cyrus could not believe his good luck.

"What is your name, please? I am Cyrus."

"Loren. Hi."

"And where are you from, if you don't mind my asking?"

"California. L.A. I like it back there, in L.A. New York's okay but the weather's too cold for me. Life is easier in California. 'Sides, my little girl is back there."

"You have a daughter? How old is she?"

"Three years old, come May."

A silence fell. He felt a useless sympathy for this woman. To have had a child and been separated from her at such a young age—obviously she had suffered more than he had realized at first, when he mistook her for a sort of teenybopper. The reverence he felt for all mothers added a refinement to his physical attraction. "What brought you to New York?" asked Cyrus.

"To learn to be a fashion designer."

"Is that what you are doing now?"

She seemed embarrassed, or reluctant to talk. "I take courses."

"At FIT?" he asked.

She made no reply, but kept looking impatiently toward the door. Finally the black woman he had seen before came in and began conferring in whispers with Loren.

"What are we doing?" Cyrus asked.

"We're waiting for Millie. She needs to get some perfume. 'Scuse me a second." Loren jumped up and left the room.

Cyrus looked at the black woman, and then looked away. The mattresses were bare and felt dirty, as Aberjinnian had warned. Who knew how many bodies had copulated on them without their being disinfected? It made no sense to be waiting for a third woman (was Millie the Italian girl?) to put on perfume. Something began to seem fishy. Ashamed as he was to think it, the fact that the woman lying beside him was black made Cyrus suspect that they were all prostitutes. The management may have paid them a flat fee for a night's work, or by the trick—why else would so many pretty women be in such a place? It did not seem possible that they would all have come here just to indulge in sexual experimentation, when they could get countless lovers on their own. The men were certainly bona fide customers, but the women must be ringers. That would certainly explain why the blond had been reluctant to answer about her line of work.

He shivered in the cold air and tried to arrange the towel around his shoulders. There were no blankets, unfortunately. Not even a light bulb; the only illumination came from the broad crack under the door.

"Are you cold?" Cyrus asked the black girl.

"No," she replied. Her face had something meek and stolid about it. She had ears that seemed to be carved to points, as in an African mask. She was young looking, about nineteen.

"Could you tell me your name, please?"

"Yvonne."

"That's a pretty name. Mine is Cyrus."

She smiled and they lapsed into silence.

The blond returned with her chubby little friend, Millie. "Lie back," Loren ordered him. "Relax."

He did what he was told. The Italian girl got astride him with her massive breasts in his face, the black woman kneeled alongside his hips, and the blond stationed herself by his feet. She began running her hands over Cyrus's lower legs.

"This is strange," he said, starting to sit up, having the urge to laugh at his own helplessness.

"Relax. It's the 'new thing,' " said Millie. "Like the sign says."

"Don't I get to participate?"

"We'll do it for you," said Loren.

The black girl, Yvonne, put his penis in her mouth and began sucking it. The blond girl was stroking his thighs in an absent, barely attentive manner. He wished it were she who was sucking his penis. He had been so attracted to her, thought he would be making love to her, and now she was far away, down by his feet, he could barely see her. Meanwhile, Millie began swaying over him like an elephant. He pressed his mouth against the generous nipples and into the surrounding flesh, fighting off a fantasy of suffocation.

"You like it now? See, you got everything. A black girl, a blond and a brunette!" Millie croaked.

"Why don't you come in her mouth?" advised Loren.

Now he was certain they were prostitutes. He recognized the slogan of the trade: Hurry up, come. But it seemed a waste of manpower for all three to be ministering to him. "Don't I get to make love inside you?" he asked, looking straight at Loren reproachfully.

"No, I'm in my period," she said. "Just lie back. This'll be really good."

"This'll be the greatest!" chimed in Millie.

He did not lie back completely, but sought out Loren's golden hair, patting it while closing his eyes to concentrate on the sensations in his groin. He was worried that they would get impatient with him for taking too long, and so he tried to hurry the excitement, to ejaculate for their sakes as much as for his. Though this was the first time he had "slept" with three women, the novelty meant nothing to him erotically; all that mattered was to connect these indifferent mechanics to something romantic. That was why he kept petting and stroking Loren's hair, as much as to say "Good girl, good girl," pretending that she was sucking him and not the other.

"Stop with my hair," ordered Loren.

Cyrus began squeezing Yvonne's hand as he sensed his ejaculation approaching.

"Don't bite so much! Enough biting," Millie cried out.

"Sorry," murmured Cyrus, relaxing his teeth from her nipples. He sat up empty, bemused. It was over.

The promised land of pleasure, of Cythera, which Aberjinnian had dangled before him, had once again proven to be a mirage. His first orgy. Now he could go back to his stoic pastimes, expecting less from life. Cyrus smiled at his moment of delusional vanity: surely this trio had not done it for their own pleasure, or because he was so irresistible that three women would fight to serve him at once.

Cyrus went into the shower. He soaped himself well, drenching his hair and body in a long hot downpour. That felt good. Loren passed by his stall as he was drying himself.

"You don't have to go home," she said. "You can stay around and swing with someone else later."

That was thoughtful of her. She must have sensed his disappointment. Still, he had had enough for one night. He headed into the locker room to dress. When he got there he bumped into Millie and the redheaded woman he had noticed before.

"Hey, you two meet each other? This is Shelley. She *likes* you," Millie said to Cyrus with the mischievous glee of a tattling child. Surprised, he looked at the redhead. A faint smile of acquiescence appeared on her face; then she left the room, perhaps out of shyness at Millie's statement.

Unsure what to do next, Cyrus stared confusedly at the lockers. He had not imagined he would be reentering the ring so fast. But then again—why not? He might salvage the evening, and he was certainly attracted to the woman. As for Millie, she was all right after all, decided Cyrus—a good samaritan. He thanked her for the introduction as he left the locker room.

The red-haired woman was standing behind a U-shaped bar near the reception office. She had an upturned nose and a small mole by her left eye. She was wearing a sheer beige camisole, with nothing on below. The delicate swelling of her hips and her curly reddish-brown pubic hair excited him.

"You're Shelley?"

"What? They call me Red. I'm so smashed I don't even know my own name. I can fix you a good drink though. I'm good at bartending."

"Thanks. I'll have a Scotch and soda."

"What's your name?" she asked.

"My name is Cyrus. Cyrus Irani."

She nodded, looking nervously at the liquor bottles, all of which seemed to be down to their last third.

"I can do it," he offered, reaching his hand out toward the Scotch.

"Let me do it! Unless you don't trust me."

"I trust you." It seemed a strange word to use so soon after meeting someone; but in a way he meant it.

Shelley busied herself with the glasses and ice cubes, gaining confidence. "Do you know there are only two bars in New York City that have women bartenders?"

"I would have imagined there would be more."

"One is in the Village, naturally," she said, "around where I live. And the other is on the Upper East Side. But I don't like to go into those Upper East Side pickup places, you know? They're like meat markets."

"Yes, I know what you mean," he said. It seemed odd that she should disapprove of singles bars but frequent sex clubs.

When they finished their drinks, she suggested they go back into the communal room. Walking into it, Cyrus noticed that there were many more people now, as it approached midnight. They chose a spot off by themselves. He sat on the cracked wrestling mat in such a way as to have his leg touching hers: her thigh was very warm, he noticed, almost burning up. She showed her approval of the liberty he had taken by pressing herself more tightly against him. Cyrus realized that he had been preparing all his life for these sudden leaps in amorous intimacy, by the sexual dreams he had from time to time in which beautiful strangers would beckon him into their robes without any leading up to it.

He rested his hand against her white shoulder, feeling deliriously expectant. As though to test what was possible in such a situation, he placed his hand on her pelvic bone, his long articulated fingers pointed toward her coral pubic hair. He grazed her bush, which was feathery, as if recently shampooed.

"Let's talk first."

"Of course."

"I like it better if we talk. It puts me more in the mood."

"Yes. I feel the same way."

"The music's maybe too loud, but otherwise everything's perfect," she said, looking around. Cyrus wondered what she saw in this barren loft that seemed to her perfect. "I come here to relax sometimes, because I don't have much time to. . . ." She trailed off.

"Unwind," he offered helpfully.

"Yeah, to relax. I work two jobs, so I don't have time to play dating games and do a lot of socializing.

"Wait a minute." She dug in her pocketbook for a cigarette. "I'm an office manager during the day. Which I hate but it pays the bills. It's lots of responsibility and it gets nervewracking. . . . And three nights a week I'm a cocktail waitress. But what I really consider myself to be—is an actress. Acting's what turns me on. Lots of things turn me on: I like to smoke, I like to get high, and I like to make love," she said, the last in a tone which was partly defiant, partly self-conscious. "But the biggest thrill for me is. . . ." She trailed off again. He waited.

"To be onstage in front of people?"

"That's right. You got it. I'm taking acting classes now at HB Studios."

"What are the lessons like?"

"Never ask an actress a question about acting because she'll give you a twenty-minute answer."

"Go ahead: I'm interested."

"Well, my teacher is very unusual. He doesn't criticize that hard, he's very supportive, and he has interesting exercises. He makes you have an objective for everything. So like, every line has to have a purpose behind it. Like if I say, 'I don't like chocolate cake' . . . No, that's not a good example. Anyway, one time you say a line and it's whiny, like complaining, because you want to manipulate someone into feeling sorry for you. The next time you say it sulking—well, that's too much like whining, I said that already. Fear is another good one. Or you say it bragging, so that people will be impressed. Like right now I'm trying to show off. That would be my objective."

"It's natural to show off, when you first meet someone," Cyrus said.

"The other thing he makes you do is to think of everything like in terms of a verb. Because onstage, you have to be active. You can't just let things happen inside yourself. You have to come up with a gesture so that everyone can see it. Which is good for me because I'm very, like, inhibited sometimes. I don't mean inhibited sexually, which I'm not, but, like, I don't like to speak in front of groups of people. It's complicated to explain." She lit a joint, offered it to him, and continued. As he listened, he saw himself retreating into that gentle, tolerant, energy-preserving manner that came over him when he was starting to get bored. Perversely, he kept plying her with questions, although the way she talked depressed him. It was starting to have a numbing, anaphrodisiac effect. She was a type of woman he knew well, who was insecure, had a low opinion of herself, probably very little talent, and yet could not rid herself of the notion that she should have her moment of fame and her picture in *People* magazine. New York was filled with people like that, whose desperation for celebrity was both comic and a genuine tragedy.

Cyrus pulled himself up short: Who am I to feel superior? Aren't I equally a failure? He sighed, then froze, like an animal at the sound of a hunter's approach—only, in his case, the tense stillness was provoked by a fear of impotence. Were he to pursue these thoughts of failure and mediocrity he knew he would be sunk in pity: for himself, for her, for everyone else. To make love in a few minutes, he would have to work his way back to desire.

Fortunately, there was something about her that had never stopped appealing to him, pulling at him. He was touched by the brave self-exposure of her halting words and her lower body. He stared at the tracing of blue veins along her skin. Her legs were shapely, long and creamy below the knee, with the barest bristle where she had shaved closely. The feel of those bristles against his palm aroused him. Unconsciously, his hand began rubbing in a widening circle over her knee.

"Let's go where it's quieter," Shelley suggested. She had picked up at the same time both his increasing ardor and his faltering attention to what she was saying. They stood up. "See if that room is empty." She pointed to a door against the back wall.

Cyrus approached it and rapped gently. He pulled open the door, half expecting to see a couple in any Kama Sutra position. There was no one using it. "All clear," he said. He lifted Red up from the judo mat, and was tempted to go further and carry her over the threshold, but that romantic gesture would certainly have been in bad taste. Still, he felt a tremendous affection for her, now that she had allowed them to go off by themselves. Cyrus congratulated himself for having been patient and waited for the woman's cues—the sign of an older man's experience.

The cubicle was as bare as the other one, but it had a window, through which the bright aura of the city entered. Though there was no overhead light bulb, he could see Shelley clearly. He waited for her next move.

She lit a cigarette and sat back. "Now tell me all about Cyrus."

"There is very little to tell."

"Oh, you allow me to talk my head off and then you don't say a word about yourself? That's not fair. Come on, what do *you* do?"

"I'm a . . . writer," he said, surprising himself. He had not meant to lie, but the thought of telling her about his rug business seemed impossible at that moment.

"Do you ever write plays?"

"No, I'm sorry to say."

"You should write a play for me to be in."

"What kind of role would you like?" he asked teasingly.

She put her fist against her cheek, then said with frustration: "I don't know, I can't decide."

"I mean, would you like to be an ingenue, an evil landlady, or a femme fatale—?"

"I'm trying to think. I don't like Shakespeare. Chekhov's okay. . . . I'm trying to think of what we did in class. We did a sketch called *The Boor* by Chekhov that was fun for me. A comedy! That's what I'd like."

"Ah, but comedies are the hardest thing to write."

"You should write one for me, just so I can act in it."

"I don't think I can write a comedy," said Cyrus. "But maybe something else. Why don't you—why don't we lie back on the bed?"

"Okay. I just wanted to finish this cigarette first," she said, sounding a little wounded.

"Please, take your time." He was sorry he had pushed things. Now she would think he only viewed her as a receptacle for his penis. Well, to be honest, what was the point of this club anyway? He waited in silence while she finished her cigarette.

"Close your eyes. I'm opening the door a little, so I can see what I'm doing." She poured the contents of her purse onto the mattress.

"What are you looking for?" he asked.

"Drugs. Legitimate drugs—for my sinuses. I have terrible congestion. It's a tube and you just squirt it in your nose. Maybe I left it in my big bag in the locker. I have to go to the bathroom anyway. I'll be back in a little while. . . . Don't worry, I'm not stalling. I promise we'll do it when I get back."

"That's fine; take as much time as you need," said Cyrus. She left. He no longer felt impatient. He had regained the invulnerable sense of calm acceptance which had settled upon him earlier. Cyrus remembered other times he had waited in bed for women to finish their bathroom preparations and join him. When he was younger, at the start of his sexual life, the delay had seemed interminable. He had even wondered if the woman was purposely tormenting him by taking longer than she needed. Later, the wait had grown easier; now, he even came to cherish these anticipatory moments alone.

Cyrus crept to the window to look out. The view was not of the street but of the backs of buildings. There were bright electric lanterns on the brick wall facing him, and a fire escape close by. A mound of snow had not yet been cleared in the courtyard below. What a strange night, he thought. He lowered himself again to mattress level. As he wrapped the towel around him for warmth, the condom he had rolled inside it fell out. He ripped off the edge of the foil in preparation, telling himself it would be better to do this now than fumbling in the heat of passion.

There was a knock. "I'm coming in," she said. "Close your eyes." This modesty charmed him. He held out his hands for Shelley to descend. When she lifted off her chemise, she was completely naked. Her breasts were beautiful, bluish white and swollen, with soft, flesh-toned, almost colorless nipples: a dimple in the center of each nipple. He reached for them.

"Wait. I'm going to have to insist that you use one of these," she said, handing him a rubber.

"I was going to. I brought one of my own, see?" Cyrus showed her the packet. There was a momentary defensiveness in the air, on both their parts, but it quickly faded. She lay back on the bed. He busied himself with the ritual of the condom, which no man could look dignified doing. Then he began kissing her foot. It was small and cool. He moved slowly up her body to her lips, and she returned his kisses, at first timidly, then with genuine feeling. Her tenderness surprised him: it felt exactly like being kissed by someone who cared for him. Cyrus placed one hand over a soft nipple, feeling the inverted cleft pucker and rise, and with the other hand he sought out her clitoris. She was already gushing. She pushed him by the head to suck her breasts.

After a minute she said, "Go inside me."

"Not yet." He wanted to prolong the unimaginable pleasure he was feeling. As he was running his fingers from her vagina to her clitoris, she cried out and came.

"Please, come inside me!"

He kissed her gently on the cheek and slid on top.

"You're so big and hard," she said, grabbing his erection.

It sounded so silly that he wondered if this might be profes-sional flattery. But it was impossible for her to be acting; she seemed so caught up. As he prepared to enter, she said: "I'm warning you, I'm really tiny. That's what I meant, you're so big and it's going to be very tight."

"Don't worry, I won't hurt you."

"I'm not worried."

They started moving together, not elaborately, just patiently, yet he already sensed that it was going to be very good. He was making love to her with an expressiveness he had been able to feel only with a few women in his life—those he had actually loved, or come close to loving. He found her mouth and their kisses seemed uncanny, as though they had known each other for a long time, had even reached an understanding, like a married couple, beyond the first passion. Every movement was right, every variation perfect, so much was he able to trust her response.

Her legs tightened around his back. "Tell me when you're coming so I can come at the same time," she whispered.

"All right." He sought out her breasts, lifting himself a little so that he could stroke them all the while. She began to moan and kiss his face with little fervent maternal pecks. She touched his head solicitously. "Tell me when you're coming."

"All right, I will." He started going faster. A tension pulled down through his center, as though he were about to divide in half. He felt something gurgling and bubbling inside him, like burnt sugar. "I'm almost there," she said and he said "I am too." He wanted to make sure she came; she did, and then he ejaculated inside her.

For the next few moments he shuddered like a twitching horse. His head fell back against her, and she patted his hair consolingly. Could she have any idea how unusual this was for him, this deep orgasm which cleared out everything that had been inside?

He waited for his penis to bob up out of her, small again, then shifted his weight and rolled off.

She kissed him on the lips, circumspectly, as though reverting to shyness. "I know men don't like it as much with a rubber, but that was very good for me. I hope it was good for you."

"That was wonderful." His gratitude to her was so total he did not want to spoil it with words. A physical wholeness spread from his still-tingling groin. His nostrils picked up the acrid odor of seminal release mixed with her momentarily pungent vaginal fluids—a smell that caused him to think of cats mating, and that made him feel a youthful vitality he had given up on. "Did I hurt you?" he remembered to ask.

"No. Why should it have hurt? Oh, you mean because . . ."

He nodded, then lapsed into a reverie, looking at her. Cyrus's silence and his almost holy concentration on her body seemed to make her nervous.

"We should be going back . . . ," she said.

Why? he wondered. He wished he could stay this way for hours. Did they really have some sort of obligation to the rest of the group? He resisted the idea that she might be in the management's employ, reasoning instead that her fidgeting to escape was because she feared developing feelings of attachment to him and then getting rejected.

"Just let me touch these again," he said, reaching for her breasts.

"They're very sensitive. They're not that big, but they're sensitive. I'm very sensitive all the way from here to here," she said, tracing the muscle from her nipple to her side. He continued to squeeze them softly: he was fascinated with these breasts, and his fingers were taking a memory-print of them.

"They are certainly that big," said Cyrus, "they are beautiful breasts. In fact—I'm sure you know this—you have a beautiful body, Shelley."

"Thank you."

"You are really quite a beautiful woman."

She pouted dubiously. Her profile hung with a certain sadness over her long, graceful neck. Why did she think he was merely flattering her? He had never been more serious in his life.

She started to stand up. Cyrus wondered whether to ask for her phone number—if dates between club members were ever made on the outside. But something held him back: maybe just his having gotten used to following her lead. When she said nothing, he followed suit. The seconds were running out, he knew he might be squandering an opportunity, and yet the words would not come. Perhaps it's for the best, he thought. This magical experience is a gift, meant to be just what it was. To try to build on it further would be to spoil it; one must respect its self-enclosed character.

Cyrus stood up alongside her. They embraced one last time.

"I hope I see you again sometime," he murmured.

"You can call up here after two in the daytime and find out who's going to be in. You get to know some of the regulars after a while. So, if you want to see me again, you can find out ahead of time if I'm going to be here—just ask for Red."

"Thank you! Thank you for everything." Cyrus let her leave first, then stooped down and picked up his used condom. He walked across the judo mats alone, filing past the socializing groups whom he fastidiously refused to look at, wanting to preserve the uniqueness of his experience. For the third time that night he showered.

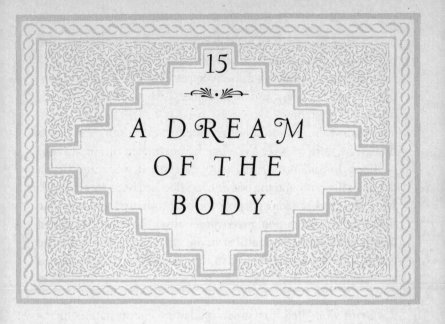

15

A DREAM
OF THE
BODY

THE FIRST OF THE MONTH had again rolled around. Cyrus went
to his bank and withdrew all but the last two thousand dollars
from the savings account. The bank officials had turned down
his loan request. He called Aberjinnian to find out if any buyers
had turned up.

"In all honesty I haven't had a chance to get to it yet," said
Aberjinnian. "Do you want me to return the slides?"

"No, please hold onto them a while longer. Maybe I could
make a presentation to the Rug Fanciers Club."

"They don't like to be pressured by dealers. Their meetings
are mostly show-and-tell among themselves."

"I could give a scholarly talk, which just happened to show
my rugs as examples."

"That might be possible." Aberjinnian sounded irritated and
rushed. "I will get back to you on it in a couple of days." Cyrus
hung up, thinking that if nothing happened in a week's time, he

would take his chances with the regular auction houses. The problem was becoming a matter of indifference to him. If worse came to worst, at the last minute he could call up certain whole-sale dealers he knew and simply accept whatever they offered, no matter how low.

Meanwhile, he could not get Shelley off his mind. It was as though he were in love. Yet when he questioned himself further he knew he did not actually love Shelley; it was more that a dream of the body and the body's happiness had been reawakened. No longer did it seem possible for him to marry someone like Scherezade, who excited no passion in him. The swing club had taught him again the truth of desire. It had touched him like grace. The whole experience, in fact, had left an oddly religious afterglow, with the bare matted room reminding him of a mosque.

Cyrus wondered how much the tawdry circumstances them-selves had contributed to this lingering intensity. He had a fantasy of descending into the pleasure quarters of New York (such as they were) and becoming like a heterosexual Cavafy, experiencing all the bitter poetic joys of bought love. The older he got, the more unable he would be to attract women to his bed; what else was there in store for a man like him? On the other hand, he could not really imagine immersing himself in that life, given his sexually cautious temperament, the danger of catching a dis-ease, and his knowledge that for every romantic encounter like the one with Shelley there would be ten of the other kind.

Cyrus still did not know what to make of her. She had seemed so unlike a prostitute—and yet, he remembered that last glimpse of her, wandering through the halls of the swing club with no apparent intention of going home soon. Either she was still "on call," or else (and he liked this possibility even less) she was a customer like him, who had not yet had her fill of sex. Could it be that what had affected him so powerfully was for her merely a warm-up, an appetizer? The most benign interpretation was that she used the place as a combination athletic and social club, and she had not gone home because she still wanted to chat with her friends and hang out. But he remembered Millie's words ("He ate me good an hour ago") and felt depressed. If only he could understand the real workings of the club, if he could discreetly question the receptionist about its employment policies. Now Cyrus's fantasies took another turn. He would befriend the girl at the desk, and find out everything. He would even have her call whenever Red showed up. But there was probably more than one receptionist: would he have to make friends with all of them? Or he could frequent the swing club for a month every night, making sure he ran into her again. Impossible: not only would it be too expensive, but he could think of nothing more deathly to the spirit.

Supposing Red were, after all, a part-time prostitute, just as she was a part-time cocktail waitress. He could go down into that underworld just long enough to lead out his own Eurydice. He could offer to settle a certain sum in her bank account (which he did not have) in return for her moving in with him. Or they might even get married. To rehabilitate and marry a whore had always been the sentimental dream of a certain intellectual type . . . the yearning of a bookish renunciator for the mysteries of the flesh, combined with a masochistic streak, since these liaisons rarely worked out. Nevertheless, such transactions occurred with frequency in the Orient, thought Cyrus. A man would buy out the contract of a brothel prostitute, or a geisha. But what would he find to talk about with Shelley, day after day?

A FEW DAYS PASSED; the image of Shelley's body would not leave his thoughts. He would give anything to sleep with her again, just one more time. Oh, why hadn't he asked for her phone number? Stupidity, shyness. Or was it some misplaced respect for the Aristotelian unities of catharsis? At least he knew that she took acting lessons at HB Studios (as did half of New York); it might yet be possible to track her down.

One evening, finally giving in to the urge, he took the IRT train down to Greenwich Village. He had decided to leave a little note on the bulletin board of the acting school which said: *Shelly (Red), call Cyrus ("the writer"). I very much want to see you again*, with his work and home numbers on the bottom of the card.

HB Studios were on Bank Street just west of Abingdon Square. He had always liked walking around that area, with its narrow twisting streets, old Federalist-style brick townhouses, the meat-packing plants, the briny-smelling docks and the river. It had been overlooked until the recent realty boom which left no Lower Manhattan neighborhood unsqueezed, but he still got the feeling of a quiet zone off the beaten path.

As Cyrus approched the address he had written down on a slip of paper, he saw several young people in stylized punkish clothing whom he guessed were acting students, draped over a Buick. It was parked in front of a slender gray townhouse that looked as though it had once been a firehouse or a stable. He wondered what he would say to Shelley if he saw her among them. She was not. He thought of asking the students, who were apparently on their break, sharing take-out salads as they slumped over the car, if anyone knew her or if she was in class right now. But their cliquish boisterousness intimidated him into not speaking.

Just then the heavy front door opened; three laughing students, closer to his age, were leaving the school, and Cyrus slipped in through the open door, grateful to be able to avoid the inter-com. Confronted with a door to his right which said QUIET PLEASE! CLASS IN PROGRESS, a staircase that led up to what he guessed were the school administrators' offices, and sounds of normal conversation and tramping up the stairs from below, he headed toward the basement. Somewhere in the last few moments he had lost all self-esteem, and felt himself trespassing where he had

no right. If anyone had questioned him about what he was doing
in the building, he would have fled without a word.

The basement walls were stripped to brick, painted white. A
narrow room held lockers, benches, a pay phone and soda and
fruit juice machines. Several students were chatting about their
work, but what caught his eye were the others, walking alone in
circles, pacing and muttering to themselves, gesticulating with
their arms thrown out, then looking down at scripts held in their
hands. They reminded Cyrus of the patients in the day room of
the psychiatric ward where he had stayed after his nervous breakdown. Ever since that time, he had had a periodic nightmare
that he was returning for more institutionalization and the patients were absurdly gleeful to have him back.

Not wanting to appear to spy on their private soliloquies, he
turned his gaze toward the placards on the wall. IMPORTANT: ALL
STUDENTS MUST NOW PAY IN FULL TO REGISTER, one said, and
Cyrus speculated about the sequence of events that must have
gone into making such a sign. Another read: THIS IS AN UN-
PROTECTED AREA. PLEASE TAKE YOUR BELONGINGS WITH YOU.

He found himself staring at a short young man who was tying
his sneaker laces with an intensity that made Cyrus wonder if it
was life or a theater exercise. Suddenly the man caught Cyrus's
eye and said: "Are you working with someone? Do you need a
partner?"

"No. Excuse me," said Cyrus bashfully. "I am not a student
here. I am only trying to get in touch with someone who studies
here. Do you have a—a—a message board or something like
that?"

"Sure. It's on the stairway between the first floor and here.
You passed it on the way down—didn't you see it?"

"No, I must have missed it. How stupid of me. I'm sorry to
have bothered you unnecessarily."

"I can show you," said the young man, bounding with panther
energy toward the stairs.

"Please, I don't want to trouble you. . . . You are very nice to go out of your way like this . . . ," Cyrus repeated as he caught up with his guide.

"I guess it is kind of dimly lit. Easy to miss if you didn't know it was there."

"Thank you so much!" said Cyrus with a little bow. "I am very obliged to you for rescuing me."

He waited until the student had disappeared before turning around and pinning his embarrassing message on the board. Then he stepped back and quickly scanned the forest of index cards with offers for apartment-sharing, baby-sitting, selling stereo equipment, tutoring French, rides to California, exercise classes and so on. The chances that she would see his note in this thicket did not seem great.

What a fool I'm being, he thought to himself as he left the school building. Still, he had done all he could for the moment; there was that comfort.

A FEW DAYS LATER Eddie dropped in at the store. Cyrus had not seen his nephew for several months; the boy looked older, more streetwise.

"Uncle, can you do me a favor?"

"What is it?"

"Can you loan me a hundred dollars? Because if I don't have it, I'll be in some bad shit."

"Why do you need the money right now?" said Cyrus, staring at Eddie's denim jacket with a black India ink stain over the pocket.

"It's a long story; I don't want to go into it."

"If you don't tell me anything, I can't loan you anything."

"I can't explain. It's like what they call in the movies a debt of honor," said Eddie with a broad grin.

"Is it for drugs?" asked Cyrus.

"No, man! Everybody acts like I'm into drugs or something.

My dad got so mad when he found a little pot in my room, right away he wants to have me committed as an addict. Can you believe that?"

"I had heard," said Cyrus, cautiously. "It's also my impression that you have a drug problem."

"See, that's what I mean! You don't understand, you're just blaming me without facts. That's what pisses me off. The whole family is like in a fucking conspiracy against me: Grandma, my parents, now you—"

"Let's go back to the beginning. Have you asked your father for the money yet?"

"We're not talking right now, he and me. Okay, look, if you won't loan me a hundred, how about fifty?"

"Because you are my only nephew . . . I will loan you fifty dollars, yes, without any questions."

"That's really awesome," said Eddie, pounding his fist into his other hand. "You're the greatest, that's really cool."

"But you must pay it back to me within six weeks. If you don't I go to your father and I tell him the whole story."

"That's cool."

Cyrus rang his cash register open. He took out two twenties and a ten. "Six weeks, remember, you promised. Since you spoke of honor before, this too is a debt of honor. I am having my own financial problems right now."

"I know. I heard Dad talking to Mom about it."

"You *know?*" Cyrus's eyebrows raised of their own accord. "And you came to me anyway to borrow money?"

"It's real important. I didn't know who else to ask." Eddie slipped the folded bills into his jacket pocket. "Don't worry, you'll get your money back. I'll be thankful forever! I really mean it."

Cyrus smiled dubiously. When Eddie affected sincerity, it usually came out sounding like the opposite. "Where will you get the other fifty dollars?"

"I'll think of something. Maybe I can work as a delivery boy for Food Emporium. I know some guys that can get me in there."

"You know," said Cyrus, appraising this other black sheep of the family with a perverse fondness, "you will come to a bad end if you keep this up, borrowing money and so on."

"I know. But this is just a stage I'm going through," the teenager said with surprising knowingness, giving him a rakish smile.

"Let us hope," replied Cyrus. "Otherwise you will end up like me." He said good-bye to Eddie, and the doorbell tinkled as his nephew left.

What was fifty dollars less anyway, when he would soon be thousands of dollars in debt?

THE EVENING HAD finally arrived for his dinner date with Marge. At six-thirty Cyrus pulled the grille across his shop window, locked up and went next door to the pet shop. He had already composed his face in a convivial expression for the hours ahead.

Marge was in front by the parrot cages. She had on a cream silk blouse and a long Mexican parti-colored skirt; around her shoulders was a nut-brown woolen shawl, and she was holding a small suede purse. Cyrus had never seen her so dressed up; it made him nervous.

"I'm ready. I just have to lock the door."

"You look very pretty tonight," said Cyrus, offering his arm.

"Thank you, sir."

He could not tell how much he was expected to act like a real date, but he decided he would at least fulfill the part of a gallantly attentive gentleman, which was never inappropriate. At the restaurant, Cyrus quickly pulled out Marge's chair for her, and lit her cigarette. Marge's friend, the owner, came over to their table and made a twenty-second fuss over them, instructing the waiter to bring them a free half carafe of wine.

"Everything looks so yummy," Marge said, glancing over the

menu. "I better watch it or I'll be twice as much a blimp as I already am."

"But you are not so overweight, Marge."

"Please, I've been fat all my life," she replied.

The matter-of-factness of this statement gave Cyrus pause. He looked down at the menu: "I wonder what I will have. . . ." Just then their waiter came over.

"What can I do for you special people tonight? You people look *famished*," he giggled, as if it were all too absurd a masquerade, this business of ordering food. His limbs were so loose he appeared to be falling backward. They settled on enchiladas verdes and chicken tacos.

"Grr-reat combination!" he approved.

When the waiter was out of earshot, Cyrus said a little ironically: "He seemed to be in a cheerful mood."

"He's just trying too hard. He'll get over it."

Cyrus felt chastened. Maybe she thought he was making fun of the waiter's homosexuality (was he?), and maybe she was especially sensitive to that sort of prejudice. "Will you have some wine?"

"I shouldn't," she said, "but what the hell."

"So. Tell me your news. I am all ears."

"Okay. Well—I'm giving up the pet shop. Leaving the city. And I'm moving to Newton, Massachusetts."

"That is a shock. I will miss you—I can't tell you how much. What is taking you off to Massachusetts?"

"My fiancé. We're getting married."

"Congratulations! I didn't even know you had a fiancé." Cyrus shook his head at her: naughty, naughty, you were holding back. In fact his blush came from having so misread the situation. If he had misjudged Marge this much, he wondered, what else in his life was he seeing all wrong?

"Oh, sure. Didn't you ever meet Howard around the shop? He hasn't come down much recently—that's why I've been going out of town on weekends. I've sort of been commuting to Boston."

"Wonderful news, Marge. I am very happy for you. How long have you been seeing this man?"

"Oh, it seems like forever. Three and a half, four years? I met him at the rent strike against Columbia. Since then he's been getting his doctorate at MIT. So we've been postponing living together until his schooling was finished. Which is in May. Then I'm packing up and getting the hell out of here."

"What about all your monkeys and your puppies? You are planning to move them too?"

"No, there's a pet store up on 120th Street. They're willing to take them in. I lose on the deal but it's worth it."

"Tell me more about your fiancé. I am very curious about him."

"Oh, he's a sweetie-pie. He's kind of stay-at-home, studies all the time. He was a math prodigy when he was a kid. But then he ran into the sixties and dropped out. Made a big mess of things. Then he met me on the upswing and—hey, what can I tell you, he's been going great ever since. It's hard to describe Howard, he's got an offbeat sense of humor that comes out once he's gotten to know you."

"I would like to get to know him. He sounds very smart. And he also cares about you, I assume."

"Oh, he's crazy about me. That's never been in doubt. I'm telling you, it makes a difference. I've had some boyfriends in the past who were really hostile pricks."

"Yes. So," asked Cyrus, "what will you be doing up in Newton, Massachusetts?"

"I don't know, I'm not sure yet. Maybe help Howard out. He's thinking of starting an engineering consulting firm. Whatever it is, it won't be another pet shop."

"Why? I thought you liked pets."

"I do, but gimme a break."

Their food arrived.

"Well, I wish you, of course, every possible happiness and

success. But I have to tell you this, things will be lonelier on the block without you."

"Thanks, Cyrus. I know I'll miss you. You've been a real— friend." Marge put her hand over his. "That's why I asked you to dinner tonight. I just wanted you to know that you've made a difference in my life. You're a good man. And I appreciate all the help you've given me."

"Please, I have done nothing special."

"Don't argue. Anyway, let's change the topic, this is getting sappy. You'll never guess who I ran into in Boston."

"Tell me, please."

"Kathleen."

"Who?"

"You know, Kathleen, our ex-neighbor! She sends her best regards to you, she made me promise twice that I would. I bumped into her at Quincy Market outside the basket shop. She lives in Boston now."

"But I thought she had moved to Rochester."

"Well, it turns out she didn't like Rochester, plus one of her favorite brothers lives in Cambridge, and she felt she could get better medical care in the Boston area."

"How is her health?" Cyrus asked, leaning forward.

"She was in a wheelchair this time. But she says the illness has stabilized, so that's good. We didn't talk much about it. You know how it is: I was with Howard, and she was with her brother, and we were all going off in separate directions. But we took down each other's phone numbers and we will stay in touch. Now if *you* ever get up to Boston, we can have a whole reunion of the Amsterdam Avenue gang."

"I would like that very much. It would be something to look forward to."

"So tell me about your plans," asked Marge.

"Nothing so exciting as yours. I will continue as before. Running my shop, selling rugs."

"What are you going to do about the rent?"

"I am trying to sell my private rug collection. If that happens, I can hold on until the end of the year."

"And after that?"

"After that we will see," Cyrus said. He shook his head at Marge's pitying face. "I will manage. I think in the end that I must move. I have finally come to the conclusion there is no other way."

"Whoopee! I'm glad to hear you finally talking sense. Don't go into debt for those creeps."

"Lately I have even been thinking about—you will laugh at this, but—even moving into the bookstore around the corner. I have the feeling MacCourt is ready to pull out."

"He's been sick a lot lately, hasn't he?"

"Yes. He has liver trouble. Poor man. In any event, I wonder if I wouldn't be happier selling books. I have always had a sort of fantasy about running a bookstore in which my favorite authors were kept permanently in stock. That way the shop would be a reflection of my own personality and reading tastes. Does that sound egotistical?"

"No, sounds great. I would love a bookstore like that. If it's really what you want, hon, go for it!"

Cyrus winced inwardly at this canned-optimistic expression, but was pleased with Marge's approval of the idea. "Well, we'll see. I haven't spoken to MacCourt about it yet."

When the check came, Marge snatched it away. "This one's on me."

"I thought you said this meal was free for both of us! I would never have agreed to your paying, Marge. Please, can't I at least give you something for the tip?"

"Put away your money. This is my treat."

ONE DAY CYRUS WOKE UP with the taste of despair in his mouth. All that had stood between him and his sorrow was gone. This

was not only a depressed mood but logical despair, based, it
seemed to him, on sound reasoning. Those glimmers of a solution
that had been leading him on—it suddenly struck him that none
of them would work, not this or that compromise, not love, not
the old way of life, not a new life. The business was going under,
there was nothing he could do to stop it. Even that one daring
hope he had kept for last—suicide—seemed too gawdy and beyond reach. For five months he had been trying this door or
that, secretly waiting for some unforeseeable miracle to rescue
him or allow him to continue as before. But none of the options
had worn the desired face of inevitability, and his will was as
much in pieces as ever. Only now his stomach and his chest felt
charged with pure anguish, from the moment he first opened his
eyes until nightfall.

"You must change your life." He kept repeating Rilke's line
as he swept up the shop. *Du musst dein Leben andern*, sweep,
sweep. What made the little poet so sure it was even possible? I
have run out of expectation that anything good will ever happen
to me again, thought Cyrus. Oh, I don't want to live any more!
I hate myself. Who cares about you? Stop complaining. You
must be a good little soldier and carry on with stoicism and
dignity.

THE FIRST BALMY SATURDAY IN APRIL brought out throngs along
Columbus Avenue, strolling and window-shopping, sitting in
outdoor cafés, walking their bikes toward Central Park, gathering
in thick clusters around the street entertainers. The crowds spilled
west to Amsterdam Avenue. All day long Cyrus ran up sales. It
turned out to be one of his best days of the year; the register
bulged with checks and six hundred dollars in cash. He decided
to stay open two hours later than usual, till eight-thirty.

Arnie had called earlier to say he might stop by, and at seven
he came into the shop, just as Cyrus was walking a few other

customers to the door. Arnie was wearing his old oatmeal sweater with the tear in the sleeve, but he seemed more upbeat than usual. "Boy, you got a regular parade out there."

"So nice to see you, Arnie. How have you been?"

"Not so bad, not so bad. I sold one of my inventions."

"Does that mean you can retire?"

"Means I don't have to work so hard the next six months. Means I can buy a few things. Hey, you got any new rugs?" he said, partly in jest.

"No, I'm sorry." Cyrus thought for a moment. "But I tell you what I can do. I can let you see the rugs upstairs in my apartment. These are things I have been collecting over the years for myself."

"Oh, boy, your own private stash."

"I will give you the key because I cannot leave the shop alone now. I am expecting more customers. Here." Cyrus handed over his key ring. "This one will let you in the apartment. And—if there is anything you want to buy, I promise to let you have it for a very fair price."

"Are you sure you want me to just walk into your place alone? I mean," Arnie chortled, "supposing I'm really a burglar or an art thief."

"I trust you're not."

"All right. But we can do it another time if you'd rather. I might feel funny poking around your goodies without you being there."

"Please, there is no reason to worry. I am glad to let you have a look. Just don't build them up too much in your mind before you see them, or you will be disappointed. These are just a few old rugs that happened to strike my eye."

"That in itself is interesting to me." Arnie pocketed the keys. "Well, thanks! I'll take good care of these. Be back in a little while. What's the apartment number?"

"Three-E."

"Three-E, three-E. . . . Oh, I almost forgot. Here's your final installment." Arnie took out his wallet and handed the rug dealer forty-five dollars, then went off. The store was empty for the first time in hours. Cyrus yawned and sat at his desk, thinking maybe he would lock up earlier, rather than wait until eight-thirty.

A few minutes later the shop door opened. A dark-skinned Hispanic youth of slight build, around Eddie's age, wandered in with a comb stuck high in his hair. He seemed insecure as he looked around. Maybe he was just getting interested in rugs, Cyrus thought, or had wandered here from uptown and had lost his bearings in the neighborhood. "Can I help you with something?" Cyrus approached the customer.

He sensed the boy's fear as he came near him, and was eager to assure him by his manner that he was not prejudiced but would assist with street directions or in any way he could. When Cyrus had gotten around three feet from the boy, he held out his hands palm-upward and repeated: "Can I help you? Are you lost or something? . . ."

The kid took a gun out of his windbreaker and motioned Cyrus to retreat toward the desk. "Give me your money."

A long silence followed.

"I will not. I will not give you my money," said Cyrus.

The boy was trembling. He seemed either inept or inexperienced at holdups. Part of Cyrus involuntarily sympathized, but for the most part he found himself rigid with outrage.

"Gimme your money!" the thief cried out, in an almost whiny voice. "Now! Look, I no want to do this but I got no choice. We run from Castro Cuba and there no jobs here."

"You want me to feel sorry for you when you are robbing me? This is not the way to solve your problems."

"Come on! If you no hand over the money I gotta shoot, I gonna kill you. That's the way—"

"Kill me if you wish. I will not give you my money."

The youth stared at him incredulously. He looked over his shoulder, to see if anyone was entering behind him. Cyrus thought he might have been considering the possibility of just turning around and leaving. He decided to wait the boy out. "Come on, I mean it, I gotta shoot," repeated the robber unimaginatively, looking sideways and whipping his head back. It seemed as though nothing were going to happen one way or the other; they were at a calm, eerie standstill. Then, like an afterthought, the boy pulled the trigger. Cyrus screamed in pain, and the thief ran from the store.

16

EPILOGUE

IT WAS ARNIE who found him and took him to the emergency ward. The bullet had struck the shoulder just above his right breast, no more than six inches from the heart. Because it had pierced through the muscle and hit a joint, an operation became necessary. The doctor at Roosevelt Hospital who performed the debridement said it could have been much worse: had the bullet shattered the bone, it would have taken a year to heal. This way it would require only six months: ten days' hospital care, two months' convalescence at home, four months of stiffness and partial use.

Cyrus's mother came to the hospital every other day, giving up temporarily her volunteer work at the burn center. Arnie stopped by during the first weekend, and Marge brought a basket of fruit. Cyrus was glad there were not more visitors. Most of the time he slept, woozy from the medication, conveyed by a procession of murky, turbulent, epically interlocking dreams.

Freddy offered to take care of his bills and close down the rug shop. Cyrus was too weak to do anything but accept. He was grateful to have an older brother who was such a good business-man. In very little time, Freddy had enlisted Aberjinnian and both had disposed of the inventory. They paid off Cyrus's debts, netting him an additional nine thousand dollars from the stock's sale. He would not even have to part with his private collection, which was one consolation. About the loss of the business itself, he felt resigned and numb. It was all happening above him, like configurations of angels or cherubs disposing of mortal destinies in a Renaissance painting. Though he would have liked to have kept his shop, he felt tired, and there was an undeniable relief in not having to worry any more about the monthly nightmare of meeting the rent. It had all been taken out of his hands.

Cyrus was sent home with his arm in a triangular sling, which he would be wearing for the next six months. His shoulder throbbed constantly; he could not raise his arm yet any higher than his nose; he could move it laterally only with difficulty; and even the simplest everyday tasks such as dressing himself or eating or locking the door required a certain amount of advance planning.

At home he watched afternoon soap operas, and read books on Indian miniature painting, a new interest. Now that the weather was warmer, he strolled every afternoon in Riverside Park, one day following Riverside Drive all the way past Harlem, past the medical center, and up to 180th Street, where he climbed to the Cloisters. He was leaning over a railing on Cabrini Boulevard, looking out at the Hudson and the Palisades, and down at the wooded area below, when a solitary Puerto Rican youth ap-proached him. The blood drained from Cyrus's face and a spasm went through his spine; immediately he drew back sideways to protect his wounded shoulder. The youth of course brushed past him harmlessly, but Cyrus felt a column of air vibrating along his front shoulder for minutes afterward; and it took some time to get his heart to stop pounding.

In the following days, each time he went outside he noticed that he would react with the same instinctive panic whenever someone Spanish-looking and young approached him at fairly close range. How silly, he thought, to generalize that way. Supposing the robber had been black, or a redheaded Irishman, or an Iranian like myself—would I also cringe whenever I passed by one of that group? At the same time he could not deny his fear: he was like a lab rat who had been given a powerful electric shock.

Cyrus often relived the trauma of the holdup. Why hadn't he simply let the thief have his money? Whether it *was* unconsciously suicidal, or an obedience to some stubborn need to stand his ground, what disturbed him in retrospect was that he seemed, back then, to have reached a point of indifference as to whether he lived or died. He would have to change that.

A few weeks into the convalescence period, his brother visited him and broached the subject of what he wanted to do next with his life. Cyrus asked if he would look into the possibility of taking over MacCourt's used bookshop. Freddy opposed the idea: "Why do you want to stay a storekeeper, getting robbed and shot at? I won't let you." Cyrus insisted. Freddy made inquiries, and came back with the distressing news that MacCourt had died. The relatives had no interest in seeing a bookshop perpetuated there; they were already talking to the Strand about selling the whole stock for next to nothing, just to get rid of it. Meanwhile, the realtors already had a new tenant lined up. There was something evasive about Freddy's intonation when he reported this that made Cyrus wonder if there was not a little more to the story, if perhaps his brother was—maybe not lying, but oversimplifying. Cyrus realized he would never know how seriously Freddy had tried to press his suit.

He resigned himself to the inevitable: going to work for his older brother.

✻ ✻ ✻

EACH DAY NOW, he boarded the IRT train during rush hour and rode downtown to West Twenty-eighth Street. He had never had to be pushed and shoved in these morning subway cars during all the years he had had his own shop, and he disliked it, especially when someone brushed against his tender shoulder. But there were compensations to working downtown: he felt as though he were coming out of a long hibernation. He enjoyed leaving the office to go to lunch, a part of the river of pedestrians, or meeting clients around town in the late afternoon. He would walk to his appointments whenever possible, and it seemed to Cyrus that he was getting the city back. New York was opening its glories to him again, by the one sure way it let itself be appreciated—on foot.

The job took awhile getting used to. It was a large Middle Eastern import-export operation, with woven handbags, luggage, costume jewelry, cotton blouses, copper vases, sheepskin coats, area rugs, mirrors, incense, music boxes, toys and other novelty items. Cyrus wished he could have more respect for the goods they peddled. On the other hand, it was a job: it gave him financial security, health insurance. And he had evenings and weekends to himself, to read, go to concert series or visit museums. He even had enough free time to finish some of the essays on art he had begun years ago, if he ever felt like taking them up again.

Cyrus had worried most in the beginning about making a costly clerical error, and Freddy humiliating him. But working for his brother was not quite as bad as he had imagined. The best of Freddy came forward in his work life: his business acumen and responsibility and concentration. Cyrus thought his older brother was even making a touching effort to be diplomatic with him. There were still times when Freddy's belligerent, overbearing side manifested itself, especially toward the end of a workday. At such moments, Cyrus remembered why he had always kept his brother at arm's length. But he had run away from Freddy for so long that now it made him feel stronger to be facing that difficult relationship daily, like staring into a furnace and not melting. And Freddy had changed a little too—become subdued, chastened, toned down, as the result of his son's disappearance. Eddie had run away from home, and was living somewhere on the Lower East Side, that was all anyone knew. If the trouble over his son had left Freddy with a defeated air, Cyrus had to admit that he preferred his brother sad rather than manic; it made it personally easier to be around him.

IN THE HOSPITAL he had had a dream. He dreamt that he was talking to an old Zoroastrian woman whom he deeply respected. She too felt an immediate rapport with him, and was telling him how glad she was to have finally met him. He leaned forward and whispered in her ear: "But I have so much to learn! I never really gave Zoroastrianism a chance. I am too ignorant of my own religion even to have the right to reject it."

"You want to understand Zoroastrianism?" she asked. "I will explain to you the essence. There is the world that we see"—and she elongated her body to the right in a sort of flowing, t'ai chi movement—"the world of matter, the flesh and the five senses. Then there is the world"—and she pulled up her spine, coiling and uncoiling from her upper body—"of the spirits: all those forces that we share the world with, but that remain invisible to the untrained eye."

This explanation, at once banal and hopelessly mysterious, struck him in the dream as making perfect sense. Somehow her accompanying movements had driven in its meaning. The old woman went on to explain other precepts that he could not remember on awakening. But the dream left him with an urge to study with a wise religious teacher sometime in the near future, and a peculiar confidence that something might come of it. It seemed that at last a space had been cleared inside him, and that now he would be able to make progress, even rapid progress, in spiritual matters.

Nevertheless, Cyrus was reluctant to put his dream-inspired optimism to the test. He wanted to interrogate his sentiments further. Examining himself, he saw that he was a man without roots, with a spirit that was merely drifting along unanchored, and he worried about what lay ahead of him if this condition were to continue for the rest of his life. Until now, he had confronted the world in a spirit of stoicism and forbearance. But this no longer seemed to be enough; his stoicism was growing stale, he needed a philosophy of life that was more nourishing and substantial.

At the same time, the word "religion," which kept coming up again and again in his mind, bothered him. To the skeptic inside him it suggested unquestioning obedience and mental suicide. In order for him to be drawn into religion, any religion, he would have to make contact with its intellectual traditions. He would have to find that part of its theology which was still alive, still profound, ethically complex and in creative flux. It would not do for him to begin at the point of faith: he knew now that he could not expect such heroism from himself. Since he was a man who lived in his mind, he would have to approach this at first through the mind.

Occasionally Cyrus asked himself if he wouldn't be better off studying a religion other than Zoroastrianism, one whose sacred texts were more intact. Buddhism, for instance, with its appealing meditational psychology; or Judaism, with its unbroken tradition of textual interpretation; or Catholicism, with its fascinating history of saintliness and worldliness; or Islam, with its wonderful Sufi mystical literature. Why Zoroanstrianism? The answer came: because he was Zoroastrian. If he followed any of these other quests, he would be like a tourist, enchanted and distracted by the exotic but finally homesick. He needed to return home, to the rituals of his youth, to his "roots," weak as they might be. Assuming that all religions possess a similar core, he simply had to trust that if he were patient and serious about it, Zoroastrianism would yield him enough spiritual sustenance to nourish his deepest self.

The resolve to pursue Zoroastrian studies was linked in his mind with another decision he had been arriving at. This was to marry Scherezade and raise a Zoroastrian family. Since she was already certain of her religious faith and knew how to perform the rituals, he would come that much closer to the heart of it by living alongside her. He would absorb it by osmosis. Moreover, Zoroastrianism was a very domestic religion: many of its practices centered around the home, raising children and seeing them through initiation. Were he to remain a forlorn, ascetic bachelor, the gates of this optimistic, family-centered religion would most likely remain closed to him.

Of course he realized that he could not marry Scherezade simply because she was orthodox; that would be using her. But he felt himself a decent enough man that, if they were to make a life together, he would certainly come to love Scherezade and take good care of her. As for the problem of sexual attraction, it had receded in importance. Whether the scare he had gotten from the shooting had altered his thinking, or whether he would have changed anyway, the excitement of lust no longer seemed as crucial as having a wife who was sweet and dependable and faithful.

The woman from the swing club still troubled him from time to time, though with decreasing force. She had never called. Maybe she had never seen the note, or she had tried to call when he was in the hospital. Just as well, he told himself (not always convincingly). One day he happened to be walking on the same block where the club had been, and he noticed that the New Thing sign was missing. In its place there was a laminated placard:

CMA   Spiritual Development Class

Through CMA you become the predominant creative force
in your own life. Instead of reacting to life
as it unfolds, you learn to harness the power
of the individual to create the life you really want.
Learn: Shiatsu Meditation / Laughing Practice / Healing Prayer
and more   one flight up

Cyrus smiled darkly to himself: "Laughing practice . . . I
could use that." It seemed that the god who watched over him
was playing another of his tricks by causing the swing club to
vanish, and with it any last hope of tracking down Shelley.

ON THE SECOND SUNDAY EVENING in August, Cyrus set out for
the fire temple. He had phoned ahead of time to learn when the
Gatha Society would be meeting next. Though he still did not
feel quite ripe for this spiritual test, he could not reasonably put
it off any longer.

The subway to Queens smelled of singed rubber and was
broiling; it had been his misfortune to get onto an old, un–air-
conditioned train. Cyrus took off his suit jacket, worried that his
white shirt would soak through at the armpits with perspiration.
He was unsure whether or not Scherezade would be attending
the meeting, but he had prepared for running into her by dressing
up. Now he unfastened the top shirt button with his left hand
and loosened his tie; he could tighten it up later, before entering
the temple. The train was filled mostly with blacks, he noticed.
He traded neutral glances with a stolid black man a little older
than he, who had white sideburns and a U.S. Postal Service
satchel on his lap. When the first seat became available, Cyrus
sat down and pulled from his pocket a folded magazine page: it
was the big Sunday crossword puzzle, which he had not gotten
around to doing yet. He immediately began filling it in, to calm

his nerves. The puzzle was three-fourths solved by the time he reached his stop; he put it away, thinking he would try to finish it on the way back.

There was a welcome evening breeze, and the streets were lush with summer smells from the rosebushes on the freshly cut lawns. Cyrus could not help remembering that the last time he had come this way it had been snowing.

The main door of the temple was closed; he went around to the side door and found it ajar. From the quiet downstairs, the place seemed deserted; he wondered if anyone else had shown up or if he had gotten the date wrong. He climbed the stairs to the prayer room, and began to hear a few voices. Three men were waiting around, much more casually dressed than he, in short-sleeved shirts or Lacostes.

Meher greeted him warmly. "Please come in, welcome. We are expecting some more people, so we will just wait a little while." Cyrus went over to the water cooler in the hallway. Meher took him aside when he came back, and whispered: "As you are a new member, please stay for tea afterward. I would like us to have a little chat alone."

"Certainly, thank you," said Cyrus. Eventually he would be asking Meher for his sister's hand, so this might be an opportunity to achieve a friendly footing with the man. Cyrus took a seat a few chairs away from the nearest person. He wanted to quiet his mind before receiving the teachings. Each time the door behind him opened, he turned around, half-expecting to see Scherezade. When a dozen or so people had arrived, Meher, who was in his white robes, came to the front. Cyrus had expected the old priest to do the teaching, and had a moment's disappointment when he realized that Meher would act as their spiritual guide. But that was foolish: what difference did it make if Meher was younger than himself?

"The topic of today's talk will be: 'If God is not all-powerful, what is the use of God?'" Meher gave an ironic smile, letting the paradox sink in. "God, whom we call Ahura Mazda, is utter goodness, from which only goodness can come. All bad comes from Angra Mainyu, the Hostile Spirit. The Hostile Spirit existed in the beginning, along with Ahura Mazda. In Zoroastrian thought there is a profound sense of antithesis, of opposition. Or, for want of a better word, dualism. It would be very good if we Zoroastrians could cease to be ashamed about being called dualists, and take pride in it. Zarathustra did not teach a thoroughgoing monotheism. That is a distortion of Western scholars and Zoroastrian liberal reformers who want the religion to seem as close to Judaeo-Christianity as possible. It is true that the religion acknowledges the *unity* of the divine will, which is the essence of monotheism. But Zarathustra saw divinity everywhere. He saw a divinity in the fire. He saw a divinity in the trees. Ahura Mazda brought these lesser divinities into being, just as many lamps can be lit by one lamp."

For the next hour, Meher spoke about the Seven Creations (the Heptad), the hierarchies of spirits, and the division of time into three epochs. Try as he might to concentrate, Cyrus's mind began to wander. He could find no way to make these distinctions relevant to the hunger that had brought him there. He felt as though he were back in graduate school, taking notes. Perhaps if he were patient and drenched himself in it, for months and months, he might be able to go beyond this boredom. A little voice of despair told him that he was wasting his time; he had neither the temperament nor the sustained will nor the simplicity to pass through the arch of spirituality.

When the sermon was over, Meher handed out mimeographed sheets. At the top of the page was one of the Gathas, Zarathustra's songs, rendered phonetically in the Roman alphabet; below this were two translations, one literal, one poetic, by someone named Taraporewala. The group read together the top part, and Meher drew connections between the individual words in Avestan and their English correspondences. Cyrus found this philological part rather interesting.

Afterward, when the meeting had broken up, Cyrus stayed behind. Meher went into the temple kitchen to make some tea, and they took it into the library on the first floor.

"So, how did you find this first session?" asked Meher.

"I particularly liked the part when we studied the Gatha."

"The Gathas are amazing. If one wrestles with the Gathas, they have such a sense within them, of inner coherence. . . ."

"Yes."

"I can never get enough of the Gathas. But we will talk about that later. I see you are still wearing a sling."

"Unfortunately. You heard about my accident?"

Meher nodded. "Awful city."

"Sometimes it is awful, yes. But so is every place."

"I wonder. Anyway, I am glad to see you walking and about."

"I am very happy to see you too. How have you been?" asked Cyrus.

"Fine. I am working hard."

"But *your* health is good?"

"Very good."

"And how is your family?"

"Thank God everyone is fine."

"Your father is still alive, isn't he?"

"Yes, he is back in Karachi, and he is doing all right," said Meher.

"I am very glad, very glad. And how is your mother?"

"She too is well, thank God. Thank you for asking. . . ."

"And your sister?"

"She is fine. You may not know that she is going to be married?"

Cyrus felt a cloud cross over his heart, and his throat constrict with shame. Somehow it was not a surprise. "You mean Scherezade?"

"I have only one sister."

"No, I didn't know. My mother told me nothing about it."

"This happened only suddenly, in the last week. We received

an offer from a family in Lahore. He will be coming over in a few weeks. I met him once—a very nice chap."

"I am glad to hear it. Well, then you are to be congratulated! And please extend my wishes to Scherezade for every happiness in life."

"Maybe you would like to come to the wedding."

"I would be delighted. I would be honored."

Cyrus drank slowly, savoring the bitterness of the well-brewed tea.